I0828633

A Realm of Sea and Smoke

Krystal Harding

Book Cover by Get Covers

Images from: Vecteezy.com and Canva

1st edition 2026

Paperback ISBN: 979-8-9904093-4-7

Contents

Pronunciation Guide

Pronunciation Guide

Characters

Luna Cromwell Embros: Luna Crom-well Em-bros

Damian Ashford: Dam-ian Ash-ford

Bastian Ashford: Bas-t-ian Ash-ford

Valyn Halloran: Val-in Hal-lor-en

Niklaus Adair: Nik-louse Ad-air

Fennik Elrod: Fen-nick El-rod

Elijah Elrod: Eli-jah El-rod

Undas: Un-dahs

Vanalli: Va-na-lee

Erina (Lilliana): E-ree-na

Tanis: Tan-is

Harold: Hair-old

Cassandra Halloran: Cass-an-ra Hal-lor-en

Penelope Ashford: Pen-el-ope Ash-Ford

Scarlet Ashford: Scar-let Ash-ford

Marie Elrod: Ma-re El-rod

Nora Adair: Nor-ah A-dare

Talissa: Ta-lis-sah

River: Riv-er

Claye: Cla-y

Ignis: Ig-nes

Voxis: Vox-es

Lumina: Lu-mean-a

Zekon: Z-con

Illisandra: Ill-e-san-dra

Otius: O-tee-us

Zephir: Ze-fear

Milara: Me-lar-ah

Undine: Un-dine

Jasmine: Jazz-min

Victoria: Vic-tor-e-ah

Alstrom: All-strom

Beatrix: Bee-a-trix

Elenor: Ell-e-nor

Marcloff: Mar-kl-off

Elucia: E-luc-e-ah

Alric: Al-rick

Valmor: Val-more

Aralia: A-ral-eah

Arthur: Ar-ther

Miharu: Me-har-roo

Mina: Me-nah

Celia: Seal-e-ah

Ishtar: Ish-tar

Luther: Lou-th-er

Rafael: Ra-Fiel

Westley: Wes-ley

Patrick: Pat-rick

Creatures and Daemons

Ithika: Ith-ick-ca

Lyria: Leer-rhea

Ophelia: O-feel-ia

Ritmer: Rit-mer

Hilmer: Hill-mer

Realms and Cities

Floria: Floor-e-ah

Fildery: Fill-dur-rey

Mirith: Meer-rith

Hildaria: Hill-dar-e-ah

Mirith: Meer-rith

Solaria: Sol-are-ah

Valhime: Val-hime

Daglidell: Dag-li-dell

Endora: end-door-ah

Anchora: Anchor-ah

Celetsia: Cel-es-tea-a

Altaria: All-tear-e-ah

Doria: Door-e-ah

Oakenhall: Oak-en-hall

To all those waiting in the darkness

We gotta make our own light

CHAPTER 1
PROLOGUE

1,000 years ago

The War of the Roses

Ash and blood covered almost every inch of the battlefield, body parts and corpses strewn everywhere. Blood still trickled down my face, a distant throbbing in my skull reminding me that I had a huge gash on the top of it. I moved more bodies, rolling them over to see the young faces of those we broke bread with last night. Hundreds of men and women were now dead. Maybe a few hundred had survived this last assault from Hellis, but I was split up from my mates. I was split up from my family.

Rage settled in me as I combed the field, finding more dead than living. The few living folks I came across, I moved back to camp so they could be seen by the remaining healers. I need to find Lumina; she could find the living quicker than me. I knew this would be dangerous; I knew there was a chance we could all be split up. But I made that call. One I am starting to regret. I know they haven't died. I can still feel them, even though it's faint.

"Talissa!" A young woman came running up to me. Her blonde hair danced behind her as she ran. The silver and gold eagle-winged helm she wore kept the rest of her features from me, but I knew who she was. She stopped short in front of me, leaning on her knees to catch her breath. "They found Voxis and River. They're making their way back to camp now."

"Any word on the others?" I asked her. She looked at me with weary eyes. I'll take that as a no. "We can't stop looking for survivors. Head to camp and let Voxis and River know that I won't stop looking for the others. They're free to join me when they are up for it." Without a word, she turned and left me standing amongst the piles of our dead. Tears slid down my cheeks as I looked out across the land. Countless lives lost, and for what? Marcloff won't stop once he takes our land from us. He will make us his slaves. But is being a slave worse than being dead?

Fire and light spark up ahead, a pulling sensation in my chest has me running towards it. That better be Ignis and Lumina, I swear upon the stars they better be alive! The ground rumbled beneath my feet as I tried to avoid every limb and head that I came across. *Claye!* My heart thundered in my chest, threatening to explode out of me. My feet couldn't take me fast enough. I watched as a flare of light crested over the hill in front of me. Lumina must have found people still alive; she wouldn't let them go back to the healers at the camp if she could handle it herself.

I reached the top of the hill, looking out over the sea of blood and bodies. My heart sank at the sight of our loss piled in with the dead from Hellis. My eyes snagged on the sight of Ignis and Claye, stacking the dead from Hellis and lighting them ablaze. Lumina was indeed healing those on our side who were still living. I watched as healed soldiers helped lay out our fallen in rows, so many rows. Making my way down the hill toward them, I notice how the soldiers look at me. Some bow slightly while others downright drop to their knees in praise. It's unsettling. I am not one of the old gods who needs to be worshipped to feel alive.

As if the wind sang my arrival, Claye and Ignis both looked directly at me. Tension sweeping from their faces briefly before they went back to their tasks. Lumina watched me cross the field, her eyes examining every detail of my body that she could see. "I'm fine." I lied as I got closer to her. I had a few cuts and scrapes, the gash in my head, a few bruises I feel forming under my armor, but other than that, I am physically fine. It's the mental aspect that isn't fine.

"Have you seen River or Voxis?" She asked, turning her attention back to a young woman whose arm was gashed wide open. She was doing a good job of healing the injured quickly, but I heard the young woman speak up.

"Please don't take away the scar. I never want to forget how lucky I am today." She said as she closed her eyes, waiting for some sort of pain that she assumed was coming. Lumina took a deep breath and dimmed her light. Within a few minutes, the gaping wound on the woman's arm healed, leaving only a faint pale scar as requested. The woman thanked Lumina, then got up and joined the others in caring for the dead.

"They all asked to keep their scars. They all want to be reminded of the battle here, the lives of friends and family that they have lost, and the reminder that they are lucky to be alive." Lumina said as she watched a group of soldiers, women and men, carry bodies across the battlefield. "Was he here today?"

Lumina looked at me as she asked the burning question. I'm sure they all wanted to know. I tried not to think about his face, the face I searched the battlefield to make sure he was not among the dead. "Yes. I could feel him. This is becoming too risky. I can't let him continue to play on both sides. It's going to get him killed."

Ignis rested his gloved hand on my shoulder. "He made the choice. He knew it was best that he stay our eyes in Hellis. I know it's hard, but he's the reason we are still standing today. I caught a glimpse of him earlier as he took out the catapults and the orc-like beasts in the back of the line. I don't know what Marcloff is creating in Hellis, but I don't like it," Ignis said as he wrapped his arms around me.

"He's right. We need to prepare for creatures we have never seen before." Claye said as he dusted off his hands on the exposed fabric just above his greaves.

"How do we prepare for things we have never seen before?" Lumina asked. Her blonde hair was matting to her face with sweat and blood from those she had saved.

"We trust that he can get the information to us before the next fight." Ignis said with a serious tone in his voice. "Let's get back to camp. The bodies of our dead need to be buried, and the only priest we have is hiding in his tent like a child. Poor bastard thinks he's safer in a canvas tent than out on the battlefield."

"No one said he was smart." I retorted. "My father thinks Otius isn't thinking things through. I'm starting to believe him.

Something has got to give or else there won't be people to protect in a year."

The grim realization of the lives lost hit me like a ton of bricks. We've lost so many. How can we keep going?

You keep going by keeping the love alive inside of you. I love you, little goddess. I'll be with you soon.

DEATH IS COMING

WHEN THE SEA RISES

CHAPTER 2
LUNA

"Who the fuck do you think you are?!"

Well, that wasn't how I was expecting my morning to begin. I could hear Talissa screaming down the hallway at someone. Valyn rolled over, placing his arm under me, pulling me in tight. "Does she realize it's way too early in the morning to be yelling like that?" He whispered into my hair as limbs moved around me. The bed was enormous enough for all of us to sleep, but we all stayed close to one another knowing what daybreak will bring.

"Something tells me she just doesn't care," I replied, trying to pull the blankets up over my head. I do not know who she is bitching at or why she is bitching at them, but the sun isn't even peaking over the horizon yet. She needs to go back to bed and start her day over again.

"Do you want me to go see what's going on?" Niklaus offered, his voice sounding so groggily. We all had finally crashed around midnight last night once we arrived at Solaria. Fennik had elected to stay behind in Floria to help with the Crimson Army's training and rebuilding his home. I wanted him to come with us just for the night, but he knew his people needed him. It's not like we will all be separated for long, at least I hope not.

"That's probably not a good idea, Nik. We don't know who she's talking to. You don't want to get blasted by accident." Damian muttered as he grabbed my leg and wrapped himself around it. "Besides, do you really want to set Luna off by leaving?"

A thrumming coursed through my body at the thought of him leaving and getting hurt. "Calm down, princess. He's not going anywhere," Bastian said from somewhere below my waist. I honestly do not know how we all fall asleep in basically a pile of limbs and flesh, but it works.

Four of my mates have spoken. I knew I was one short. Where the fuck is Valdis?! I shot upright and searched the room for any sign of life from him. Nothing. A pulse surged through me as Ophelia slipped from my fingers and onto the floor. *Find him.* She didn't need any more instructions than that as she took off through the door and down the halls. Everyone slowly untangled themselves and looked around the room.

They began speaking, but I wasn't listening to a word they were saying. My sole focus was Ophelia as she slithered through the halls searching for my missing mate. A hand slipped its way onto my back, slowly sliding down my spine. I blinked and refocused on the surrounding room. Each of my mates just watched as I took each of them in until I finally landed on the face attached to the hand that was lovingly stroking my spine.

"Valdis, I swear to all the stars above that I will hurt you if you ever vanish like that again!" I snapped. His violet eyes met mine as he smiled.

"So now I have to tell you when I go to take a piss?" He smirked, shrugging his shoulders. "Alright, noted. Now come back to bed." He tried guiding me to lie back down, but my focus shifted back to Ophelia to tell her to come back, but I froze. Standing in the hallway were Talissa and a large man. One that I recognized from my brief time in Celestia. Fuck.

I pull Ophelia back, but she refused to leave Talissa alone with him. I didn't blame her. His granite eyes reminded me of the stones on the shores of Doria. Dark and unmoving. His jet black hair was slicked back, showing the small wrinkles in his forehead from the disapproving look on his face. He looked as cold as ice and like he was about to strike her. That wasn't about to happen in my mate's home. I blinked, refocusing myself, and tore from the bed. The silk from my nightgown dragged behind me on the floor as I ripped open the door and stalked down the hallway.

As I followed the halls to where Ophelia stood poised beside Talissa, I heard clattering and commotion behind me. She looked at me as I rounded the corner with pure panic on her face. "I know who you are, but you were *not* invited here. Leave." I say sternly as I stand next to Talissa. The footsteps that were rushing behind me came to a halt as they froze in their place. I remember how they looked when they say Undas for the first time.

"I can be where ever I please. You would do well to remember that." He puffed his chest out and gave a look like I was expecting to bow to him and apologize.

"Like I said, you were *not* invited here. Now get the fuck out." I said with more command. He turned his attention to my mates instead.

"You would do well to keep her in check," he replied to them. The disapproval on his face was clear, with his scrunched nose and raised eyebrows.

"And you would do well to remember you are a traitor to your blood. Either leave on your own or I will remove you. Do not speak to my mates. Do not speak to my aunt." Ophelia slipped from our sides to get between my mates and the traitor before me.

”If you know who I am, then why do you test me? I could remove your life from you with one snap of my fingers.” He let out a deep laugh that made my blood boil. My mates looked like they wanted to move, attack him, but they didn’t move. Growls tore from their throats, but no words. Talissa remained frozen in place. Was this fear? “Say my name then.”

“Go fuck yourself, Otius.” I spat. “You can’t harm me. Not like you think you can, but feel free to try.” I threw him a challenge. One that he would either take or one that he would walk from. I hope he takes it. He turned to me and smiled, waving his right hand. A gentle wind went through the hallway, well what I thought was a gentle wind. The force of his power hurled Talissa and my mates into the wall. Yet I barely felt anything from him.

“My turn.” I locked eyes with him with a wide smile on my face. Smoke and ice formed around his feet, climbing up to his knees. His eyes widened, the whites stark against his tan features. I let the elements climb higher on him as a scream tore through the hallway.

"STOP!!!" I could hear my mother's voice clear, but I kept my eyes locked on Otius. The fear in his eyes as he looked at me made me proud. Talissa rested her hand on my shoulder.

"Luna please. Stop. You'll kill him." She whispered as I heard more commotion to my other side. My mates had all gotten to their feet and were stopping my mother from reaching for me.

"I will not let him hurt you or anyone else. I gave him the option to leave, and he refused. We both know I can't kill him; he's a god." I said flatly, my eyes still locked on him as he fought against the ice. Before I could continue the ice climbing up to his throat, fire erupted from behind him, melting away my progress. For the first time since laying eyes on my great grandfather, I blinked. Undas was stalking through the hall towards us. Rage and fury on his face.

"My granddaughter told you to get the fuck out of her home. Leave. NOW!" He roared, shoving past my mates and mother. "This is your last chance. Or would you prefer to be stuck in clouded ice for eternity? I wouldn't put it past her."

Otius scoffed as he looked past Undas to me. "This is not over child. You will learn to submit to your elders." Without another word he spun on his heels and left.

"Go fuck yourself!" I yelled at him, flipping my middle finger high in the air. Tension eased as Otius left us, but I felt eyes on me. "What?" I snapped as I took in the room.

"What the hell was that all about?!" Niklaus exclaimed. I guess I didn't really fill anyone else besides Talissa on what I found out.

Oops.

CHAPTER 3
LUNA

Undas walked with me down the hallway and into the library. The rage had subsided from our unwanted guest, but I still felt a charged energy to me I couldn't place. The library was quiet; the books sleeping on their shelves. Undas walked over to the enormous fireplace, snapping his fingers to ignite the wood inside. I fell into the chair next to the fireplace as he paced back and forth.

"Should I ask what brought all of this about?" Undas paused and looked over at me. I shrugged my shoulders. My eyes stared at the embers as they danced to the song of the crackling wood. "Luna, what happened?"

"You should ask your daughter. She was the one yelling at him, asking him who he thought he was. I sent Ophelia out to look for Valdis. He wasn't in bed when the altercation was going on. My overreaction to him in the bathroom turned out to be a good thing. Ophelia essentially made it to where Talissa was, and I saw Otius, and stormed out. Who does he think he is, though? He needs to realize that he is no longer the strongest in these lands." I say, my focus never leaving the fire.

"Otius wants Talissa to go back to Celestia. He wants to keep her in a cage, essentially. He fears losing her again, but after your display of power, he will turn his focus to you." Undas finally took a seat on the couch across from me. The large arch windows behind him held the picture of the world, still sleeping under a pink starry sky.

"He can't control us. He can't cage us. It won't end well for him if he tries." My words were cold and distant. My blood turned to ice at the thought of being in a cage, useless as my mates fought without me. I refuse.

"None of us wants that for either of you. Talissa wouldn't have barked back like she did before. Otius was always the one who would force his children to do things they didn't want to do. He always did what he thought was best. That was until he made your grandmother stand trial at the Grand Holy Court. Your grandmother and I didn't see eye to eye back then. Otius had told my father about Vanalli's mistake and my outburst. My father forced my hand to enact the Union Law. A law of the gods that one is to be enslaved to the other until amends are made. I never wanted that. But Otius thought he was doing the right thing by forcing his daughter to take accountability for her actions. He never imagined that we would fall for one another and that our mating bond would snap into place. Maybe one day we can tell you the entire story." Undas looked at the fire, admiring the flames. He let out a sigh. "Fear makes one see things that do not exist. Fear makes one do irrational things that they wouldn't normally do. You would do well to remember that."

"Fear will never go away. It's how we handle the fear that we have that makes the difference between losing everything and everyone we love or succeeding. I know better." I said, turning my gaze to meet my grandfathers. His eyes were loving and kind; the smile that graced his lips was genuine. I wish I had him around me my whole life, but I'll take the time I have now. It's better than none at all. "How is Vanalli doing?"

"Her parents are back from the supposed dead and have been a giant pain in her ass since. Not including my own parents being home as well. It's been tough." He brushed his hand across his face, pinching his nose before looking back at me. "There still is no word on Melody. Allura has been worried, she feels like she betrayed us and wants punishment. Otius is all for it, but your grandmother and I do not want to punish her for actions that were out of her control. She never would've done it if she wasn't possessed. Vanalli has been self-punishing herself for not noticing the change in Allura."

"Talissa and the others are leaving for Hellis shortly after daybreak. I plan on going with them, I want to check in on Vanessa. I hadn't seen her since before the mess in Floria. I'm pretty sure there is a meeting or six I have probably missed." I said jokingly.

"She's been busy doing some recon of her own. Not saying that she hasn't missed you, but she's been busy. With her help, Talissa should be able to get into Minaris without being detected by Marcloff. I wish you two wouldn't do reckless things, but I know there is no stopping either of you." Undas let out another sigh and part of me felt bad for causing him stress and worry.

"She doesn't want me to keep with her. If she had her way, her mates wouldn't even be going with her. I wouldn't put it past her to keep them in Infernia with the rest of the Noire family and taking off. If she does, should I try to go with her?" I asked him, waiting patiently for him to think about his options..

"No. You have your mates that will need you to return to them. Talissa is smart and strong. I just have to trust that she is going to make the smart decision." He looked back at the embers, then to the door behind me. "Speaking of your mates,

I'm sure they are ready to break down that door and come in here to make sure you're not getting scolded." I huffed. He wasn't wrong with them being at the door, but they knew I was fine. Valyn has been inside my head this whole time, listening in.

"If they wanted to or felt the need to, they would be in here already. They know I am safe. Aside from wanting to know what all of that was about, they are fine." I looked past Undas at the rising sun and let out a sigh. "I thought I had a little more time to sleep, but the sun is done sleeping, as am I."

I rose from the chair and looked back at my grandfather. He looked tired, exhausted, really. His skin was paler than usual. I could tell sleep had been eluding him, probably for much longer than I even realize. "I'll fill you in on everything that happened in Celestia if Talissa hasn't already. Just know that I do not trust Otius. I don't know much about Illisandra to form an opinion on her yet. But if she really does follow his orders and his beliefs, then she is no better in my eyes." I sat back down in the chair and filled him in on Otius's betrayal of those in Celestia, the poisoning of the water to keep everyone weak and unable to return to Cerulia. I told him what Marcloff disclosed about Otius and the old gods, taking over Cerulia and claiming it as their own. The look of horror that graced his features was hard to look at. I finally told him about Marcloff, saying we were the bad guys, not them. Their gods abandoned them when our kind arrived. I know my mates could hear everything. I could hear their worry and fear as if it was wafting into my head like a buzzing white noise. "Now you know. I don't trust Otius, but I don't trust Marcloff at his word either. Hopefully, Alistar or Zekon have some answers for me. If not answers, they might be able to point me in the right direction."

I rose once more, but this time I didn't look at the god broken on the couch behind me. I opened the door to see my mates standing there, staring at me. The hollow wind that filled these halls moments ago still echoed through me. Otius only stands thanks to Undas. I hope he thanks him.

CHAPTER 4
VALYN

I watched as Luna walked past us, back down the hallway to the room we had been sharing. She didn't look at us like she used to. The warm smiles we had grown accustomed to seeing was nowhere to be seen. I looked into the room as Undas got up from the couch and smothered the fire. Luna dropped a truth on us that I don't think any of us would've thought about before. If Marcloff is right, then have we always been the bad guys in their stories, even before the war?

You had nothing to do with the war. You weren't there. Your father was, my father was. But you, your brothers, Valdis, and myself were not. Get that thought out of your head. Her voice echoed in my head, and I knew she was speaking directly to me. Not to the others. I watched as Bastian and Damian moved out of the way, letting Undas pass freely between them.

"Do you believe what Marcloff said?" Damian asked Undas before he could reach the end of the hallway. Undas turned back to look at us, a man in utter defeat.

"If he is right, then we have all been living a lie. If what he told Luna is true and not just a way to have her second guessing herself, there is only one person I know who has the answers. And I might just rip him limb from limb to get them." Undas's voice turned dark. A sinister expression flashed in his eyes before he turned from us and stormed out of the house. I looked at the others before making my way back to the room. Luna was inside already getting herself dressed, damn it.

"No fun time this morning, Princess?" I teased her as I grabbed my shirt from the floor by the bathroom door. I remember exactly where I threw it last night when we get here. She looked at me with a sense of sadness in her eyes. "I'm teasing my love. This morning has been chaos enough. It's not like we won't have other opportunities." I wrapped my arms around her and pulled her tightly into my chest. Her vanilla and citrusy scent circled around me, mixing itself with my own. It was her way of making sure I wouldn't forget her when we parted ways shortly. "If you think I will forget what you smell like or what you look like, you have another thing coming."

She looked up at me, a tear slipping down her cheek. I softly brushed away the stream from her cheek before pressing my lips to hers. Her hands reached up for my hair, and she let out a vicious growl before pulling away from me. "Grow. It. Back."

I couldn't help but laugh. She was so cute and very territorial about my hair. Well, not just mine, but all of ours.

"I will grow it back once I know I won't be on a ship for long periods of time. Long hair and the salty sea air do not mix well." I said as I ran my fingers through her hair. I gently tugged at the few knots that were at the ends. "You might want to get your hair trimmed too. I know you love your ponytails, but your ends aren't doing well."

She swatted my hand away from her and stuck her tongue out at me. "I haven't brushed my hair in I don't even know how many days. Once I get a brush through it, it will be fine." She protested as she rummaged through a bag that someone had brought here. I couldn't remember who grabbed what when we left Mistveil. A hole began forming in my chest at the thought of home. I wouldn't be there for quite some time, but she will be there practically alone. My heart sunk at the thought of her alone there when she returns from Hellis.

"Valyn, if you convince her to cut her hair short, I will fight you." Bastian said as he entered the room. The somber expression that was on his face moments ago had vanished. He was trying to put on smiles for her. We all were at this point. Leaving her alone was the last thing any of us wanted to do. As much as this whole thing was her plan so we could protect our people and ready our armies, I still didn't like it.

"She can cut her hair if she wants. It's not our call." Niklaus said as he followed behind Damian and Valdis who were bother talking quietly amongst themselves. I looked around the room at everyone. Niklaus and Luna bantering about her hair, Bastian grabbing the hairbrush he found in his bag and pulling her toward him so he could brush her hair. Valdis and Damian looking over maps and something else on their phones. I hadn't even looked at my phone once. I took in the whole picture. Everyone happy. Everyone smiling, even though the smiles weren't wide with joy. We were trying to make the best of the situation.

"We should get some breakfast before Talissa decides we need to leave now and we end up missing food. I can't go without food today, I might kill someone." Luna complained as Bastian began braiding her hair. I watched as he twisted the strands of hair together before tying them off at the end with a small black band.

"Since when could you braid hair?" Damian asked as he finally looked over at what everyone was doing.

"I've been practicing on my own hair. Let's just say, braiding her hair is much easier than my own." He laughed as he gave her a kiss on the top of her head. The braid was surprisingly neat, kept together with no hairs out of place. I was impressed to say the least.

"Alright, food. Now." Luna said as she stalked for the door. I shook my head and looked at the others. Worry filled everyone's eyes. We can't lose her, not again.

CHAPTER 5
LUNA

The walk through the halls was quiet, no one daring to speak too loudly. The sound of our boots on the marble announced our arrival at the kitchen before we arrived. River and Ignis were already sitting at the table with Voxis. Talissa, Lumina and Claye were nowhere to be seen. I glanced at River for some indication that she was alright, but he just smiled at me. I guess that was the only acknowledgment I needed.

"There's bacon and eggs on the stove. Coffee is brewing in the kettle. I hope you don't mind us making use of your kitchen. We just like to cook," Voxis said from her seat. I nodded my thanks and headed for the stove. The smell of the bacon was heavenly. I loaded up a plate and placed it in front of Valdis. He raised his eyebrow as he looked at me. I just turned back and started making more plates for my mates. I hadn't noticed Voxis move from the table. "Take as much as you want. There is plenty more that can be made if necessary. Talissa, Lumina and Claye already ate, so don't worry about leaving any for them."

"Thank you. I really appreciate the food." I placed eggs and bacon on my plate and took my seat between Damian and Bastian. It was my normal place since the day I met them. I wish Fennik was here with us one more time before we had to leave. Eventually, I would see him again, but today Valdis filled his seat. We all sat quietly and ate our meal. River and Ignis chatted amongst themselves as Voxis took a seat by us.

"Are you ready to go to Hellis today?" She asked me. River and Ignis stopped their conversation to listen to my response. Valdis quickly took a sip of water from his cup.

"Of course I'm ready. I need more answers than just going and meeting my other uncle. Finding a library or get the answers from Zekon or Alistar upfront would be best, but I don't expect it to be that easy." I glanced at Valdis. He just nodded his head at me. He understood I needed the truth just as much as everyone else.

"I hadn't heard that story growing up. You would think that if that was the truth, I would've been told stories, in school or at least by my parents. Something is missing. Something that we are not aware of," Valdis suggested softly across the table.

"No offense, but does it matter? Who's to say that he isn't speaking his truth? To him, we are the enemy. I doubt he hasn't made history in his city saying exactly what he told her. You might not know about it, but those in his city and the ones close by might all believe what he's telling them. I was a soldier, I followed the orders I was presented with. I trusted those above me. Maybe I shouldn't have, but there is no turning back now." Ignis spoke from his seat at the other small table.

"You're not wrong. He could very well have followers believing what he told me. The only way of finding out is by getting knowledge from Limbris. It's just getting it out without him realizing it." I said as I popped a piece of salty bacon into my mouth. Everyone looked at Valdis. "Don't even fucking think about it. Marcloff knows he's my mate. You think I would let him put himself in danger? There are other ways."

I let Ophelia out to play once more, her dark body shimmering with the lights from the ceiling. Voxis let out a shudder as Ophelia slipped between the chair legs, inspecting everyone. "Are you sure that thing won't eat one of us?" Voxis questioned as she watched Ophelia gently wrap around Bastian's leg. She knew who belonged to me and was just as curious as the rest of my little pets. Each one wanted to greet them officially, but I wasn't about to let them all out now.

"Ophelia won't hurt anyone unless I tell her to. You're safe, Voxis." As if I gave Ophelia the okay, she slithered her way over to sit beside Voxis. It was cute how she just wanted to get love and affection from her. Voxis just looked down at her with hesitation, but it was River who reached down, giving the little shadow snake exactly what she wanted.

"Daybreak will be here before we know it. If we are all leaving together still, you might want to hurry. After this morning's intrusion, I doubt Talissa wants to stay here any longer than she already has." Ignis piped up as he cleaned his plate in the sink. Glancing over at Damian, he rephrased, "No disrespect to you. We just don't trust him."

"No disrespect assumed. After witnessing what happened, I don't blame any of you. Just know that my homes are always open to you all. Maybe Daglidell would be properly suited for you in the future. The Gods don't seem to venture there unless they have to." Damian offered, returning his attention to his plate. We all would leave shortly, but he would have to stay here and deal with any fallout from this morning. I swear if Otius steps foot back in this house, I will find a way to rip him apart and stop him from healing for a thousand years. A soft caress in my mind allowed me to let down my walls for the moment.

I can handle whatever comes my way. You just make sure you come home to me in one piece. Damian's deep voice lulled over the conversations happening in the room. I focused on his voice, following the light that tethered our minds together as one.

I will always come back to you. I just need you to promise me you will go to Daglidell yourself if Otius pulls some shit. I pleaded with him, trying not to imagine him fighting off my great grandfather alone. Not saying he couldn't, but it wouldn't be a fair fight.

That is a promise I can keep, my little Luna. Stick close to Valdis while you're in Minaris if you go that far with them. He paused before looking up over at me. *I mean it Luna, come back to me whole. I rather you stay with me, but I know better than to ask you to.*

A promise to you on the stars. I will return to you—to you all in one piece. I corrected myself, letting everyone in on my thoughts. Multiple waves of light and love funneled around me as they all understood what I meant. I wish Fennik was here. I know he can hear us, but it doesn't make it any easier. Refocusing on the room in front of me, I realized Ignis and Voxis had left the room, leaving only River left.

"We will look after you while you're with us. Just know that we don't expect you to be by our sides the whole way. We can do it ourselves and honestly, we need to. Zekon will be ecstatic to know that he has a niece though, especially one as exceptional as you." River tussled my hair before heading for the door. Today wasn't going to be easy, but we had to get started. If not, the goodbyes would kill me.

CHAPTER 6
TALISSA

Lumina and Claye refused to leave my side after I returned to our room. Voxis had brought us food before heading with River and Ignis to the kitchen to eat themselves and to make food for Luna and the others. It meant a ton to me the way they treated Luna as if she was always a part of our lives. I hadn't seen Ophelia watching Otius come at me. I didn't even feel her presence. Lumina has been fussing over me since I returned. She could tell I was anxious, checking me for cuts and scraps after I told her about Otius' little power play.

"Was Luna hurt in the exchange? Do I need to go check on her?" Lumina asked once she was satisfied that I was not about to bleed out on the floor. There wasn't a drop of blood to be seen.

"She wasn't phased. It knocked her mates on their asses and into the wall on the other side of her, though. If they were hurt, I'm sure she would've healed them within seconds of the injuries." I said as I began packing the little things that we had with us. My mother had stashed away our belongings at Firehearth manor, sending some stuff with my father when he met us here last night. I was grateful to them for bringing us clothing and some other necessities I wouldn't have thought of.

"What did she do to Otius in return?" Claye questioned from the bed. His curiosity was piqued the moment I told them she stood up to him.

"She began covering him from the feet up to his waist in a smoke filled iceberg. If my father hadn't shown up when he did, I'm sure she would've trapped him inside of ice." A shudder rocked through me at the thought of my niece putting our grandfather on ice.

"No white flames?" Lumina asked. She was fiddling with some books that my father had brought. Some new medicine books, some historical accounts of what we had missed while we were away. Lumina lit up when she saw the leather-bound tomes.

"No. Honestly, I don't know if she doesn't know how to use it or not. It was just wise that she didn't expose that to him. That is something she needs to keep him from finding out." I sighed, zipping up the navy blue duffle bag my mother had sent for us. Each of us got one, a different color for each of us. Once

I finished with my bag, I moved onto Voxis and Rivers. Ignis had already packed his before breakfast.

"What did Otius want from you?" Claye asked hesitantly. I know they wanted to tread lightly when asking me questions, but they deserved to know.

"He wanted us to return to Celestia. He said it wasn't safe for us here. The biggest mistake he made was saying Zekon would want it that way." I clenched my fist around River's favorite faded grey t-shirt. He was wrong. The pull of Zekon's bond on mine was getting stronger every day. I knew he was waiting for me to come to him. "I might have lost my temper and yelled at him. I think that's why Luna sent Ophelia to check on me."

The door suddenly pushed open, startling me from my folding. Voxis and Ignis came into the room with a somber look on their faces. I looked past them for River, but Ignis just shook his head. "He wanted to let Luna know she didn't have to babysit us. She's needed in Mistveil and Mirith, not putting herself in danger with us in Hellis. Valdis should be enough of assurance that we will be alright."

"She has a meeting with Vanessa in Infernia. Seeing us off was just a bonus plan for her." I replied as River entered the room. I finished packing his bag and looked at everyone. "I feel like us coming back here might've been a mistake." I confess.

"Why do you say that?" Voxis asked, grabbing my hand as she led me to the bed. I took a seat next to her and tears started flowing down my cheeks. Her soft, tan fingers brushed away each tear. The love and worry in her eyes were clear.

"Otius followed us back. I know all of my grandparents are back, but he did damage. A lot of damage. In Celestia and during the war. How can I leave Luna knowing that she will have to deal with him?" I sobbed out. Voxis pulled me into her chest and ran her fingers through my hair.

"Luna is stronger than you give her credit for. She will be okay. Not only that, but do you really think Milara and Zephir will allow her to deal with them alone?" She reminded me. Luna wouldn't fully be alone here when we left, I kept forgetting there were others here to protect her.

"We should probably get ready to leave. Not that I don't want to stay here longer, I just know this is going to be taxing on all of us." River said as he grabbed his bag. "Thank you for this, sweetness."

Pulling back from Voxis, I wiped my eyes and smiled at them. "I think you are right. It's best we get heading out sooner rather than later." I slipped my feet into some sneakers that my mother had sent. They were weird feeling, cushiony yet firm. It was so odd. I can almost bet money on the fact that she has never worn shoes like this in her entire life. I pulled myself together and gave them the biggest smile I could muster. "Let's go."

Without another word, we each grabbed our bags and headed out. I looked at the room once more taking in the calmness we all shared here last night. Probably the last calmness before the chaotic storm ahead of us. I took a deep breath in before closing the door and following everyone down the hall to the main entrance.

One day we won't always be rushing off to the next disaster that needs to be fixed. I just have to keep reminding myself what's at the end of the tunnel.

Little Goddess, please tell me you've come back to me.

CHAPTER 7
LUNA

The rest of the morning was a whirlwind of getting our bags packed, phone calls to family, letting them know where we were going and how long we would be gone for. Talissa and the others were already waiting for us in the main hall of Solaria's grand castle. This place was like a maze, but somehow, they knew where to go and how to get around. If it weren't for Damian, I would've lost my way to the bathroom.

"We're ready to go when you are," Talissa said as she gave me a big hug. Everyone was doing their greetings, and as I noticed, their goodbyes. We wouldn't be seeing each other for quite some time. I looked over at Bastian as he chatted away with Ignis. The smiles they had were bright and welcoming. Ignis and Damian were talking together in a corner while Niklaus and Lumina were examining a potted plant by the front door. Valyn and River were laughing it up about something with Valdis and Voxis, leaving me and Talissa to our own devices.

"Do you think things will ever get better for us?" I asked her as she looked around the room at everyone. Seeing the same things that I was seeing.

"Wars come to an end, eventually. They may not end how we want them to, but they do end. I just hope this time we are all on the right side of things. I know you worry about what Marcloff said to you. It's had me rethinking a few things myself. Just learn the facts before jumping into the ocean. You never know what lurks in the darkness." Her words, although ominous, made sense. I don't know all the facts, but I'm determined to do everything I can to ensure things are done correctly this time.

"Not to break up the party, but we should probably get going before Milara gets here, guns blazing from Otius' outburst this morning. I already see Valhime being blasted to rubble and I for one do not want to be here when it happens." River said, as he and Valyn wrapped their arms around us. I knew we had to leave. I just wanted to be selfish a little longer.

Princess, the sooner you do your duties as dual princess, the sooner we can get back together. Valyn's words carried into my mind.

I know. I just don't like the idea of us being apart. But, you're right. "Let's get going. The sooner we get to Infernia, the sooner you guys can go find Zekon." I announced to the room. Everyone gathered their things, gave hugs, and said goodbye to each other. An unspoken promise of safe returns lingered in the air between us all.

Bastian pulled me into his chest, running his fingers through my ponytail. "Please be safe, princess. Don't be reckless." He gave me a deep kiss, biting at my lower lip. I returned the kiss with the same passion as he had.

"I promise I will be as safe as I can be. I can't promise that if shit hits the fan that I won't go full psycho, but I'll try to not intentionally cause issues." I gave them my best grin as Niklaus pulled me into his arms. Another kiss, an unspoken vow, another crack in my heart as he let me go. Damian was next, a throaty growl slipped between his lips as he pulled me closer to him.

"If there was time, you wouldn't be vertical right now," I could taste the hunger in his words as he kissed me. I could happily go back to bed with all of them and say fuck todays plans. However, this was important, and our time to be selfish hasn't come yet. He released me into the arms of Valyn, my sweet summer prince. I tugged at his beard and pulled him closer to me.

"Promise me you will be careful. We saw how the seas were when we went to Floria, don't get lost in them. Please." I said as he pulled me tighter.

"I will be as careful as you will. I'll see you when you return. I love you, my little Luna." Valyn kissed me gently, leaving me longing for more. He released me to Valdis. "Keep her safe. She is your responsibility until she returns to Mistveil." Valyn's warning was anything but subtle. Each of my mates stood and waited for me to leave with the others before heading to their own realms. None of them wanted me to have to watch them leave. I appreciated them for that.

Valdis squeezed my hand as we crossed the threshold of Solaria and into Infernia. "Welcome to your home away from home, my love."

CHAPTER 8
LUNA

Bright sunlight danced with the wind and leaves as we made our way through the garden next to the Noire family home. My last time here wasn't what I expected, but then again, I didn't know the truth back then. Sapphire blooms and fire blooms were everywhere in the garden, mingling with belladonna and nightshade. The beautiful colors of reds, blues and greens were so beautiful, yet so deadly. Then again, the most beautiful things in life were the most deadly.

I watched as Talissa and the others looked around the courtyard, waiting for something to happen, but nothing did. Stones crunched under the wheels of a car coming up the drive. I watched as a black sedan pulled up in front of the manor. The driver looked like the same male from my first trip here. His smile and nod in my direction confirmed my suspicions. I waved back in a kind gesture as he opened up the back passenger door.

The tall, blonde bombshell of a beauty that was my sister-in-law stepped out from the back seat with a devilish grin on her ruby red lips. The glow from the morning sun radiated off of her, basking her in a golden hue that matched her hair. Behind her, my oldest brother-in-law crept out of the back seat. His glowering disposition was one I barely missed, but it was the sandy brown-haired male that jumped out behind him that had me smiling again. Kieran must be visiting home as well.

"Who are they?" Lumina leaned in and asked me. I smiled at her as she looked back at them all. Gabrial was looking everyone up and down like he was about to fight some of the men, while Vanessa took in the women of the group. Not in a bad way, but more of an intense interest kind of way.

"My sister and brother-in-laws. Gabrial can be grumpy, but he'll come around." I said as I stepped around the group to embrace Vanessa. "How are you holding up?" Vanessa gave me a tight squeeze before letting go.

"Well, we have a meeting in about an hour with Valmor in the main meeting room. As for the rest of your company, they can wait in the foyer while we are in our meeting," Vanessa said, glancing over at the group behind me. She leaned in and whispered. "There is another coming with him. I'm not sure if

Zekon is sending someone else or if he's coming himself. I don't want them to be seen until we know who it is."

"Do we have reason to worry?" I whispered back, hugging her once more to disguise our conversation.

"I don't know. Zekon has been very secretive since Marcloff's attack began in Floria. I have a feeling he might try to do an internal takedown of Limbris before anyone else can get hurt." She let me go and plastered a fake smile on her lips as she addressed the group. "Let's get you all inside and comfortable. Princess Luna and I have to get things ready for the meeting."

With that, she turned from us and walked toward the house, Kieran and Gabrial flanking her on either side. Valdis extended his arm for me to take as we made our way to the front door. The cherry oak had a moon and star insignia on it, much different from the first time I had been here. This whole place looked different, if I am being honest with myself. The stone exterior was now painted a greyish white, the shutters that accented the windows were now black. I wasn't sure I even recognized this house as the same from my first time here. Footsteps crunched into the rocks behind us as the group followed closely. I glanced over my shoulder as they took in the home before them and their surroundings.

"What was Hellis like before?" I asked, halting their movements behind me. Talissa looked at her mates, then at me.

"Nothing like this. It was emptier and colder. This place is thriving and looks just like home. I know you told me they were just like us, but I guess I just didn't believe you," Talissa said, looking out over Infernia as their morning sun crested over the mountains. Hellis was like a whole different world compared to Cerulia. One with its own sun and moon. Sometimes I wondered if we were even on the same planet as them.

"I've heard the stories, but I can only imagine what you all experienced firsthand," Valdis spoke softly as he opened the doors. The large room was brightly lit by the rising sun's rays coming through the back window above the staircase. My cheeks heated at the thought of Valdis's first time seeing me in my underwear was him throwing me over his shoulders and carrying me down these same steps. "I can do it again if you wish." He leaned in, whispering in my ear.

"No thank you!" I yelped as I quickly walked through the room towards the meeting room. I could hear his laughter following me down the hall. I rounded the corner to come face to face with the meeting room door. The same door I was carried through last year. What a difference a year can make.

"You can enter you know." A gruff voice came from behind me. I turned to see my other father-in-law standing behind me. King Alistar Noire of Infernia. His smile was warm and inviting, one that he had always given me, but one he rarely gave his son.

"I know, I'm just thinking about the first time I was here and how much life has changed since then." I replied. I reached for the door, but it was pulled open as my fingertips grazed the cool iron knob. A small ripple of shock fluttered across my face as Vanessa stood there in the doorway.

"You really need to start treating this place like home and not like you are a guest. This is your home from home." She ushered me in as her father followed behind me. Gabrial and Kieran were already in the room acting like security guards in the corners. "Will you two go find somewhere else to be? No one is going to come out of the fucking shadows to attack us and if so," she turned and waved her hand up and down at me. "We have a literal goddess who could turn them to ash with a snap of her fingers. You two are no match for her."

Gabrial grumbled something under his breath before pushing away from the wall with his boot. "You don't have to rub it in that we are inferior to her. Maybe we just want to feel needed, did you think of that?" He vanished through the door without another word.

"He didn't have to be so cruel, but he is right. We know she's the strongest of us all, but we do like feeling like we can help." Kieran gave me a hug then vanished out the door behind his eldest brother. I glanced at Vanessa. I could tell Gabrial's words hurt her, and I'm honestly surprised that she didn't stalk out of here after him to give him a piece of her mind.

"They will be fine and so will you." Alistar said to his daughter as he took a seat at the table. "We have business to attend to before my brother arrives."

"Are we sure he is coming?" I asked, taking the seat next to Vanessa. She threw herself down into the chair closest to the window, staring out it into the courtyard.

"I think so. He won't make his presence known until the others have laid eyes on Talissa and made sure that she is indeed alive again and no tricks are being played." Alistar slid a piece of parchment across the table to me. "This is the rundown of the two he is sending in his place. Valmor is a good person, his parents weren't the most helpful back in the day, but he chose the right side in the end. As for Rafael, he's decent. He was one of Marcloff's go to men during the first war but defected to help Talissa when his wife died by the hands of Marcloff."

I couldn't help the gasp that escaped from my lips. "He killed his wife?" I exhaled, my voice nothing above a whisper into the void. Alistar simply nodded his head. A tear slipped down my cheek.

Before we could say anything else, the door blew open forcing a strong gust of wind to enter the room. What now?

CHAPTER 9
LUNA

Papers were flying everywhere about us in the room; flames licked at my fingertips as I rose up from the chair. Vanessa was up and at my side within seconds of me leaving the chair, but it was the deep sigh from behind me that kept me from launching at the two dark figures as the entered the room.

"Do you two have to always make a mess when you enter a room? Or is the theatrics a part of the whole presentation?" Alistar's voice was calm yet laced with a deep annoyance. The wind died down to a deep musical laughter that filled the air.

"I'm sorry!" The one man laughed as he came into view. He was tall and built like a damn ox. What the hell was he eating? He smiled widely at me before grabbing my hand and placing a kiss to the top of it. "I do apologize, Zekon is one for the dramatic flair. It does have a tendency to rub off on those of us around him though. My name is Valmor, and you must be the goddess who has been causing quite the stir in Hellis."

I looked at the man before me. Bright eyes as silver as the full moon on a cloudless night, but specks of moss like green reflected in the light from the room. "Good morning. We weren't expecting you for another hour or so. Please," I waved at the seats at the table. "Have a seat, I'm sure we can make arrangements for drinks and refresh—" Before I could finish with the princess pleasantries, the other male pushed past Valmor and took a seat at the far end of the table.

"Do forgive him, he is a little cranky first thing in the morning. Isn't that right, Rafael?" Valmor glared at the other tall male. His eyes pierced into me as I took in his golden eye and the scar that ran over it. His other eye was a pale blue, lifeless and creepy.

"My apologizes." His ability to fake sincerity was astonishing. His words seemed sincere, but the rolling of the eyes said otherwise. He was annoyed at being here and honestly, I was fine if he just left. He didn't need to be here in the first place. My annoyance must've struck a chord with Valdis.

Is everything alright? Do I need to come in there and make my presence known? I let out a deep sigh, stupid fae male possessiveness.

Everything is fine. They just arrived early, and one is being a bit of a dick. Don't worry about it, I can handle anything that comes my way. So chill captain dominance. I retorted back down the bond so he would just calm down and not start a war within the house. If I had to keep my mouth in check and not tell this dude off, then he needs to keep his head on straight. His laugh rumbled through the bond, but that was the last I heard from him.

"It's fine. I am used to rudeness. My first time meeting Valdis was pretty bad; he wrecked my wedding." I giggled out as Vanessa stared at me with shock. "To be fair, he knew I was his mate long before I did. In hindsight, I'm glad he wrecked the day. It turned out so much better later on."

Valmor just stared at me, mouth agape. Rafael stood up from the chair and walked over to me. "I don't like people. They lie and have a tendency to treat others they aren't familiar with, like trash. I just expect the worst from others. However, you don't seem to treat our kind with disrespect. I was unaware of your relationship with Prince Valdis. I'm sorry." Rafael had a softer tone to his voice that didn't match his features.

"I understand that. Where I grew up, I was the outcast. I had three friends aside from my siblings who treated me like I was human and not some abomination, all because my hair is naturally blue. I learned how harsh people could be at a very young age, and I promised to never judge someone based on appearance or their past. We all do things we aren't proud of in time of distress and need. Think we can start over?" I replied, extending my hand to him. "My name is Luna Embros. You are?"

He looked at my hand for a long moment, then to Valmor, a smile crept upon his lips, enhancing a little dimple on his left cheek. Grabbing my hand with a firm grasp, he replied. "My name is Rafael, Lieutenant to King Zekon. It's a pleasure to meet you."

"The pleasure is all mine. Now, with that out of the way, please have a seat. We have some information and ideas that we would like to discuss." I released his hand and headed back to my seat. I could hear my mother's voice singing praise in my head that I didn't lose my shit on him for his disrespect.

"You did really well," Vanessa whispered as she took her seat next to me. I glanced over at Alistar, who also gave me a small smile and nod of approval. Vanessa then cleared her throat so the entire room could hear her. "I know my uncle has reservations about making his plans known to anyone outside of his inner circle. I don't blame him. With Talissa back from the dead, maybe he will be willing to help us end this war for good this time. I don't think anyone wants the amount of loss and bloodshed like before."

I watched as Valmor soaked up every word that Vanessa was saying, watching her with intense interest. Oh lord, I hope he doesn't think he has a chance with her. "You've come so far from the little girl who I watched grow up. Your uncle would be very proud of you if he could see you at this moment." Valmor said as Preena came into the room with drinks and bowls of fruits and what looked like fluffy eggs with trays of bacon and sausage. Her cart was filled with food that, for a moment, I got distracted. She placed a plate in front of me and smiled.

"Thank you Preena." I said with a smile. Her smile was wide as she nodded her head and began placing plates in front of everyone else. When she was done, she nodded her head and left the room. Plates were filled before anyone began speaking again.

"If Talissa is back, then why isn't she in here with us?" Rafael asked as he popped what looked like a blueberry in his mouth.

"She is with her other mates. We were unsure of who would be with Valmor and not to be disrespectful, but we weren't sure if we should trust you or not." I spoke bluntly, which he seemed to respect. He shrugged his shoulders and continued eating without another remark. "She is here. They all came here but are keeping their distance until the time comes for them to see Zekon."

"Zekon isn't here. He couldn't leave Minaris. With Marcloff being injured by your little stunt in Floria, Zekon has been dealing with people trying to quickly defect from Limbris. We don't have the space for all those trying to escape from him. Those who are old enough to remember the first war and how Marcloff got those to follow him do not wish to go through it again." Valmor spoke with sorrow and a painful reminder of what truly happened.

"Zekon didn't tell me any of this when we last spoke." Alistar interjected, glancing between Valmor and Rafael. "How can we help?"

"He is working with King Raynor currently since he has the space to take people who genuinely don't want to be a part of this war." Valmor spoke and my heart just broke. There were plenty of places on Cerulia where they could live in peace if people could just give them a chance.

"What about the mountains? I'm sure the Mitos runs beneath the surface as well. Maybe we can set up camps to help house those who wish to be free," I sputter out, not thinking about what that would truly mean. "Why not take down Marcloff from the inside?"

"Because we have tried that. During the first war, there were about fifty of us who tried to take him out while he was in compromising positions. Only the joke was on us. He didn't sleep, and he never took a lover to bed. We fell short on options, and all we have to show for it is the ten of us he let live. With the constant reminder of what we had to lose to stay in line." Rafael spoke softly, his voice trailing off as he spoke of the loss they had to endure. The room went silent, forks scraping on plates the only sound that filled the empty space.

"I'm sorry. I shouldn't have suggested that." I finally broke the silence in the room. Pushing my plate from me, I glanced at Vanessa. She was staring off into the glass of wine that she had been swirling during the last bit of the conversation.

"You don't need to apologize. You were just making a suggestion. How would you know what we tried before?" Valmor said as he crossed his fork and knife across his plate. I just nodded my head as I kept my focus on Vanessa.

"What is it?" I whispered into her shoulder. Icy cool air swirled around us for a moment before she broke her stare into the glass.

"You need to get back to Mistveil. Now." Vanessa stood up from the table and looked at everyone in the room. "Talissa and the others will go with you to Minaris to see Zekon. Hopefully, he can trust them enough to bring them up to speed. I need to call your grandmother. Shit's about to hit the fan." And with that, Vanessa quickly excused herself from the room, leaving us all looking at one another.

"You should listen to what she said Luna. Get back home. Quickly and safely. I'll inform Valdis and the others of your departure." King Alistar said gravely. I guess that meant I wouldn't be seeing Valdis before leaving.

"I'll escort you to the gate, your highness." Rafael stood up from the table and waited for me by the door. I quickly hugged my father-in-law, bowed to Valmor, and excused myself. This wasn't good.

CHAPTER 10
RAFAEL

I watched as Princess Luna walked ahead of me. Her blue hair dancing down her back as she walked. The morning sun had gotten higher in the sky since we first arrived, but the rays danced in her hair, shining on her silver highlights that glistened, adding depth to her hair. She intrigued me, the way she carried herself, the eyes that were both wise and young and the boldness she had to tell everything to me bluntly. Most wouldn't have dared, but no, this princess had balls bigger than half the men Zekon had in his army. She is more than just a princess, more than just a simple goddess. She was something so much more.

She glanced over her shoulder at me, then quickly back in front of her. I wonder if she was talking to Valdis, if she had mastered that part of a mating bond. Maricel always would send me her little laughs through our bond to remind me she was thinking of me and waiting for me to come home. I miss that sound. What I wouldn't give to have her back. I quickly shook off the thoughts of her before they could break me again. It's been over a thousand years, yet I still pine for her as if I just lost her yesterday.

"Are you alright?" Luna's voice carried back to me on the wind, as if her words were meant only for me to hear. She had stopped walking as we came up to the stone and wooden doorway that would take her home from here.

"I was just thinking of my wife. Sorry if I projected." I replied, folding my arms behind my back and standing straight as if waiting for an inspection from Zekon.

"You weren't projecting. I can just feel people's emotions more than I used to. It's a little jarring when my worry is pushed aside by such a deep sadness. I'm sorry if my suggestion earlier brought up terrible memories." She was apologizing as if there was anything she could've done to stop me from thinking about Maricel.

"I never stop thinking about her. And I never plan to. Losing her and my unborn, were the breaking point that I needed to switch my blind loyalty and faith in Marcloff. It also has made me the person who I needed to be. I may not have been able to save them, but I can save others now." I watched her analyze my face. I couldn't tell if she was trying to remember the details or just trying to read my mind, but it was very uncomfortable.

"Losing someone so close to you can kill you, too. Considering you are still standing here before me tells me how strong your heart is. It also tells me you aren't done yet and nor is your love. Maricel was what you needed. Maybe there is someone out there who needs you now. Even if it's just as a friend and nothing more." She extended her hand to me, and again, I hesitated to take it. I don't know why. One deep breath after another, I finally grasped her hand in return. "I'd like to call you my friend in the future. Maybe even help you when you are in the darkness. Think about it."

Before I could respond, she let go of my hand and headed through the doorway back to her home.

"I'd like to be your friend too, Luna."

The entire walk back to the house had me deep in thought. The girl I saw inside of the house at that meeting was levelheaded but emotional. Someone who would do anything to end the suffering of innocent people who didn't ask for this. Yet, the woman I just saw off was so different. She spoke as if she had lived for centuries and had more knowledge of the world and its people than any book you could find in a temple or library.

"She's a goddess," Valmor said as I made my way up the stairs and onto the patio.

"I could gather that much," I retorted, a little annoyed that he would act is if I couldn't tell that from her looks.

"No, Rafael, she is *the* goddess." Valmor rephrased his words with emphasis. "I didn't realize who she was when we were first told of this meeting. I knew she was Valdis's wife and mate, but I didn't know she was Talissa's niece."

Shock rippled across the surrounding shadows. "You mean she—" He nodded his head. I had heard rumors that one day there would be another in Talissa's bloodline who would become the Goddess of All. Time, space, the elements, becoming the bringing of death and destruction and life and restoration. That she would be stronger than Talissa, but without the need to take from her mates as if they were batteries. "Why didn't they tell us?"

"Fear that we wouldn't come. Talissa is indeed inside with the others. She's ready to go when we are. I might have you follow Luna, though. We need to make sure that she isn't a ticking time bomb waiting to implode." Valmor was thinking like an advisor, not a friend. He sees her as a potential threat, but I'll take the chance to get to know her better.

"Fine, I'll come up with some reason to show up uninvited." I replied, stalking back down the steps. "Tell Talissa I said hi. I'll see you all soon."

Valmor waved as he turned and walked back into the house. They would leave without another word, and I would follow orders until I am told otherwise. I guess for now, it's off to Mistveil.

CHAPTER 11
LUNA

Shit had indeed hit the fan while I was gone. Harold was yelling at someone in the hallway as I made my way through the halls toward my room. I could hear him complaining about someone coming over unannounced and inviting themselves into our home while we were away. I heard the other deep voice, calm yet threatening, dance through the halls.

I pivoted the corner to see my other father-in-law face to face with Otius. Fucking bastard followed me. "Get the fuck out of my house!" Harold yelled at him once more. "I don't give a fuck that you are here, or the title you used to have. You are no longer the ruler of these lands. Your great-granddaughter is, and she is not here!"

Otius looked over at where I was standing and smirked. "Seems to me she has just returned. And she's done so alone this time." I rolled my eyes as he tried to push wind at me to knock me on my ass.

"Did we not learn before that you can't move me that easily? When will you just give up?" I asked as I crossed the room and stood between Harold and Otius.

"When will you learn to have respect for me?" Otius sneered at us, irritation flaring his nostrils.

"I don't respect those who use fear as a control tactic. That's what Marcloff does, and if what you claim is true, you aren't like him. Or is what he told me true, and you invaded this land and stole it from his ancestors?" Harold looked at me with wide eyes. I guess no one filled him in on that little tidbit of information. The rage that filled Otius' face was evident.

"How dare you accuse me of being a monster!" He bellowed at me, trying to make himself look larger than he really was. I just rolled my eyes. This is annoying, and I am already over it.

"You poisoned your granddaughter and her mates while they were in Celestia. You wanted to keep them and the other gods weak and unable to return home to their families. You are a monster, so why wouldn't I look into Marcloff's claims?" I shrugged my shoulders before turning my back to him. "King Harold, is Athena around? I have need of her skills."

Harold looked at me with wide eyes and nodded. "She should be around here somewhere. I'll go find her." With that, Harold took the hint and got the hell out of the room. Athena was always lurking about. It wouldn't shock me if she was sitting in the shadows as I turned on my heels to face my great grandfather.

"You really need to learn to stop showing up unannounced. These homes are not yours; you abandoned these lands and have no claim since your replacements have already been born and took hold. Go back to Celestia. You're no use to any of us here. Even if you were, we wouldn't want your help." I glared at him, holding my chin up high as I looked him in the eyes without flinching.

He raised his hand as if he was about to strike me. I refused to flinch or back down. I met his enraged gaze with a smile. I could feel the energy in my body vibrating, begging to be unleashed on him. Shadows darkened around us as he brought his hand down towards my face, but the hit didn't land. A black band of shadows formed around his wrists. Not one of my makings. "Tsk, tsk. That is not how we treat women these days." A deep voice echoed off the surrounding walls. My heart wasn't dancing, so I knew it wasn't one of my own, but who—

"Who the fuck are you?" Otius howled, fighting against the restraints of the shadows. I turned to see the striking golden and grey eyes meet my gaze. Rafael gave Otius the wickedest of grins.

"You don't have a right to ask me who I am. Rumors of your betrayal reached all the corners of Hellis and Cerulia. You're only here to try to bully your way into power, like you did before. I won't let that happen. I also—" He paused, stepping up beside me. "Won't let you lay a finger on the eternal one."

Eternal one? What the hell was he talking about? I watched as Otius paled as he looked back at me. "Don't think for a second that we are done here. One of these days you won't have a dog to watch over you and it will just be you and I." Otius seethed through clenched teeth. Rafael released his shadow bands, dropping Otius' hand. "Consider yourself warned."

With that, Otius stormed from the room through the front doors and out into the courtyard beyond. "I wonder how long he will sulk knowing that he doesn't have the sway over the people like he used to." Rafael said from beside me as we watched Otius get consumed by a ray of golden light. I looked up at Rafael, taking in his features now that he was a little closer to me. His scar looked like, at one point in time, he would've been in an immense amount of pain. His smile, though wicked, revealed a dimple and sharp canines. I guess the fae and daemons weren't really all that different in features. Well, most of the ones I met, at least. "If you have questions, just ask. It's better then you trying to concoct your own ideas in your head."

I turned away from him and looked down the hall towards my room. I really should get stuff ready for my trip to Mirith. The Hildaria region hasn't been in too badly of shape, but I needed to talk to Nox about the dragon riders and if they could help us scout out the other realms for Marcloff's troops. Hurried footsteps halted my thoughts. Harold had rushed back into the room, my heart now pounding like a drum. "What's wrong?"

"Valyn is at the Mor. Someone launched an attack on his fleet. His mother is already on her way there, I told her I would follow once I collected you." Harold's words were rushed as he looked between me and Rafael. I caught his eyes flicking around the room looking for my great grandfather.

"Let's go. Rafael, you can make yourself at home. I need to see to my husband." I said by way of dismissing him, but he cocked his head to the side and sighed.

"Princess, I think it would be wise for me to go with you. My scent is faintly lingering on you from my harrowing rescue, last thing I need is one or all of your husbands and mates to want to kill me without explaining." Rafael had a very valid point. The scent was faint, the smell of licorice root and fire filled my nose and settled my thrumming heart just a bit. Oh dear gods, don't let the fates be a dick and place another in my life. I can barely keep up with the men I have as is.

"I may not know who he is, but he's right. Let's go." Harold ushered me for the door with Rafael right on our heels. I couldn't feel Valyn's injuries. Was he injured? Was someone else injured in his place? Questions swirled through my mind as I climbed into the back seat with Harold. Rafael took the front seat with Gus, Harold's personal driver. The houses and trees all blurred together as we barreled through the streets of Mistveil. People going on about their day, as if chaos hasn't been ensuing for months. I guess we do have a better handle on the situation here, but for how much longer?

As the car rolled to a stop, I was already out of the backseat and running through the front doors of the Mor. Maggie was already standing there waiting for me, a grim look plastered across her beautiful face. Oh no.

CHAPTER 12
VALYN

The window across the room was wide open, letting the smell of the sea waft from the window out into the mountain air. I could barely open my eyes. My right eye was burning so badly from me trying to open it, I just gave up. I could hear low chatter from outside of the door; two females and two males. I recognized my wife's voice immediately and the rage that filled it. Only my mate could make worry sound like a threat of death to all if I'm not okay. Maggie and my father's voices were clear, arguing about retaliation and how long I'll be down for. Then the other male voice chimed in and was sounding like a voice of reason, calming Luna's threats of death and violence. I could sense her washing away the raw emotions before I heard the doorknob twist and smelled her scent swirl around me.

"I'm going to fight you all. You understand this, right?" She said as she took her spot on the hospital bed next to me. I felt her melt into me as she traced circles on my bare chest. I could feel the tears stream down her cheeks and land on my chest. Her body shuddered from the cool breeze that was now trickling in from outside. A more random event with the seasons changing. Summer was finally peeking its head out from behind the pollen and flowers of the spring. I was hoping to be home in Doria for the solstice, but that might not happen.

"I'm sorry I worried you." I whispered, placing kisses on the top of her head. She grabbed my hand, entwining our fingers together and squeezing me tightly. "Victoria is here too. She wasn't as badly injured as the rest of the crew or myself. I think I have Jasmine to thank for that."

"They're mates. Of course, her pendant would protect her." Luna spoke so matter-of-factly. Like she could see the teethers of fate woven between everyone. For all I know she could see what our eyes couldn't. Maybe this new power she gained has given her the gift of sight.

"I doubt that, but they love one another in their own special way." I retorted, waiting for her to confirm my suspicion. She just huffed, going back to tracing little circles on my chest. A soft scent struck my nose, that doesn't belong to anyone of us. "Luna, my sweet darling. Whose scent is that?"

"His name is Rafael. He is part of Zekon's army. Bit of a dick, but he came to my aid when Otius showed up, starting some shit at the house." She replied so nonchalantly. Her fingers not missing a beat. "Before you go freaking out, I am fine and so is everyone at the house. Rafael came here with us to make sure you're alright and introduce himself. I also have questions as to why he followed me to Mistveil, but I'm glad he showed up when he did."

"Your great grandfather was at our home?" I said, the rest of her words sinking in slowly as the room spun. We should have protected her, but someone else was there to help her instead. That wasn't sitting right with me. She nodded her head, keeping quiet so I could process everything. "Who was at the house when you came back?"

"Your father was face to face yelling at Otius. It was a sight to behold honestly. I didn't think he would've yelled at him the way he did. I'm proud of him for standing his ground though." She said as she looked up at me, her face slightly blurry to me. "I stepped in between them the moment I heard the yelling. And I sent him looking for Athena. Rafael showed us as Otius was about to strike me. Dude seriously doesn't get that he is not a threat to me, and that I am the bigger threat in that relationship. He needs to just fuck off back to Celestia and leave the clean up from his bullshit to us. He had no issues leaving it to Talissa before, so why does he give a fuck now?"

I could see the storm clouds in her eyes, the bright light that danced in her chocolate brown eyes. She was already plotting that mans death over a thousand times in her mind. Probably also figuring out how to make all of those deaths happen in reality. Curse of the gods is never truly dying, but in her eyes that could be a torturous blessing. Part of me feels bad for the old god, the other part of me wants her to tear his throat out. The door opened again. The sound of boots scuffing across the marble floor had me trying to sit up and protectively hold Luna close to me. I didn't recognize the person—that was until the scent wafted over to me.

"You must be Rafael." I said, a bitter taste filled my mouth as I spoke his name. "Thank you for protecting my wife when we could not. We are indebted to you." He was more blurry to me than Luna was. Shit, is my eyesight going to be fucked up for much longer? I blinked my eyes quickly, trying to get my sight to focus on the stranger in front of me.

"Why do I feel you are not as happy that I was there as you claim to be?" His deep voice rumbled through the foot of the bed, leaving me feeling a vibration from my feet up to my chest. My vision slowly focused on the behemoth of a man at the foot of the bed. Holy shit. Scars littered his body and marred his face. A warrior indeed.

"I am grateful, just wondering why you were there to begin with." I said bluntly. No hiding my skepticism about his timely arrival when Luna needed someone there for her.

"Easy, Valmor sent me after the princess left our meeting. He wanted to make sure she was alright seeing that her uncle and my king happen to be related. I am here to offer assistance until I am recalled back to Minaris." Rafael was blunt. I guess I could respect it, but it didn't mean I had to trust him. "Look, I get you don't trust me and, to be frank, I don't care. I have more skin in this war than you do. I am here at request of my commander and the advisor of Minaris. I follow my orders until I am told otherwise. Like it or not, my orders now are to stay with the princess and aid her however I can."

Yeah, he was really going to piss me off and annoy me. Luna cleared her throat to get my attention. "If things are getting bad enough that a Prince of Cerulia is getting attacked, then we really could use all the help we can get." I let out a sigh. I know she's right and I should look at this arrival as a gift, but something doesn't seem right.

"If you're worried my intentions with the princess are anything but added protection, I can assure you that is not the case. Princess, your father-in-law wanted a word with you if you have a moment." He stepped from the end of the bed to the side opposite of her. Reluctantly, she sat up on the bed and pressed a kiss to my lips.

"I'll be right back. I need to make sure everything is alright." With that, she was gone from my side and out the door, leaving me alone with Rafael.

"I don't know you. Part of me doesn't want to know you. What I do want to know is why my mate has a faint scent of you on her. I get it, you were there for her, but she doesn't need protection like most women you know." I positioned myself up on the bed so I could get a better look at him. He watched my movements without moving away from the bedside.

"Look, you know nothing about me and I get the need to protect what is yours. I am here on orders. The only thing you need to know is that I won't let anything happen to her. I've suffered greatly at the hands of Marcloff and I don't want what happened to me to happen to anyone else." Rafael glanced back at the door as he spoke as if he could see her all the way out in the hallway wherever she was standing.

"It's not my place to ask or pry. I'm sorry you went through the suffering you have, but we have gone through so much with Luna over the last year. Thinking we lost her and that she died was the worst gut wrenching feeling ever. I wouldn't wish that pain on anyone else." I could feel her fingers mentally caressing my mind as I spoke of her death and eventual rebirth. It was a lot on all of us and I truly meant it. I wouldn't wish that empty hollow pain on anyone.

"She died?" Rafael raised a brow at me. Fuck. I don't think I should've opened my mouth. "Is that why Otius is back on Cerulia and not sitting in his golden castle in the stars?" I half choked on spit when he referenced Celestia like it was a glorious heaven. From the stories I've heard from River and Lumina, it was nice, but there were no golden castles or spires that took over the lands. At least not where they were. They made it seem more like it was a cozy cottage life village. I can't imagine what others believe of the Gods resting place.

"It's not my story to tell—" I began, but Rafael abruptly interrupted me.

"Were you there when she died?" His curiosity was piqued, and he was glancing at the chair in the corner. I waved my hand at the chair, gesturing him to grab it. To my surprise, he grabbed the chair with one hand and lifted it above his head before placing it down next to the bed. I guess I was lucky that he didn't scrape up the marble floor with dragging it, but dude come on.

"Yes, I was there, but again. Not my story to tell. There is so much that happened that day that it's hard to replay without the thought of losing her all over again engulfing me in sorrow." Rafael seemed on edge suddenly, fidgeting with his hands and staring at the door. "Something wrong?"

"I know you said it's not your story, but it is. I wasn't there for my wife. She can't tell her story anymore, so I have to keep her memory alive." Rafael gripped a small silver locket that was hanging on a chain around his neck. I didn't realize that he had lost his wife. Maybe even his mate. He could know exactly what that feeling is like, and I just made him relive it with my worry and fear.

"I'm sorry. I didn't know." Taking a deep breath, I thought of my words before speaking. "We each have different mothers. All our mothers loved Luna, except Fenniks' mother, Marie. She believed Fennik shouldn't have had to share a mate with his brothers. They had a bit of a falling out, but Luna refused to let Marie stay in Floria once the news of Marcloff's forces invading Floria came to our shores. Luna, Niklaus, Fennik and I all went to bring her back. However, when we arrived, she doubled down and ended up attacking Luna, stabbing her in the chest. Luna was going through another changing, one we did not know was coming. Luckily for us, she wasn't gone from us for long. It felt like an eternity, and it was the most painful thing I've ever lived through."

"Anytime we lose a mate, it's like our hearts are being ripped from our chests and we can't breathe or see straight. When Maricel was taken from me, it was a reminder and a warning. A reminder that everything I loved could be taken from me, and a warning that I had nothing left to lose except my life. I was Marcloff's right hand, but his greed and obsession became too much for most of us. We tried to kill him before the war got as bad as it did, but we got caught. The death of Maricel and our unborn were my punishment for betraying Marcloff. I should've taken her somewhere safe before we made our attempt, but I wasn't thinking straight. I just wanted to get it done and over with." He paused and closed his eyes; a deep sigh left his lips before he continued. "I left that night after being discarded by Marcloff in my empty home. I carried my wife's lifeless body with me all the way to Infernia and begged them to let me help them and bury my wife. Alistar wanted to send me to the dungeons, but Talissa and Zekon wouldn't let that happen. I joined them that night, and have been loyal to Zekon ever since. They allowed me to bury Maricel and our unborn son. Luna thinks that I may have another mate out there, but I don't know if I'm ready to find love again."

I couldn't help the tears that ran down my cheeks. I was so worried about this man with Luna that I assumed he had ill intentions. Rafael wiped a single tear from his eye as he gazed out the window. "I am so very sorry. Nothing I can say or do will take away that pain or bring them back to you. But, if Luna thinks there might be someone else out there for you, I'd listen. I met her before her changing; both of them. From human to fae, then fae to goddess. I never could've imagined my life being tethered to someone so much more powerful than me or my brothers. But I listened to my heart and for once, I believed in a life I never thought I could have. If you are truly here to assist us, then I will take all the help you can give."

Rafael looked back at me, extending his hand out. "I swear on my life that I am here to make sure that she stays as safe as I can keep her. I'll be here to lend you my power and my strength. On this, I promise."

I grabbed his hand in return and shook it. A vow to protect my mate. A promise to keep her safe. I'll take it.

CHAPTER 13
LUNA

"He needs his rest, Harold. You can't expect him to hop out of bed and get back aboard a ship to go hunt the daemons who did this to his him and the others. He could lose the sight in that eye!" I could hear Cassandra chastising her husband as I made my way to what I could only describe as a healer station. Healers bustled about the halls, glancing at me as I passed them. Their white robes adorned with a small silver circlet on their head with what looked like a small opal dangling on their forehead. Each kept their hoods high on their heads as they made their way in and out of rooms carrying bloody bandages out, replacing them white clean ones. Linens and robes were carried into different rooms as they cleaned up the room from the poor souls who were no longer occupying them.

"There is no time, though, my love. If we don't get Valyn back out to sea, the daemons could make way to Doria." Harold was doing his best to prove his point, but Cassandra wasn't one to change her mind once it was made up. Not even if I were to interject.

"You sent for me." I interrupted before Harold could dig his proverbial grave any further. They stopped arguing momentarily as Cassandra turned from her husband to embrace me. "I'm sorry for the intrusion. Is everything alright?"

"Valyn and the others were attacked by a group of sea daemons. Sirens and what we can only assume to be the vicious sea wyvern Noro." Harold spat her name out like she was some wretched creature that was out for blood.

"Noro would not harm Valyn unless they attacked her or her newborn. Considering she left us alone on our way to Anchora, you can take her off of your list." I retorted, anger flashing in my eyes. Something akin to fear flashed across Harold's face, but it quickly vanished. "Do you think Valyn could really lose his sight?"

Cassandra nodded at me before looking down the hall as Maggie made her rounds. "Maggie said there is a chance he could regain full sight, but it's not likely. He might already be blind in that eye. Valyn doesn't remember what happened after the boat went into the sea. I fear my son is not ready to leave that bed, but his father thinks he is and should be back out on the sea."

"He is strong, my love. You know this. Victoria will be ready to go soon. You know he won't let her on the ship without him at the helm. Regardless of what anyone says." Harold was right, and Cassandra knew it. Valyn was strong willed and hardheaded, but he was also understanding.

"Maybe I can help, or at least talk to him. If he wants to go back out to sea, I will go with him. I'm sure my mother and father would understand my need to be with him during this time." I offered some type of option to stop them from bickering again.

They both looked at each other as soft footsteps sounded off the floor behind me. "Good evening Princess Luna. I wasn't aware that you had made your way here." Maggie embraced me in a tight hug before looking at Cassandra and Harold. "I have some bad news. Valyn has suffered a partially torn optical nerve. He is already complaining of blurry vision. I fear he got here too late for us to catch the damage before it had gotten that bad."

"Your healers can't reattach it?" Harold asked, but the resignation in Cassandra's eyes told me everything I needed to know. She saw this coming. She knew that his vision was being stolen from him.

"We have repaired it, your highness. That doesn't mean that the damage hasn't already been done. Even with our abilities, we can't snap our fingers and fix it like it never happened. We are just not that blessed. I'm sorry." Maggie continued speaking, but I couldn't hear a word she was saying. A vibration shock waved through my body as I stalked down the hallway back to Valyn's room. The door was ajar when I stopped in front of it, taking a deep breath. I can do this.

I pushed the door open and stared at my mate, ignoring the daemon sitting in the chair next to the bed. "Luna, what's wrong?" Vayln's concern should worry me. It should worry me, but all I feel is rage. The thought of him not being able to see with both of his eyes is unimaginable. I refuse to let that happen. The room darkened with each step toward the bed I took. Slowly, the night sky took over the room, stars bursting across the floor beneath my feet.

"Holy shit! What is going on?" I could hear the daemon shouting from what sounded like under water. I just watched as my summer mate sat as still as stone on the bed as I approached. He put up his hand as if stopping the daemon from coming back to the bedside or interfering with what I had to do. I felt eyes on me as I moved onto the bed, cradling my mate's face between the palms of my hands. I could feel the coarse hair of his beard roughen against my skin. He pressed his cheek into my hands and let me feel him relax, his way of assuring me that he was not afraid of what I was about to do. It meant more to me that he trusted me and believed in me.

"I'm going to fix you," I whispered into his ear as I placed a trail of kisses from his cheek to his lips. His eyes were closed, but I knew which one had been damaged. A long red scar slashed across his right eye. "Open your eyes." With that simple command, he opened his eyes and smiled at me. His turquoise eyes, normally bright and lively, were now dull with the one going foggy. I wasn't about to let him lose his sight. I told him I will fix this and I will.

"Leave the scar." The only thing he said as he closed his eyes again. I pressed a kiss to his lips and dug deep down for the white flames to burst up to the surface. I could feel the pure fire and rage fill me as I pressed a kiss to his eye. White flames exploded from my body, snaking its way out of the room and into the rooms of all the living in need of healing. I could feel the pain and sorrow of those who had died and the heartbreak of those who had been left behind.

This was more than just Valyn and his crew. The pain and hurt threatened to consume me, the flames burning brightly as they reached the last room; that of a small child. My heart thundered in my chest as the child lay there barely breathing, his mother crying while holding onto his little hand. The father pleading with the healers to do more for him. I let the flames wrap the child up in a soft little blanket, slowly feeling my way through the poor boy. His heart was failing him, his body too weak to fight off the infection that was spreading. He wouldn't make it through the night if I didn't help him.

His mother let out a gasp, her eyes wide with fear as she watched her baby boy get plucked out of bed by the flames and brought to me. The parents followed, keeping close to their son, who smile weakly at them. He was too young to accept this fate. I wouldn't allow it. The flames gently carried him through the room to me as I turned from Valyn. His parents halting in the doorway as I wrapped their son up in my arms.

"It will all be okay now, little one. You have so much more life left to live." And with that, I placed my hand over his tiny failing heart and let the flames repair him. Bit by bit, the flames gently worked their way through his body, killing off the infection and wrapping around his heart to repair the damage he was born with. Color flushed his cheeks, his bright blue eyes opened wide with wonder as he took me in. There was no fear in him. This strong little boy would live a long, healthy life. Be damned if I would let anything but that happen.

"It doesn't hurt anymore." His voice sounded so strong as he looked from me to his parents. "Mommy! Daddy! It doesn't hurt anymore!" I placed the child down on the ground and watched as he ran into his parents' arms. They hugged him tightly and cried. The heartbreak they felt earlier was gone. All I could feel now was joy and love in its place.

"Thank you! Thank you so much, your majesty!" His mother cried out as I slipped from the bed and onto my feet. Gracefully, I made my way past those in the room watching the show and knelt down next to the child.

"What is your name?" A smile crept across my face when I saw his eyes roam my face. Taking in whatever he saw with wonder and awe.

"My name is Tulan," he replied with a bow. I ruffled his short, wavy brown hair and gave him a big smile.

"It's nice to meet you, Tulan. My name is Luna. You go out there and live a nice, long, and healthy life. Go out and play. You deserve it." Before I could stand, Tulan wrapped his arms around my neck and gave me a big hug. A feeling of warmth and relief flooded me at that moment. His parents kept bowing and uttering their thanks, but the only thanks I needed was right here in my arms. The strong beating heart of the child that needed to live.

CHAPTER 14
LUNA

Everyone was chattering about the boy's miraculous recovery, people looking at me not with fear or suspicion but with admiration and excitement. Tulan's smiling face will stick with me for years to come. Gone was the sick little boy that I just happen to stumble upon, and in his place is the child who now has a full life ahead of him. Hopefully, one I can make better for them all.

"Are you alright, Princess?" Valyn asked as I sat next to him on the bed. I looked him over. His eye was no longer cloudy, but the scar remained. I nodded, as I looked back at Tulan. He was waving at me as him and his family left the room. I gave a small wave back and a reassuring smile, although doubt was beginning to take root in my mind. What if I did the wrong thing? What if I can't fix the world outside these walls for him? For any child that needs a safe future. "You'll see him again. I can feel it."

"Did I do the right thing?" I asked, my voice barely a whisper. Valyn grabbed my cheeks and made me look at him.

"In what world would you think you did the wrong thing?" His thumbs stroked my cheeks as tears slid down them. I haven't felt this heavy before in my life, like a weight was pressing down on my chest and I couldn't breathe. "Relax my love. Take a deep breath. In through the nose, out through the mouth. Good girl. Do it again."

I closed my eyes and took a deep breath, slowly releasing the air that filled my chest. I followed Valyn's commands as my heart slowed to a steady pace. Am I having a fucking anxiety attack? I mean, I've had them before, but nothing like this. I took another deep breath for good measure. Why do I feel guilt for saving his life? Is this a warning that something bad is going to happen? Did I throw off some type of balance?

"I've never seen something like that before." Rafael's voice cut through my thoughts. Opening my eyes, I watched as he slowly made his way back to the seat beside the bed. "Everyone in the Mor is healed. Not a single person shows any sign of illness. Broken bones, mended. Those on deaths door, walking out as if they just had a cough. Have you done that before?"

"Not that I can recall. I mean there was the white flames in Floria, but that just healed the land and removed the daemon corpses." I said, quickly covering my mouth. "I'm sorry I—"

Rafael raised his hand. "I know you're not about to apologize to me for killing the scum that have attacked innocent people." He raised a brow at me, and I felt so small. Why was I about to apologize for removing the rotten corpses from the land? They deserved to die. Or did they? Did they buy into the gaslighting delusion of Marcloff?

"You said you and others tried to overthrow Marcloff. You left. How many of the others stayed out of fear?" Rafael looked stunned by my blatant question. Valyn squeezed my hand as if silently warning me to tread lightly.

"Too many. I had nothing left. No one left he could hold over me to keep me there. The others had more family, children, parents, wives and husbands. I was used as a warning to those who would make the choices I did. He punished the others differently. Why do you ask?" Rafael said through gritted teeth.

"If they stayed out of fear, does that make them any less than you? They're following orders to kill so their families don't die. That doesn't make them scum. They're being tortured, maybe not physically but one hundred percent mentally. If you had more family in Hellis, what would you have done? Stayed or still left?" I pulled my hand away from Valyn as I stood up. I could feel the rage coming back to me. Marcloff is using his people as pawns and threatening to kill them if they don't obey. That's not a leader; that's a conqueror.

"That is the price of being the Goddess of All." A gentle voice cut through the rage. I turned to see Illisandra standing in the doorway. Her lithe body draped in a blush dress that covered all the way to her ankles. She gracefully made her way into the room and smiled at me. Her eyes were like the sun, bright orange with flecks of obsidian throughout. It was slightly unnerving to be in her presence. "May I sit?" She gestured at the other chair in the room. I looked over at Valyn and Rafael, both looking frozen in time; unmoving. "They won't have any issues with my being here."

Illisandra walked over to the chair and took a seat, looking at the chair across from her. I sat down, unsure of why neither of the men were moving. "What did you do to them?" I asked, wary of whatever she was actually capable of. I knew nothing about my great-grandmother except that she is mated to Otius and was an accomplice to his plan to keep my aunt and her mates in the afterlife.

"No one told you what my powers are, did they?" She let out a sigh and looked past me. The light reflecting off of a small, pink, star-shaped mark under her left eye, gave me pause. It wasn't like the freckles that Talissa and I have. It was something else. Her long silver-blonde hair cascaded down the back of the chair, barely touching the floor. She adjusted herself in the seat as if it were uncomfortable for her to be in. These chairs were plush and bouncy. I don't know how she wasn't comfortable. "I guess I can't really blame them for not telling you. Everyone thinks Otius is the one who can control time, but they're wrong. My husband is the god of myth and creation. Can you guess what my powers are yet?"

She looked past me to Valyn and Rafael, who still had yet to move. I glanced around the room and noticed that the dust that would normally dance in the sun was suspended motionless in the air. The clock on the wall stopped ticking. The birds outside the window were suspended above the ground, unmoving. I gasped. "You're the Goddess of Time?!"

Illisandra chuckled and smiled. "Of course. I don't know where history took the power from me and granted the title to your great-grandfather, but it's always been mine. But now that you know my secret. I am here to talk to you about yours."

I looked over at her with hesitation. If she were the Goddess of Time, then why the hell hasn't she fixed things? Turn back time and stop this stupid war from happening. I also picked up on her mention of my not-so-secret secret. "What do you want to know?"

"I don't want to know anything. I want to talk to you about what your title means. What being the Goddess of All truly means to the world as we know it. You just saved a little boy's life, who was knocking on death's door. If you had been a moment later, he would be dead and gone from your grasp. Or would he have been?" What the hell was she talking about?

"He would've been lost to me if I hadn't saved him. There is no option for me once they have crossed the threshold into death." I said with certainty. Well, at least I made it seem like I was certain, but what if I wasn't? What if I could drag someone back from beyond and give them life again? Would that make me a death god or a god of life and creation?

"Your mind is spinning, child. I need you to just focus. You have your great-grandfather in a panic. Not even your grandmother has the strength that you do. My sweet child Vanalli has the same white flames as you do. Otius is the only other who possesses the ability to use them. Neither of them, however, has brought someone destined for death back to the side of the living and then some. That boy will live a much longer life than was planned out for him by the fates. Your nature as a human, as fake as it was, was to question things, become strong and independent and fight for yourself but also be a caregiver, a child who would love with all their heart and then some. Someone who would destroy the world to save those they loved and in turn lose themselves in the process. When you had your first changing, you were in the throes of war. You jumped headfirst into a battle with zero hesitation and fear for your own life. After that, you overcame daemons, a troubled fae king, and you faced off against the greatest evil this universe has seen in Marcloff. Yet, you cleansed the entire battlefield and city of Floria before it fell to the decay and rot that Marcloff had spread. You destroyed the corpses of daemons and left those of our fallen alone, just buried. You didn't feel doubt or regret then. But meeting Rafael has given you doubt. Marcloff has given you doubt. I understand it all. My curse with my powers is that I can see time and every possible path forward, but I can't go back and change the past without rippling the future. Ripping you away from this world." She paused and looked at me and smiled. "Luna, I refuse to change any part of the past. If I do, you will forever be lost. Never born. And the war and world that we have now will cease to exist. You are the end goal of this world. I hate to tell you that the fate of the worlds rest on your shoulders, but it does. Your doubt is proof that you can change the world for the better. Your doubt shows that you're still alive and not dead to the world around you. Just know that you control the destiny of everyone. You can choose to lead an army of the undead into Hellis and give the daemons a chance at revenge, or you can lead an army of light into the darkness and destroy cities in the name of you and the gods. You and I need to talk more, but right now this is all I can offer you. A choice. See both sides. Your aunt came close. But you have surpassed her. It's all up to you."

Illisandra stood and pulled a silver chain from around her neck. A silver star pendant with two crescent moons on either side dangled at the bottom. "This is my blessing to you. It will grant you the access you need to my powers. Even as the Goddess of All, you still will need help along the way. You haven't fully come into yourself yet. But you're getting there. Just know I love you, and if Otius ever comes back to bother you, just continue to put him on his ass. He needs a reminder that he's not the strongest out there anymore."

She put the necklace on me and pulled me into a hug. "Thank you." Was all I could muster before the sounds of the world around me flooded into my ears again and she was gone. Valyn and Rafael looked at each other than me. "If you're feeling up to it, we should probably head to Doria. You were attacked on the way there, Marcloff must be going for the summer realm next."

"I'm ready once Maggie says I'm good." Valyn said, giving me the world's most puzzling look. *Did something happen that I am unaware of?*

I got a visit from someone I didn't know I needed a visit from. I'll tell you later. I looked at Rafael. "I'm sorry for what I said earlier. But I'm still waiting for that answer."

"If I still had family that could be hurt by Marcloff if I left, I would still be there by his side. But I would be sabotaging him the entire time. I wouldn't stay there willingly." Rafael said with such resolve that I felt it. "Maybe there are those that stayed that are doing that. I can only hope."

"Hope is the only thing we can have right now. Are you going to come with us to Doria?" I asked him as I made my way to the door. I looked back at him grinning.

"Absolutely."

CHAPTER 15
LUNA

Minutes ticked into hours as we waited for Maggie to get to us. Valyn insisted on everyone else being checked on before him. He knew we were fine; he knew I wasn't going anywhere. Rafael stood at the window watching out over the city. I can only imagine what is going through his mind. Something tells me he didn't think about those he left behind and the choices they had to make to protect their loved ones. Hell, I didn't think about it. Why didn't I think about it the moment Marcloff said things weren't as they appeared? Why did I so blindly run into war not knowing the full story? My mind began spiraling as I looked down at my hands. I've taken the life of Hilmer's. I've taken the lives of countless daemons in Floria. I took down creatures in Taiga and a fucking demi-god. Why? To what end?

"Are you alright?" Valyn asked, squeezing my hand. I looked up at my summer mate. His silver hair was still cropped tight to the side of his head, the top pulled up in a bun. His dark beard still full on his cheeks and jaw. His bright turquoise eyes still shining like the sea waters, just now a scar mars his face. He was still one of the most beautiful beings that I have ever laid eyes on.

"Physically I am. Mentally, there's so much going on in my head that it's hurting." I rested my head on his arm as footsteps sounded in the doorway. I looked up hoping to see the high priestess, but instead Valyn's almost twin was standing in the door. "Victoria!" I jumped up from the seat and ran to give her a hug. We had gotten close since our time on The Selestine. "I'm glad you're okay."

Victoria just laughed and gave me a hug. "I hear we all have you to thank for our quick recovery. I was expecting to be in here for a while. So, thank you."

"We're going to head to Doria after everyone is checked out. If Marcloff is sending an army to the summer realm, we need to be there to protect it." Valyn said as he finished pulling his shoes on. Victoria nodded and then looked over at Rafael, who was leaning up against the wall, his eyes closed like he was sleeping, but I could see his shadows dancing restlessly behind him.

"Who is that?" Victoria leaned in and whispered. I guess she didn't realize that he wasn't actually sleeping. He peeked an eye open and looked at her. Taking in the tall, silver-haired beauty that stood next to me.

"My name is Rafael. Where she goes—" he tipped his head in my direction. "I go. For now."

"Creepy." Victoria glanced at Valyn to see how to move forward with Rafael. Friend or foe. Right now, I say, friend. Hopefully, he doesn't turn to foe later. "I'll call Westley and see how far out he and Peter are. The Birkenhead should be close by."

"Did The Selestine fall?" I questioned. I wasn't sure which ship they were on when they were attacked. Victoria shook her head and left the room, holding her phone to her ear.

"We were on a different ship. Hence, that is why we were ambushed. The Selestine and The Birkenhead have the best radar systems in all the realms. We were trying to be discreet when we left." Valyn finished tying his boots before standing and pulling me tightly to his chest. "I don't think going by sea is a good idea, Luna."

"You got attacked on the sea. How else will we get rid of what attacked you if we don't follow the same path?" I pressed. He knew I was right. If there were creatures in the water that could harm innocents and not that far from shore, then we need to handle that. We can't have the local fishers getting hurt or worse, the innocent children swimming at the beaches.

"She has a point. If we want to get results and make waves, no pun intended, we need to get out to sea. The sooner, the better." Rafael kicked off the wall and stood beside Valyn.

"Prince Valyn," Maggie began as she entered the room. "You're free to go. If the others are any indication of how well your wife can heal people, you'll be just fine. Luna, can I have a moment of your time?"

I nodded. "Of course. What can I do for you?" Maggie waved her hand at the door and excused herself. I followed her lead. Clearly, she wanted to speak in private, and I can respect that. "Is everything okay?"

"I'm worried about the amount of power your expressed healing the entire Mor." She began, her eyes examining me as if she was expecting to see fatigue or some type of crack in the foundation.

"I feel fine. A little mentally exhausted, but that is just because I'm waging a war inside my head." Maggie raised her hand as if asking me to stop so she could continue.

"Do you know exactly how many people you healed today?" I shook my head. I wasn't conscious of the body count. "Two hundred and forty-nine. Not including the four dead in the morgue that sat up on tables."

My eyes went wide. "What—what did you just say?" I had to be hearing things wrong. There is no fucking way I brought the dead back. I would've felt that.

"You brought four fae back from the dead, Luna. Four fae who had been dead for several hours. You healed them as if they hadn't just been pronounced dead. Their families are currently hugging the ones they thought they lost forever." Maggie's concern seemed to grow the more she spoke. "You didn't know you brought the dead back did you?"

I just shook my head. The room began to spin, the walls suddenly too close. I started hyperventilating. How did I bring the dead back unknowingly? Is that what Illisandra meant when she said I could bring an army of the undead to Hellis's doorstep? Can I resurrect the dead? Is that even an option? I couldn't breathe. I tried to find the wall behind me but missed, falling flat on my ass. I could hear Maggie's voice, but it sounded like it was coming from above water. Like I was drowning. Victoria was in my face within moments. Holding my cheeks and forcing me to look at her, but I just looked past her. Tears fell down my cheeks like the rivers running down the mountains. I can't bring everyone back from the dead. It would throw the balance off. But what if—

LUNA! A deep voice cut through my thoughts. The smell of smoke and snow surrounded me instantly. Darkness surrounded my vision, pulling me into my mind. Just so I could see him. Bastian was there, arms out, waiting for me to collapse into him. *Deep* breath, *baby girl. Come on. One. Two. Three. Release. Again.*

I followed his instructions. Slowing my breathing down, calming myself down. Tears still flowed, but I wasn't hyperventilating anymore. I held on to him as tight as I could. I know he wasn't physically with me. I know I am at the Mor, and he is in Taiga, but for now this is as real as it's going to get for me.

Good girl. What is going on? I could feel your panic all the way here in the winter realm. Are you alright? Did something happen? Do I need to come home? He listed off every question in a rush. I wanted to tell him to come home. I wanted to tell him I needed him, but that would be selfish of me.

A lot happened. Valyn got attacked. He's fine now, and so is the rest of the crew. But I did a thing. And I don't know how I did it. I didn't even feel it when it happened. I'm messing with the balance of life and death completely by accident. I don't know what I did wrong, or how to fix it, or even if I should fix it. The words tumbled from my lips. Bastian held me, just letting me get everything out. I began explaining everything that had happened and what Maggie had just told me. *Am I a monster, Bastian?*

If you are a monster my love, then I am a daemon. Well one of the worst ones. You care so much, that is nothing to be ashamed of. As for bringing the dead back to life. You didn't do it on purpose. If they are back to their loved ones with no pain and no memories of them dying, then how is that bad?

I don't know if they remember or not. I kind of starting spiraling after Maggie told me. I didn't know I could do that. Something Illisandra said earlier rang out in my mind. *What if I could bring the dead back that were wronged by Marcloff? What if I could grant them peace even if it means they can only return to this world for a brief time. Bastian's eyes went wide. Maybe I should've kept that thought to myself.*

Could you do it, so they won't feel pain? We have rage for what Marcloff has been doing, but I can only imagine the unrest of those he wronged and those who died by his hand. But would they go back to the afterlife when Marcloff dies? He wasn't disappointed in my idea. No, he took it and ran with it.

I don't know. But—I grabbed the necklace from around my neck. *I think I know someone who can answer that question for me.*

Then go do what you have to do baby girl. I think you should probably let your guard back down and go back to Valyn. He's freaking out. Bastian put his fingers beneath my chin, urging me to look up at him. *Go save the world baby. I'll be here every step of the way. Taiga and the winter realm have your back. Let me know when you're ready for me to come home.* He leaned down and kissed me. My lips parting as a silent invite. He seized the moment and devoured my lips. His hands roamed my body as he growled into me. *That wasn't very nice.*

Soon I'll come visit you and we can do this for real. I dragged my nails under the back of his shirt. *Just be ready for me.*

Forever and always. He kissed me once more before reluctantly letting go.

Forever and always.

CHAPTER 16
VALYN

Her breathing hitched as her eyes fluttered. I probably should've given her space, but she had me panicking. Maggie was filling me in on what she had told Luna right before she collapsed. Everyone's voice was just chaotic noise, like radio static. All voices but one. I couldn't hear Luna, but I could pick up Bastian's voice crystal clear. She was at a loss about what she had done. She doubted herself and whether she was doing the right thing. I wish I could take all of her pain away.

"If she collapses again, she can't go out to sea, Valyn. We can't take the chance of something happening to her out there." Victoria was just trying to be logical, but I turned on her in that moment.

"Luna will not leave my side. We need this to end. She is our hope and our future. Probably the only person who can take down Marcloff and walk away alive. I will not treat her as if she were some weakling." I snapped. Rage bubbled in my stomach, searching for a way out.

"I'm not saying she's weak. I'm saying if she passes out again out at sea and slips off the fuck deck then what? You jump in and save her?" Victoria bit back. She was within an inch of my face before I knew it. "Not even Jasmine can keep us safe in the waters right now. Do you think she even wants me out there? She doesn't know I'm in the Mor unless someone got word to her. If she finds out, there will be hell to pay for me. So stop being fucking selfish and think about more than just you and her."

Victoria stormed off down the hallway away from us. Luna rested her hand on my arm, startling me. "Go apologize. I'll be fine. If she'd rather me not be on the ship out of worry, I can ask Nox to fly me over to Doria where we can regroup."

"It was your idea to face the sea. Clearly, we can't do it without you. We see what happens when we're not together." I tried replying with swagger, but it felt so forced. I was nervous; I worried about her mental state and what her powers were going to do to her physical being, not just mental. "I'll go talk to her. You just get checked up on. Make sure you didn't hit your head when you collapsed."

Luna brushed her lips to mine. "Go fix this." Maggie was behind Luna in seconds helping her to her feet and lightly scolding her for not sitting down when she felt disoriented.

Maggie was like a mother hen when it came to making sure Luna was safe.

I nodded at Maggie then headed down the hall to find Victoria bitching to Westley about how I have blinders on and I'm not thinking clearly. Poor Westley looked like he needed an excuse to leave. "Westley, can you excuse us? Try to find Patrick and the others and tell them we'll be leaving at dawn and to get some rest. Mary has rooms open and waiting at The Balemore for us all."

"Thank you, Valyn. I'll get right on it." He turned to Victoria. "Sorry to cut this conversation short. Please excuse me." Westley bowed, his dark chestnut hair sweeping his brows. He gave me a look of gratitude as he straightened and left us.

"I'm not going to apologize for what I said Valyn. You're not thinking like yourself right now. I get it she is your mate and she is probably the most powerful being walking the realms right now. But, what happens to everyone if something happens to her? Will you be able to do what's right by your people or will you abandon us for her?" Victoria's questions and fears were valid.

"I'm not looking for an apologize. Actually, I'm here to apologize for snapping on you. Luna understands your worries. She's offering to fly with Nox if that would make you more comfortable. As for your list of questions. If I put Luna before my people, she would be absolutely pissed at me and would lose her shit on me." I chuckled. Victoria knew I was right. Luna would rip me a new ass.

"Hehe, I guess you're right. I'm just a little shaken up I guess. It's not often the sea betrays us." Victoria turned from me to look out the window. The setting sun colored the normally blue waters with shades of orange and yellow. The sinking feeling that she's right and the sea finally betrayed us settled deep in me. "Jasmine is worried about her mother. The seas have become unpredictable and she can't reach her by phone anymore. Valyn, what if Marcloff got to Undine?"

That was not a thought on my radar. I didn't think that the Goddess of the Seas could be in trouble, or that she even walked these lands anymore if I'm being honest. "We can figure something out. Maybe we can talk to Vanalli. She might know a way of getting in touch with her."

"That would be great." She paused, took a deep breath then looked at me. "I'm sorry. I shouldn't have snapped like I did. There is just a lot going on and I've never not felt safe out at sea. With or without Jasmine's ever protective hand." I pulled my cousin into a hug. She stood there stiff as a board as I gave her a tight squeeze.

"We've never not been safe at sea. Things are in chaos right now. The sea is no exception." I let her go, clearly I've made her uncomfortable. "We will get through this like we've gotten through battles before; side by side. I can't do this without you, Westley or Patrick. We're a team remember."

"We've got your back, but do me a favor." I raised a brow at her. "Don't do that weirdness again. You barely hug me when are parents are around, let alone when it's just us." I could help busting out laughing. She was right though, I never used to do that.

"I thought you could use a hug, blame Luna for this change." I chuckled. Footsteps echoed off the floor behind me, four different sets. I turned to see Luna, Rafael, Westley and Patrick all standing there together. "Well, I guess we set sail at dawn."

Everyone nodded and we made our way out of the Mor and on our way to our evening lodging. Tomorrow is going to be the start of a long journey.

CHAPTER 17
VICTORIA

The Balemore was rowdy, with sailors given new life thanks to Luna and her powers. I walked in with the Moore brothers, both speaking quietly to one another in hushed whispers behind me. I know they're not talking about me, but I wish for the love of everything that they would just talk at a normal volume. The warm summer air entered the lobby with us, causing some curses from the other patrons who were sitting in the little sitting area at the entrance. I couldn't help but roll my eyes. If they don't want the heat bothering them, then they should move to a table further away from the door.

The woman behind the front counter was not from around here, and it was obvious from her thick accent. She was Skothi. Nothing bad at all about her people, but they were usually known as very blunt people. Something I could truly appreciate. "Welcome to the Balemore. I'm assuming you're part of the

Doria crew?" She smiled widely at us, taking a mental note of our features.

"Yes ma'am. I hope our crew hasn't been wreaking havoc this entire time." I offered an apologetic smile back at her while casting a glare at the crew who were being overly loud and obnoxious.

"Nonsense. They have been a joy here. It's nice to know what not everyone around the realms is stuck up or looks down on others for being different. Your crew has been a pleasure to have. My name is Mary, and I run this establishment. Prince Valyn has made the arrangements for you all to stay the night here. I told him if you needed more time than just the night, we have plenty of space." Mary's reassurance was the only reason my crew wasn't getting reamed a new ass right now.

"Thank you for the offer, but sadly, we are leaving at dawn. Next time I come to visit my cousin here in Mistveil, I'll come back and stay here." I offered her a smile and looked back at my men. Every was standing, not a single scratch on them. I wonder if they know how lucky they are to still be alive, and who to thank. My eyes landed on Ralph. His ice-blue eyes locked onto mine as he stood up and excused himself from the group.

Westley had stepped up to finish discussing arrangements with Mary as I excused myself to speak with Ralph. "How the fuck are we alive, Vic?" Ralph's deep voice sounded hollow. You would never have guessed by looking at him that he was cut open and gutted like a fish, barely alive only a few hours ago. I walked past him, forcing him to follow me to a small little table in the corner of the room. The rest of the crew watched my movements, silencing their loud banter as I moved. I should address them as a whole, but Ralph needed more answers than the brief gloss over. He was knocking on death's door, and he knew it.

I took the seat against the wall, looking out at everyone as they sat down and hushed their conversations to low whispers between the tables. Patrick and Westley were grabbing keys from Mary with smiles and that brotherly charm that made most of the women in the city's panties drop. I really didn't get it. Then again, I preferred the company of the women who were fawning over them. Ralph took the seat in front of me, blocking everyone else from looking at us. I took a deep breath, thinking long and hard about how much I wanted to divulge about Luna and what she is truly capable of. None of these men were there in Floria to see what she was capable of. Stories have already begun being told in whispers to children at night before bed of the goddess who walks amongst us that's here to bring peace to our lands. I thought my cousin was insane after he told me what happened. I didn't believe him until today.

"What do you know of Valyn's wife?" I asked, my voice barely above a whisper. Ralph shifted in his seat as I watched a bead of sweat dripping down from his dark black hair onto his forehead. I don't even think he has ever met her. Let alone laid eyes on her.

"Nothing. Just that she is his mate, and she is mated to his brothers and that daemon prince from Infernia. Why?" I raised a brow at him. Waiting for him to tell the truth of what he's really heard. After a few moments of silence, he relented with a sigh. "Fine, fine. What I've heard just sounds like fairy tales, Vic. That she slipped into Floria's main castle that was under siege and not only took Marcloff on head-to-head but cleansed the realm of all the deceased daemons with the white flames, leaving those fallen on our side buried with sapphire blooms surrounding them. Vic, no one is that powerful. No one has been able to use those flames since Vanalli herself walked the realms."

I shook my head. How do I tell this oaf that the Goddess he speaks of still walks the realms freely? Or that Luna is her grandchild? "Maybe you need to hear it from Valyn himself. She is the reason you're still sitting here alive and breathing—"

I stood up and looked over Ralph's head to all the eyes looking in our direction. Skepticism and exhaustion laid on everyone's faces. Desperation and fear lied there as well. "Luna is the reason we all stand here alive, and unscathed. Even from death herself. The sea tried to claim us. Something it has never done to us before. I understand your hesitation to get back on the deck and out to sea, but we aren't meant to live solely on land, and you all know it. She is going to sea with us; she wants to help us save our people before war starts to tear apart our realm like it did with the Autumn realm. Any objections?"

I waited patiently as they all took it in, looking between each other and whispering softly. Westley stepped over to us with keys in hand. "If you wish to return to Doria by sea, you have a room here. If you are too much of a coward to fight back at the sea—" He paused looking around at all of the crew. "There's no room here for you. Find a safer way home and tell your families you have left the royal navy. We owe the princess a gratitude of thanks. She didn't owe it to any of us to heal us and save us. Yet here we all are alive. She's willing to go out to sea and help us, the least you all can do is show your appreciation."

Westley stood there with his hand extended, keys sitting in the palm of his hand for those who wanted to stay. We waited patiently, observing how long everyone took before making their moves. Patrick grabbed his key first. "All hail the princess, right?" He winked at me and took off up the stairs to the rooms. I watched Yuri and Elana take one key for them to share a room. Teikan stood up, bowed to me and grabbed a key. Granth, Ralph, Rupert and Magi were still talking amongst themselves when I finally said fuck it and grabbed my own key.

"I'll know by morning who shows up to the docks and who was too cowardly to follow the oath that swore when they got their positions. Westley, take a damn key and leave the others on the table. We don't have time for anymore bullshit." I turned to the remaining crew, "If you choose not to sail with us at dawn, don't let me see your faces around Doria. And don't expect the royal family to understand how a stranger can care more for our people than those born in the realm."

Westley followed orders and left the remaining six keys on the table. One for Ralph, one for Granth, one for Rupert and Magi, one for Elsa and Lyra, and one each left for Maurice and the other for Paisely. By morning I assume that at least three of those keys will still be on the table. I left without another word, heading to my room for what will be the longest night that I've had for quite some time. I wish tonight that I wouldn't be left alone with my thoughts.

CHAPTER 18
RAFAEL

I looked so out-of-place standing in the middle of this large spare room they had set up for me. Luna laughed as she walked back into the room with her hands filled with all different types of clothing. "You can relax, you know. You're not going to get attacked in your sleep here. Just try to get some sleep. I don't know how many ships you've been on, but the Royal Navy has some pretty impressive ones." She made idle chat as she handed me a few pairs of sweatpants and a few options of shirts, all different sizes and colors. I raised an eyebrow at her as I took the garments from her hands.

"Please tell me these aren't your mate's clothes that you're offering me." I sniffed the clothes. Lilacs and some type of berry scent filled my nose, making me sneeze. "What in the seven cities of Hellis is that god awful smell?" I pushed the clothes as far from my face as possible, wrinkling my nose. Again, Luna just laughed.

"Okay, first of all, no. They do not belong to any of my mates. Niklaus and his mother design clothes, and these are a few of the samples Nora dropped off to us a while ago that Niklaus wasn't in love with, so they got put in a box and kind of forgotten about. I figured, why not let them go to some good use. Second, the smell you're smelling is lilacs and strawberries. I wasn't about to let you wear stale-smelling clothes. That would just be rude of me."

"So, you want me to smell like a woman?" I put the clothing down on the dresser by what she told me was the bathroom.

"If it's that bad, then don't wear them. But if you wear nothing in that bed, you're the one changing the sheets." She turned away from me, waving her hand above her head. "Sleep tight. If you need anything, Valyn and I are just down the hall. Dinner will be brought to you unless you want to head to the kitchen yourself. Everyone knows you're here and are expecting to see you out and about. So, don't be shocked if someone knows your name."

"I think I'll be okay. If I need something, I'll just find my way around. I'm pretty good at it." I replied as she reached the door. "Luna—" She paused in the doorway, looking over her shoulder at me. "Thank you for letting me stay here and not shoving me in the Balemore. I think I'd stick out like a sore thumb there."

She just smiled and left. I didn't need to thank her, but she also didn't need to have me stay here. I closed the door and pulled off the shirt I had been wearing since early this morning. I stood in front of the mirror and took in all of my scars and tattoos. Each one telling a story, some of love, some of hate and war, but most of sorrow. I looked at the faded blue lips tattooed on the front of my left hip. I let the memory of Maricel's lips gracing my skin, leaving her lipstick on me just so I could have them forever inked on my skin, flood my mind. To think I did it on a dare, I guess I will forever be grateful to still have some part of my love with me. My eyes moved to the twin, snake handled daggers that adorned each of my forearms. One shaded black, the other white. The black snake had a ruby eye, while the white one had a sapphire eye. My true self, with the darkness and the light in me that so desperately wants to do right and good in the memory of Maricel and our little one. My eyes landed on the final part of my body that I would never want to leave my skin. The scar that dragged from the base of my throat almost to the tip of my belly button. It was several shades lighter than the rest of me; all edges jagged from where it kept ripping open during the three years it took to heal. Marcloff left that scar on me as a reminder of my betrayal. He marked me as a traitor with this scar. He used me for my ability to listen to the world that was in shadows at all times, and my ability to kill without being detected.

So then how the fuck did he detect me that night?

Somewhere over the last few hours I had managed to stumble through the halls to find the kitchen, find a random chess board in the middle of the main room with a half-finished game on it, and stumble up to Luna and Valyn's door. I immediately needed to find some type of liquor to remedy that mistake. Luckily for me, the chef was still in the kitchen when I went back for the liquor and handed me a bottle and a glass and told me to enjoy my evening.

I somehow made it back to my room in one piece, and I'm already regretting the liquor. The room was spinning, and I hadn't even had that much to drink yet. I lifted the bottle to the light, regretting that decision immediately. Shit, I had way more than I had originally intended. I stumbled onto the bed, expertly not dropping a single drop of liquid on either the bed or the floor. That would be such a waste. Sitting there, I let my mind wander, and dear gods that was probably the worst fucking thing to do. Because here I was, sitting in the shadows watching Valyn plow Luna while my drunk ass watched. Gods, when was the last time I got off? I mean, I haven't fucked another woman since I met Maricel, and I haven't fucked anyone since she passed. But when was the last time I even got myself off?

Again, my mind fucking wandered off like the depraved beast inside it wanted. I found myself sprawled out in the shadows, completely naked, cock in one hand, drink in the other. Fuck it. I timed my strokes to his thrusts. Slow and steady to fast and heavy. With each pump, I could hear Luna screaming and moaning, and my sick ass got harder. Painfully fucking harder. I watched as she took control, pushing Valyn onto his back and sliding up and down his cock like a fucking pro. I changed my rhythm to match hers, as if she was riding me instead of my hand doing the job for me. Her tits bouncing up and down was almost the ultimate end game for me. That was until she looked at me and came all over his cock. That was the ultimate end game as I released all over my hand and stomach. I didn't even process whether or not Valyn had finished. I found myself out of my shadows and back in this too big and way too empty room.

I looked at the bottle in my hand, still a little under half full, and fucking chugged it. There is no way physically possible that she saw me in there. Gods, if she did, she could kill me from their room. I almost guarantee it. I managed to get up from the bed, fully covered in my cum, and went into the bathroom. Turning on the shower was more difficult than it should've been, and like everything else tonight, I'm chalking it up to being drunk.

After a few more minutes of messing with the knobs, I finally managed to get the hot water on and spraying down out of the showerhead without any issues. I found a towel in the cabinet above the toilet and put it on the rack next to the shower before stepping in. I let the warm water wash over me, my mind still slipping back to what just happened. Replaying repeatedly the pleasure and intensity of it all. Move for move I matched them, my eyes enjoying watching every inch of her body move on his, my ears taking in all the delicious moans and screams of her pleasure. I couldn't help it. I pumped some type of cream into my hand and stroked my cock again. It throbbed in annoyance at being at full attention again so soon after releasing, but, fuck; the images were swimming around in my head. Shadows engulfed me once more and again; I slipped into the throne of shadows this time at the end of their bed. So close that I could scent her, the vanilla and citrus of her scent whipped up with the ethereal wind that all gods have, but what I could scent even more was her arousal. And that did a number on my fucking brain. I could smell Valyn, his pineapple and sea-salty scent trying to infiltrate where her scent was potent.

I couldn't help but palm my cock harder and faster. I watched as she wrapped her lips around his cock and swallowed it whole. *Fuck. That's a gods damn talent.* I matched my strokes to her lips gliding up and down his cock. They moved around the bed, his head at the foot of the bed and hers facing the headboard. Fates are tempting me. That has to be what this is. Her pussy was within touching range if I really wanted to touch it; or worse. It looked so swollen and tight. Gods what I wouldn't give to just settle my cock inside of her for just a moment to remember what that warmth feels like. As if hearing my thoughts, Valyn pulled her pussy down on his face and devoured her like she was his last damn meal. Another thing I would give anything to do. Just to know the taste of a female losing all control on my tongue or my cock right now would be the most glorious feeling. Instead, I'm torturing myself by watching these two fuck and jerking off in the shower two doors down. Fuck it, it's better than asking if I could join in. I pumped myself a few more times before I released, once again apparently timing it with her own release.

Perfection.

The shadows consumed me then, driving me deep into the madness of my mind, where the depraved monster lived. The monster that would relish in taking what I want. A monster I didn't want to be, but for the rest of tonight, I'd let it consume me in the desire to fuck the princess. I'll let it force me to relive her fucking him over and over until morning, and I'll let it show me what it would look like if I were fucking her in his place. So come on, beast, let me bask in a glory and desire I can never physically have. Give me tonight.

CHAPTER 19
LUNA

"You're not going to make it out of here alive princess. You will pay in flesh for thinking you could take me down. No one is coming to rescue you; you're going to be stuck here with me forever." Marcloff's voice rang out all around me, chasing me through a stone crumbling castle. I ran all the way to the end of a long foreign hallway as his laugh reverberates off of the walls around me. "There's nowhere to run little princess. There's no place to hide." A loud bang shudders the floor beneath my feet as the stone begins to crumble, sending me into the endless darkness.

I jolted up out of a dead sleep, panicking at the restraint around my legs. I pulled back the sheet to find Valyn's legs were tangled up in mine. I untangled from his legs, moving slowly out of bed so I could make my way towards the bathroom. I didn't want to wake him up, he had more to do on the ship than I did. Make sure people stay alive and that we make it to Doria safe, that was the only job I had. Dawn was still far from gracing us with her presence. I did not know what time it was yet, and part of me didn't want to know.

As I made my way back to bed, I looked over at the chair in the corner of the room. I swear it felt like there was someone there most of the night. I really hope this room isn't haunted and we didn't just have a ghost watching us. I sighed as I crawled back into bed, nestling back into Valyn's arms. Feeling him pressed up against me made me feel so safe. I just hope mentally I didn't wake anyone else up with my dream. I closed my eyes, attempting to go back to sleep, until the smell of lemon surrounded me.

Are you alright baby girl? I woke Niklaus up. Of everyone else who needed sleep it was him. Studying with his mother to enhance his healing abilities has been taxing on him. I can only imagine what us being apart has done as well.

I'm sorry for waking you up. I had a bad dream. Please try to go back to sleep. I let my mind focus on my handsome blonde prince. His bright blue eyes were shining as he gazed upon me.

I've been awake, my mother has me running nighttime drills right now. She says battles won't always wait on daylight and I need to make sure that if a patient needs me in the middle of the night, I can stay awake for them. I watched him yawn, even in our little mental space here I could sense his exhaustion. *Be honest with me. Are you alright?*

No. Valyn was hurt badly. He's fine. He's safe, but I was not in a good place. Oh, and let's not forget that apparently, I can now resurrect the dead. How freshly dead you might ask, less than twenty-four hours. It's been a long day to say the least. I'm leaving with Valyn and Victoria in the morning to head to Doria to try to make the seas a bit safer and make sure the people are safe. I unloaded. Every detail of my insecurities just flew out of my mouth as if he knew what had happened.

I'm sorry, did you just say you can resurrect the dead? Disbelief sounded in his voice. *Well, that's a new one. When did you learn this? And how?*

Like I said, Valyn was injured, *and so was his* crew. *I was just trying to help, but then there was this little boy who I just felt was about to breathe his last breath and I couldn't let that happen!* I began to sob. I haven't even come to terms with that fact that if I didn't decide to save him in that moment, his life would've ended in that moment. *Am I a bad person for bringing those back to life? I didn't mean to. It was an accident.*

Niklaus pulled me tight to his chest. He felt so real in this moment, even though I know he is nowhere near me. *You're not a bad person. It's not like you're bringing back an entire graveyard of skeletons to wreak havoc on everyone.* Although *I'm sure you've probably already thought about that knowing you.* I couldn't help but giggle a little. He wasn't wrong. *Your heart is so full of love and life and the thought of letting a child die wouldn't sit right with you. I'm sure the families that were about to say goodbye for the last time thank you immensely for it. The parents of that young boy are probably beyond ecstatic that they have their son still and it's all because you love the way you do.*

He pressed a kiss to my forehead and held me tighter. *I can't stay too much longer, you know how my mother can be when I decide to slack on my duties. Promise me you will not let that thought ever cross your mind again. I love you so much. When you get to Doria, ask Valyn to take you to my room there. I want to try something.*

You have a room in his house in Doria? I gave him a look of skepticism. He just laughed.

It's technically not his house. It's his mothers, and *she gave all of us brothers a room in the house so when we vacationed in the summer realm, we all felt like we were at home. Cassandra is the most giving and loving mate. Everyone of our mothers are great, but Cassandra knew what we needed when even we didn't know. As much as I want to keep you here with me longer, my mother is already chastising me, and you need sleep. Goodnight my love. I'll call you tomorrow to check in with you. I love you to the moon.*

He kissed me once more, then slowly faded away as I drifted into a blissful slumber.

CHAPTER 20
VALYN

The songbirds decided that this morning was the perfect morning to sit outside our room and begin their songs at the crack of dawn. Luna, thankfully, was sleeping blissfully unaware of their annoying chirping. I hated moving out of her embrace, but I really needed to pee and scare off the damn birds before they woke her up. She whined a little at the subtle movements of me rearranging a pillow under her arms where I once was. She looked so cute with her hair in a messy bun, slightly drooling all over the pillow and looking like she was in a peaceful dream.

I begrudgingly left her in bed and made my way to the bathroom. The room was comfortable, but something felt odd. Like the room had eyes on me or something. It had been a long time since I had ever felt uncomfortable in the house. It almost made me not want to leave her alone in the room, but I knew I was just being silly. She was safest right where she was. I caught a glimpse of myself in the mirror for the first time since the accident. She healed me. Every cut, scrape and bruise, but I'm glad she left that scar. I needed a reminder that no matter how safe I feel at sea, it can be just as dangerous for me as anyone else.

I quickly took a piss, washed my hands and face, then headed back into the room. Luna was sprawled out completely naked on the bed, body half covered by the sheet. She was stunningly beautiful. I wish I could capture her beauty like this on a canvas. The sun kissing her cheeks; the blanket draped just right on the curves of her hips. A veritable goddess not only in body, but in truth. How the hell I got so lucky to have this woman as my mate is beyond me. The fates must see something in me I don't.

I pulled a pair of my sweatpants off the floor and decided it was wise to go get coffee for her and I. She was someone who needed caffeine to get her day started. And food. I wonder if we have any bacon left. Quietly, I opened the door and shut it behind me, leaving her to sleep for a little longer before we had to leave. I hope Rafael had a decent night's sleep, and that we didn't keep him up all night with our noise.

Walking the hallway to the kitchen I could hear laughing and chatter from beyond the doorway. The smell of freshly cooked bacon, eggs and potatoes reached my nose the closer I got. But it was the smell of roasted coffee that had my eyes perking up. I made my way into the kitchen, the chatter still continuing from behind me as I lazily searched for a coffee mug. "Your coffee is already made, Prince Valyn." Athena pushed a mug full of dark brown liquid in front of me along with the sugar bowl. "I put two spoonful's in, but if you need more, it's here for you."

"Thank you, Athena." I scooped another spoonful of sugar in and stirred it. I watched as the tiny sugar crystals danced to their doom in a cyclone in the cup. I turned away from the counter to sip my coffee, only to see the grin of Rafael sitting on a bar stool watching me. "I didn't realize you were awake."

"I couldn't sleep all that well last night, so I've been up since right before dawn. I watched the sunrise out in the garden." He looked out the window to the horizon as he spoke. "I've never seen the sunrise like this before. It's quiet, serene and peaceful. Hard to believe war is plaguing these lands."

"I wish it was actually like that all the time. No one wants war. I thought Hellis had days and nights as well." I said, sipping gently from the piping hot liquid.

"It does, but we don't get to enjoy it. We've been at war in Hellis. We don't get to wake up and watch the sunrise. We wake up, put our boots on and patrol, wondering when the next attack is going to come our way. Everyone here seems to think that Marcloff only wants Cerulia's land." He shook his head and sipped from his own coffee mug. Athena decided to quietly exit the room with a tray with a full breakfast and coffee on it. She was going to take breakfast to Luna for me, I'll have to remember to thank her for it.

"Marcloff wants to enslave everyone. Most of Hellis seems to want the opposite of him. Just to exist peacefully and possibly even coexist with our realms. Tell me if I'm getting it wrong." I took a seat at the table, reaching for a piece of bacon before continuing. Rafael did the same. "Fennik and Elijah are currently doing the same thing in Floria. Luna did what she could to help them there, but the daemon's keep coming. Attacking travelers on their way from Floria to Fildrey. The Crimson Army is doing a great job at keeping them at bay, but they've lost a few innocents along the way."

Rafael just sat there, soaking up all the words as I explained the plan that Fennik had laid out. The patrols between the capital and the second largest city in the realm. He offered a suggestion here and there, but mostly just listened. I don't know why I was so forward with him about things, but I guess it's because Luna seemed to trust him. "I can try to get Zekon to send some reinforcements to Floria if you think they would accept the help." He offered as he finished off another slice of bacon.

"If I called Fennik and told him what to expect, I'm sure he wouldn't say no. But, I also can't assume he would say yes. His realm was wrecked by daemons, his mother literally opening the door and letting Marcloff use the realm as he pleased. It might take some convincing." I offered as I to finished off the last of my bacon. Before either of us could continue our conversation, Luna entered the kitchen wearing sinfully short shorts that exposed her ass cheeks, and a crop topped hoodie that exposed her mid-drift. Rafael quickly averted his gaze back out the window as she took her seat next to me. I quickly gave her a kiss as she reached for the pitcher of juice. I grabbed the pitcher before she could reach it, "I got it Princess. How did you sleep?"

"I couldn't stay asleep last night. I kept feeling like I was being watched by a ghost or something. It was so weird." She said as I handed her a glass of juice. "Good morning, Rafael. I hope you slept better than I did." She let out the cutest little yawn before taking a sip of the juice.

"I didn't sleep well, but I'll just chalk it up to sleeping in a new place. I was just telling Valyn that I was enjoying the sunrise." Rafael was very polite, keeping his eyes mainly on me aside from a small smile to her.

"Victoria is probably playing drill sergeant over at the Balemore. We should head to the docks soon. Victoria is a stickler for timing and I am no exception to that rule." I said as I pulled Luna off of the chair and ushered her out the door mouthing the words sorry as we left.

"See you soon Rafael!" She yelled over my head.

"Yup, see you soon." He replied. I had no idea if he was ready to leave for the day or not, but I had to get her dressed before we became late as fuck and Victoria threatened to flay us like fish. I can already hear her complaining.

CHAPTER 21
LUNA

Valyn had refused to let me go back to sleep. All I wanted to do was curl back up in bed with him and sleep for another hour or seven. Did we really have to be standing out here on the dock so damn early?

"I thought you said that Victoria would be out here shouting orders by the time we got here." I said as I leaned up against a wooden post. I could fall asleep on my feet right here and then probably fall into the Selpie and drown. I quickly readjusted myself up against the post so there was no way possible I could fall off the dock.

"She normally would be here by now." Valyn checked his watch before looking at the giant ship behind us. The dock was eerily silent, no one shouting out for the morning fishing boats, no one barking orders to the merchants as they unloaded other vessels, and even weirder, there were no merchants to be seen or heard. Word of the Selestine must've travel fast for everyone to have cleared out this fast. Or maybe orders were sent to clear the docks until we could guarantee the seas to be safe again.

"Maybe she was able to get a decent night's sleep and just overslept." Rafael suggested from the other side of the dock. As Valyn opened his mouth, I could hear Victoria shouting at someone in the distance.

"I told you! You said no, everyone is loyal! Jokes on you!" She was shouting at one of the men I recognized from the Mor. Poor dude looked like he was being drug through a hell. Flanked behind them were at least half a dozen people, each looking like they have been running since the early hours. As they walked up to join us, I watched the man who was being berated look to Valyn with a pleading look.

"Vic, what the hell are you bitching about this early in the morning?" Valyn stepped up to her, looking back over the crowd of people. "Where is Rupert, Magi and Maurice?"

"Ask Westley where they are." She said as she made her way to the ship. I waved at her as she began pulling the stairs out of the side of the ship. The words on the side of the ship said The Birkenhead. I wonder if it is the sister to The Selestine. " I'll have to try to remember to ask Valyn later. "Morning, Luna. Morning creepy dude."

Rafael gave her a raised brow but shrugged his shoulders. "Morning. Need some help?"

Victoria watched him with weary eyes but pointed him in the direction of the stairs that were now protruding out of the side of the ship. He walked to the stairs and waited for her to give him commands on what to do. Two others from the original crew stepped up beside him to help him. Not that I think he needed it, but it was good to see others letting him help and not judging him.

"I held out the keys, told them they have two choices, agree to take a room and join us back at sea to pay back a debt we owe, or forgo and room and leave the safest way they think and effectively leave the Royal Navy. Looks like those three were cowards and I should've listened to Victoria and went about it in a much nicer way. My. Bad." He bit out the last two words as he looked at Victoria. Something tells me she's been boasting the I was right monologuing the entire way here.

"So basically, what you're saying is they deserted?" Valyn said as he nodded at everyone who showed up for us.

"Essentially yes. But everyone else was up and ready to go at first light. I added a bigger tip for the staff that had to put up with the crew when they arrived. I know they were just happy to be alive, but I know they were a handful." Westley spoke to

Valyn as if he was in some position of authority. And for all I know he could be. I didn't move far from the post that was currently holding me up. I really needed to lie down for a little while longer. Maybe being up all night fucking was not the smartest decision to have made. Do I regret it? Hell no. Do I regret getting little sleep? Hell yes.

"Luna come on, let's get you on board and into the captain's quarters." Valyn scooped me up in his arms and carried me onto the ship, while Westley continued to talk logistics of fuel and the best routes to take to get them out to safer waters. I don't think any of the waterways are currently safe, but who was I to say anything?

I faded in and out of consciousness as Valyn laid me out on a bed, pulled my shoes off and tucked me in. The bed was so soft and comforting that I feel asleep within seconds. Slowly I let the sounds of the waves lapping against the hull flood into my dreams, soothing me with the calmness of the waters.

Shouting from outside of the room jolted me upright in the bed. The voices sounded like they were screaming and shouting over the wind and the waves. I tried to push myself up from the bed, but my body wouldn't move. I opened my mouth to call out for Valyn, but there was nothing there. No sound came from my lips, my voice refusing to open up. Panic laced through me as I tried to thrash against the heavy feeling of uselessness.

The sky outside the small window was dark, lightning flashing through every now and then. I could hear the wood of the ship cracking beneath the bed. I tried to scream, I tried to move, but I couldn't. The wood beneath the bed splintered, sending the bed down into the water. Cold darkness swallowed me up. I couldn't move; escaping to freedom was impossible. I was going to die here, wasn't I?

Lightning flashed across the sky once more, as I looked up through the water. Long tentacles slithered around what remained of the ship. The flashing light illuminating a large creature. I couldn't see its face, I couldn't make out what type of creature it was. Fear hit me the moment a tentacle wrapped around me and the bed and squeezed. A silent scream escaped from my lips, rushing water down my throat and into my lungs. Everything felt heavy, I could breathe, panic rose in my chest. I closed my eyes and begged for the flames to consume the creature. Begged for them to save my life. But nothing came. I was powerless in the sea.

Everything slowly faded as I felt my ribs crack under the pressure from the tentacles. *I'm sorry I wasn't strong enough*, was all I could manage to send to my bonds in my final moments before everything went dark.

CHAPTER 22
FENNIK

The day was going relatively normally for me. Training with the Crimson Army had been going very well lately. Younger recruits from Fildrey have shown up more willing to help than the older mages. Everyone seemed so reluctant to go up against Hellis again. I couldn't blame them, but really, what else do they plan on doing? Hiding away in their charmed townhouses and homes? The magical protection on the autumn realm has slowly decreased since Hellis attacked Floria. Marcloff attacked our land so deeply that even though Luna healed the land, it's still trying to thrive as it once did. Sometimes the elderly can be so foolishly stuck in their ways.

I let out a deep sigh as I looked over the maps that Elijah had dropped off this morning. Things have been calm mostly. Aside from the random daemon attacks on the trails, we have things mostly under control. Despite it keeping me from being with her now, Luna would be happy with what we've done here.

Glancing out the window to watch the morning sun, a sharp pain rippled in my chest. Luna's voice broke into my head.

I'm sorry I wasn't strong enough.

Then, suddenly, my head filled with voices. Bastian, Damian, Valdis, Niklaus. Everyone was talking over one another, trying to get her to respond. Valyn's voice rang out in my head, louder than everyone else's.

What is going on? Bastian demanded an answer from Valyn. Why the hell would he know what was going on? Did I miss something?

I don't know. She's sound asleep. Valyn replied hastily. *I just checked on her the moment I heard her voice.*

Valyn, why are you with her? Valdis questioned. I was wondering the same thing. I thought he was in Doria overseeing the Hellis Gate there.

Long story short, The Serpentine was attacked on the way to Doria. I wasn't in the best condition, and neither was the crew. Luna came to the Mor and healed everyone. Valyn paused for a moment and let out a long breath. *Including the dead.*

What do you mean, including the dead?! I asked, shock rippling through my soul at his claim.

Exactly what I said. She brought a boy back from the brink of death and brought three people back to life who had just died.

She didn't do it consciously. I'm worried about her and how it's affecting her mentally. She didn't want the poor boy to die. I don't think she meant to save those who had already passed. Valyn's words landed like a hard blow to my chest, knocking the wind out of me.

Wake her up. I demanded. *Wake her up now! I know her uncle is a death god, but he is not the only one out there. If she crossed someone, even by accident, they're going to want souls in exchange for the ones they lost.*

Why would you say that? Damian asked me. I guess he really didn't know.

The fates don't like being fucked with, nor does death. Seeing as they work hand in hand more often than not, they will want retribution. Or worse. Niklaus spoke for me. We had read enough in our lifetimes to know how death gods operate. How the fates take pleasure in ripping apart lives when people change the course of their fate. *Maybe Sirus can help us out. Someone wanna call him?*

I can do better. He's here in Taiga, stuck ten feet up Holly's ass. I swear if these two don't just fucking mate already; I am going to lose my ever-loving mind. Bastian was groaning as if we were any better.

You act like you weren't the same with Luna. We all played with fire when it came to finding her as our bond. I thought mainly to myself, but I keep forgetting when we're like this, there is no privacy.

Valyn, wake her up. Figure out what's going on with her and let us know. A phone call would probably be better. Valdis demanded. I couldn't blame him, really. He was in Hellis, and the furthest one of us away from her. I can only imagine what's going through his mind.

"Fennik. FENNIK!" I blinked at the intrusion. Elijah was standing across from me, worry etched into the skin above his brows.

"I'm sorry. Mating conversations just kind of happen out of the blue. There's not much I can really do about it. Is everything okay?" I asked, trying to push the conversation in my head to the rearview. I know Luna is alive. That's really all I need to know for now. Valyn will get back to us, and everything will be alright. It has to be.

"Daemon forces have been spotted outside of Floria again. The army has been doing really well at keeping them at bay, but more and more keep coming. What should we do?" Elijah asked. It's been a long day, and I could see it on his face.

"Honestly, we need to kill them, but that will only prolonge the inevitable. They will return and keep returning until Marcloff is dead. Have you heard any news about your father?" I pressed my fingers into my upper eyelids. Things were mostly under control here. But if these daemons keep coming at us, I don't know how many more people will want to flee. And I can't blame any of them for wanting that. I just can't let Floria fall to the daemons.

"Nothing yet. Alstrom thought he had seen him the other day, but when he pursued, Alstrom said it was like he vanished into the trees themselves. You don't think the trees have picked a side in this, do you?" Elijah took the seat across from me, staring down at the map of the surrounding forests. "Gods I hope not." He whispered, mostly to himself.

I couldn't help laughing. "That would be an odd sight to see. I don't believe the trees would pick the side of the daemons trying to destroy us if that were the case, though. They would die out again, and I don't think they would like that."

"No, I have a feeling you are right about that. I don't think anyone would like to die," Elijah responded. "I'll instruct the army to destroy. Burn like usual?"

I sighed. "Yeah. I don't like it, but it makes them less likely to rise again." Before meeting Valdis and getting to know him and the others, I wouldn't have disliked killing them as much as I do now. They're only following orders from their king. Be it out of fear or actually believing him. Knowing they're more like us than we had originally thought makes this difficult; it feels more like it's hitting home than it should.

I hope the others are having an easier time where they are.

CHAPTER 23
BASTIAN

"Open the gods damn door, you two!" I hammer away at the wooden door with my fist. You'd think by now they would just learn to listen when I come knocking like this instead of acting like lovesick children. I heard clamoring inside, something shattering on the floor, and then the lock on the front door. Holly's blonde curly hair was a frizzy mess, her cheeks blushing bright pink, and she was panting pretty heavily. "It's about damn time."

"Seriously? Can you fuck off for at least another fifteen minutes? We're kind of busy in here." Holly huffed at me, trying to close the door on me. I shoved my booted foot into the doorway and looked down at her. "Go away!" She yelled. Instead, I pushed the door open and walked inside, only to find Sirius covered by a pink fluffy blanket and nothing else.

"Dude, I need you to get dressed. We have a problem." I said as Holly shoved past me, holding a baby blue blanket around her small body, before plopping down hard on top of Sirius.

"I'm in the middle of something. Whatever it is, will have to wait." He said, pressing his nose into Holly's hair as she beamed widely at me. I sighed. I really didn't want to talk about it here, but fuck it. They don't seem to remember the world is on fucking fire right now.

"No, it can't wait. You two do remember that we are trying to stop a fucking war from ripping apart the lands, right?" I huffed at them, crossing my arms in front of my chest. Holly buried her face deep in Sirius's chest like she could hide from my words. Sirius, to his credit, looked me dead in the eyes. "My beautiful wife has brought people back from death's door." That perked Holly's head up, making Sirius sit up on the couch.

"What do you mean, brought people back from death's door?" He questioned me as I walked over to the chair that his pants were hanging on. Holly was even looking at me with wide eyes. She knew the implications this could mean, even for her job.

"As in bringing a child back from grabbing a death god's hand. Oh, and reanimating three corpses that were in the morgue at the Mor." Holly jumped up off of Sirius so quick that the blanket fell to the floor. I quickly averted my gaze and tossed her the dress that was draped over his pants. "Can you two please put on some fucking clothes?"

I caught the pants slipping off the chair out of the corner of my eye. "We're covered; turn around." Sirius was standing only a few inches away from me at this point. "How the fuck did she bring people back from the dead? Did they have souls? Is she controlling them? I need details!" I honestly don't know why I didn't expect this from him.

"I don't know. Fennik said we needed to talk to you because she fucked with fate. Multiple fates if you want to be clear. He seems to think they will try to exact retribution on her. Souls for souls kind of deal. Is that true?" I asked, taking a seat at the table. Holly adjusted her glasses and fixed her hair.

"Are we sure they are living? I mean, I've heard of necromancers in Yida reanimating corpses, but that always backfires with someone's brains getting eaten or worse." She grabbed a book off her shelf and handed it to me, open with a page marked. "See? Corpse reanimation is possible, but they are lifeless. No souls. No ability to think for themselves. And without the need for food to stay alive."

I skimmed the pages, and sure enough, the necromancers had mastered this technique centuries ago. Then why is Fennik so worried? I pulled my phone out and texted Valyn.

Hey, how is she doing? I have a few questions. Were the bodies of the deceased up and moving around? What about talking? Need an answer ASAP! I tapped send and set my phone on the table before looking back at the book. It described how to perform the ritual to bring the dead to life, but something is off about this.

"It doesn't say how they reanimated the corpse. There are words and a few lines that are too blurry to read." I pointed it out to Holly. She grabbed the book and skimmed until she reached where my fingers were. Her brows furrowed together as she tried to decipher the words.

"I need to go to Yida. My colleague there could possibly give me the answers we need. I'll just owe her a night of drinking in exchange for her cooperation." She put the dark blue ribbon attached to the book between the pages. My phone buzzed on the table.

She is still sound asleep. I can't even get through to her through the bond. I'm worried about her. As for your questions, they were vertical, moving around and talking. I called Maggie to check on them, *and they all recovered from the injuries or illnesses that claimed them. I'll check in tomorrow. Right* now, *I need to get her awake.* Valyn replied.

Thank you. I'd say the best way to wake her up in dive between her thighs. That always works for me. I tapped send and looked up at Holly. "I don't think that trip will be necessary. They were moving and talking. They're alive again. Maggie just told Valyn that they all fully recovered from their life claiming injuries and illnesses." I watched as their faces dropped. For them, that answer was the best option.

"If she didn't reanimate them like the necromancers, then she committed a crime amongst the gods and, yes, the fates won't take kindly to that. Not to mention the death god she stole the souls from." Sirius said as he took the seat across from me.

"I thought there was only you. I didn't know there were multiple death gods." Admittedly, I clearly failed at paying attention in school as a kid.

"I am the one and only death god. The other death gods are more like demigods. They obey what I tell them to do or risk becoming like the souls they reap. Normally, if they lose a soul, it's because of careless handling. Not usually to the hand of life. Necromancers reanimate the bodies, but the souls stay where they belong so as not to be tainted. There's not much even I can do about necromancers. Believe me, I've tried." Sirius grabbed his phone from the half wall between the living room and the kitchen and scrolled on it. "I'll have logistics figure out who was supposed to reap the souls. I can't have them haunting my niece and causing her issues."

"Can whoever it is cause her to fall asleep and not wake up?" I asked hesitantly. Sirius slowly leveled his gaze with mine.

"Fucking Leigh. I know exactly from whom she stole the souls. My biggest pain in the ass. Give me a minute." Sirius opened his phone once more but made a call instead. "I swear to the gods she better—Leigh, what the fuck are you doing?"

"Hi boss! So, there was a mistake with a few souls I was supposed to bring home with me, and I am making it right. I didn't want to bother you with the details." A cheery voice rang through the speaker and gave me the chills. No death god, demi or other, should sound that cheerful.

"There are rules in place for a reason. You know, healers tend to have a higher success rate of resuscitating a person than human doctors do. I need you to stop stalking the person who took the souls." Sirius demanded. I hadn't heard him this stern since he scolded Luna for something during their training sessions.

"But, boss!" Leigh whined. I watched Holly death glare the phone. Her mating bond is in rare form, and if they don't address that soon, there are going to be issues.

"No buts! She is my fucking niece and a strong-ass goddess that can wipe you off the face of existence if she realizes it is someone forcing her into a living nightmare!" He growled, half jumping up from his seat.

"Fine." I could hear the huffing and pouting in her voice. Defeat. Luna always made the same huffing and pouting when any of us beat her at anything.

"Leigh, before you go. What are the nightmares you're giving her?" I thought that question was weird. Why would he want to know what her dreams are?

"I don't give them the nightmares, boss. It's their own fears that guide where they go. I just keep them in there longer, that's all. As for your niece, she's having nightmares of drowning at sea," Leigh replied before ending the phone call.

"I fucking hate that bitch," Holly muttered under her breath. Or so she thought was under her breath. Sirius just let out a small laugh.

"I don't know why in the world Luna would be afraid of drowning at sea. But she should be fine now." I felt my whole body go ice cold.

"She's on the Birkenhead with Valyn right now." I whispered out. Holly and Sirius both looked at me as I pulled my phone out to call Valyn. Luna got lucky now, but I have a feeling we haven't seen the last of Leigh.

CHAPTER 24
LUNA

I tore out of the bed so fast that I almost knocked Valyn straight onto the floor. " You're alive!" I yelled as I pulled him into me, squeezing with all my might. He hugged me tightly, placing kisses on my forehead and cheeks.

"Please don't scare me like that again. Granted, it wasn't your fault, but it still scared me when you wouldn't wake up and you know the wonderful message you sent us all." Valyn pushed stray strands of hair out of my face as he spoke. My brain hung on one thing.

"What do you mean it wasn't my fault? Wouldn't my having nightmares be my own fault?" I tilted my head sideways a little as he let out a deep sigh.

"Fennik had panicked when I told him about your little magic trick of bringing the dead back to life. He wanted someone to go talk to Sirius to make sure that a death god wouldn't try to claim your soul in place of the ones you took from them. Bastian is in Taiga,got so he took that responsibility. He got an answer from Sirius and, come to find out, you pissed off a demi-death god. Your uncle was able to get her off your back. But Bastian is still worried that the person won't let go. Especially when she told Sirius what your nightmare was." Valyn explained everything to me. I always thought my uncle was the only death god. I guess it would make sense that there's more out there.

"So basically, what you're saying is I pissed off a death god by accidentally bringing people back from the dead. And what? They haunted my ass?" Valyn let out a slight laugh as I let the thoughts of having someone haunt me stress me out.

"Sirius took care of her. I'm sure that if we have any issues in the future, he will take care of them. How are you feeling?" He cupped my face in his hands, easing my head from side to side as if looking for cuts or bruises.

"Aside from the anxiety attacks from that nightmare loop, I'm fine. How far out from Doria are we?" I remembered everything from before the nightmares. I knew we had a mission. "Has there been any sign of trouble?"

"Nothing so far. The waters are too calm, though. It's not right with the way the wind is blowing. We should be hitting some kind of waves, something. But there is nothing. It's unnerving." He stood up from the bed, reaching his hand back down for me. Valyn always made sure I was within arm's reach at any given time. It made me feel special and important, but it also made me feel like he didn't think I could handle myself in certain situations. Walking on a ship, he has me beat there by a long shot.

We walked out of the cabin and onto the deck where the crew were bustling about doing whatever job Victoria was commanding of them. The Birkenhead reminded me of the Selestine. Elegant, sleek, and most of all quiet despite the engine below deck. It wasn't anything like the pirate ships I read about as a little girl. Then again, the human part of the world, although part of Cerulia, was like its own world. Mermaids were just something I had read about and hoped to meet. Now, I'm good never seeing another one the rest of my life. But I know there are creatures out there much worse than mermaids. Noro was misunderstood, just like I'm sure others out there have been.

"How was your sleep, Princess Luna?" A tall man with messy brown hair smiled at me as we reached the far end of the deck. I think his name is Westley. I can't actually remember whether we've been introduced or if I just picked up the name from someone else.

"Luna, this is Westley Moore. He is the actual captain of the Birkenhead, but you know Victoria. Stubborn and hard-headed and not one to take the back seat and let someone else shine in her presence." Valyn said as he watched Victoria bark more orders out to the crew. Westley laughed.

"It's a pleasure to meet you. Umm, as for my sleep, I'm good to stay up for a long while now." I didn't want to admit that I was just stuck in a nightmare loop. That would be an interesting conversation. Like, hi yes, I had a wonderful sleep thinking of everyone dying at sea by the tentacles of some crazy-looking creature. Nope, I'm going to keep that inside my head and never let that out.

"If you need rest, feel free to make yourself at home. When Valyn is here, I relent my lodging to him, and as his wife and mate, I relent it to you as well." Westley saluted me, nodded and then left us.

"Okay, what was that all about?" I asked Valyn as I watched Westley walk away from us and check in on the crew. Everyone greeted him with a smile; unlike the way they greeted Victoria. Then again, Victoria enjoyed being feared; she seemed to take so much pride in her scary-girl image. I admired the confidence she had when commanding a room.

"Westley is very formal. He's a friend of mine, but you are royalty to him. He will continue to be formal with you until you tell him otherwise. Even then, expect at least another year or two of formalities." Valyn laughed as he looked out at the sea. He was right; the waters were so still it looked like we were sailing on glass. The only motion in the water was it rippling off the sides of the ship. I looked to the sky and noticed dark clouds forming on the horizon.

"Should we be worried about that?" I pointed at the clouds. Valyn turned his attention to the sky. I watched as his eyes traced the horizon, taking in the clouds, the sun slowly hiding behind the softer clouds above us.

"I'd say yes. I've seen plenty of storm clouds in my time, and none of them had a purple hue like that behind them." He looked out over the deck. "Victoria! Storm clouds ahead! Not looking friendly!" He shouted across the deck. Victoria turned her head toward the clouds. I watched her take in the sight as she turned to the crew.

"Haul ass, everyone! Storms are coming, and I don't trust that they won't bring danger with them!" She yelled across the deck as the crew began pulling at ropes and securing things to the deck.

Valyn ushered me back inside the cabin. "Stay here for right now. I promise I won't be long." He gave me a quick kiss and closed the door behind him.

CHAPTER 25
LUNA

The sound of lightning crashing made me jump as it echoed through the ship. I hated thunderstorms, and I hated being left alone during them. I could hear the shouting outside of the cabin, orders being given and received. I could make out Valyn and Victoria's voices as they carried over the thunder. What worried me most was this is how my nightmare started. However, this time I could move, and I wasn't trapped in bed.

I took in the surroundings, the dark wood paneling on the walls, the maps framed and hung, and the ones sprawled out on the mahogany desk. I wandered over to the desk and took in the map that was sitting on top of them all. It was a full map of the summer realm. Each city and town marked, along with several portals and gates. I wonder how many of the portals were temples from the olden days? I also wonder how many of them were active and where they each went. The door opened, and Valyn came into the room.

"Looking over the maps, I see," he teased as he came up behind me, wrapping his arms around my waist. "Do you have questions about what you see?"

"Just wondering about the portals and gates. Are they former temples like the ones in the Autumn Realm?" I let him in on my thoughts. "I would love to check them out if we have time. I don't want to see history get destroyed during the war. Maybe if they are in ruins, we can rebuild them." The pride on Valyn's face lit up my heart. He knew I was big on cherishing the history of our world and preserving what we could.

"Have you thought about Celvenia at all?" Valyn's question took me by surprise. What was left in Celvenia for me? The house where I grew up? The ashes of a man who raised me, yet lied to me? My friends had all come to Mistveil and Mirith. My sister was here, even if she wasn't truly my sister. No one was there.

"No," I said flatly. He hugged me tighter. "Why would you ask that? Celvenia was hell."

"Because you grew up there. That place, as horrible as it was to you, shaped you into the woman I have in my arms today. I know it wasn't the greatest place, but there has to be something about there that you miss." He pressed a kiss to my temple as he rested his chin on my shoulder. I thought long and hard about what he was saying, that I could hear the ticking of the clock on the wall.

"I miss the theatre. I miss watching my friends dance at the ballet there. And the bakery. Mildred's baked goods were to die for. Literally melt in your mouth deliciousness. Granted, the food here is much better than there, but her bakery is a very close second. Other than that, I miss nothing. The bars and taverns were shitty; the people there were complete assholes who treated you poorly if you looked the slightest bit different. Kira and Harper used to be told they would never make it outside of Celvenia because they were freaks. All because they were born with different skin colors. Virgil was considered an outcast because he chose to slum it with us instead of stay in the slightly upper-class area where his family is from. He joined the ranks of the army to get away from them. And you know my story, and Lilly's." I turned around in Valyn's arms so I could see his face as he took it all in. He didn't know what it was like to grow up unliked or unwanted.

"I didn't realize people there treated you all poorly. That isn't right." He kissed my forehead and held me tight.

"It's fine. We all left there, and we are all living the best lives ever now." I gave him a quick kiss and turned back to the maps.

"Do you think that the storms are going to cause us issues getting to Doria?" I felt him take a deep breath before he spoke.

"I have a bad feeling about the storms. When the Selestine got attacked, storm clouds like those rolled in. I think it's best you stay in here—" I slammed my fists on the table before he could finish talking.

"I am not fucking hiding in here. I am the strongest person on this damn ship, and you want to lock me up like I am the weakest. How are we supposed to work together if you keep treating me like I am a damn flower that is going to be destroyed if looked at?" I snapped. I pulled out of Valyn's arms and walked over to the window to look out. The dark clouds loomed over the sea as bright purple lightning streaked across the sky. "I'm going out there with the crew. You can stay in here and wait the storm out, but I won't."

I went for the door, but he grabbed my arm, stopping me. "I'm sorry. I'm still having issues after losing you. The thought of you being ripped from me again is unbearable. I'm sorry, I'm just afraid." Valyn sounded so defeated. I guess I couldn't blame him for being afraid. It doesn't matter how strong you are, fear can grip anyone with the desire to hold onto something or someone in fear of losing them.

"Unless someone has Otius's Blade, I will be okay. Am I worried about all the power that I have? Absolutely. But I got this. If not, I will let you know." I gave him a soft smile as I pushed silver strands from his face. It was a simple gesture but clearly one we both needed. He grabbed my hand, pressing it tight to his cheek as he took a deep breath of my scent in.

"I'll be by your side through everything. It's my job to protect you and keep you safe from harm. And so far I am zero for three. It's not a good feeling know that I've failed you multiple times." He held onto my hand as he spoke. "I don't mean to act like you're fragile. It's just my job to protect you and keep you safe."

"I get it. You and the others do keep me safe, even if it's not the way you guys originally thought you would. You all keep me as grounded as possible. Knowing that no matter how far away I am I can talk to any of you through the bond is enough to keep me alive even in the darkest of moments. We just have to face this together. Doing it alone isn't working for any of us." I gripped his other hand with mine and held it. "Let's go make sure everyone else is safe. And make sure no one is trying to be stupidly brave."

He nodded and let my other hand fall from his face. We left the room hand in hand and headed out to the deck. The storm clouds looked ominous, but unnatural. The lightning wasn't the same as normal lightning. It's hard to describe the energy it gives off as it lights up the clouds. Victoria had made sure everyone was inside, aside from her, Westley and Patrick. They didn't seem like the type of people to hide in rooms and not stay out to fight if the need arose. They turned to greet us, their faces long with worry about the impending storm.

"The seas should not be this quiet with a storm of that magnitude looming above us," Westley said as he looked up at the sky, waiting for something to fall from it.

"You would think with clouds that dark that there would be rain and heavy winds. This isn't normal." Victoria said as she made her way to the bow of the ship. Grabbing hold of a rope, she peered over the bow and into the sea. Her turquoise eyes illuminated as she focused on the water below. I had seen Valyn's do the same when he was using his powers, but hers were especially bright in the darkness. "We've got company!"

Her voice echoed across the deck as a thud shook the ship. "What the hell?" Patrick cursed as he tried to hold himself steady. Valyn reluctantly let go of my hand and made his way to the side of the ship. His eyes illuminated like Victoria's as he peered through the dark waters to see what was attacking the ship. I had a sinking feeling about what was attacking the ship, but I didn't want to voice my fear yet. If I was right, things were about to get a hundred times worse for us.

CHAPTER 26
VALYN

Luna was staying close to Patrick and Westley, luckily I knew if things went south they would get her to safety. The dark shadows beneath the ship were huge, much bigger than what we had encountered during the first attack. Something deadly was beneath these waters, and something tells me it's not alone. I watched as more shadows zipped around and twisted around the larger shadow. I realized a little too late that they were tentacles as they broke through the water and began wrapping around the ship.

"KRAKEN!" I yelled the moment I realized what we were up against. I drew my sword and sliced through the tentacle as Luna stood there, paralyzed in fear. Victoria shouted orders as the crew filed out of their lodging and onto the deck. "Don't let it wrap its tentacles around the ship! If it shattered through, we are fucked!"

"You heard him! Grab what you can and take it down!" Westley shouted, moving away from Luna and towards the others.

Patrick stayed next to Luna, speaking to her as she stood there frozen in place. I wanted to jump back and go comfort her, but she told me that she got it and if she needed me, she would make it known. I had to just be patient and know that she was okay, until she tells me she isn't.

I saw her shake her head and nod at Patrick, then she looked around. Her eyes met mine and she smiled, but she looked around again. *Where is Raphael?* She asked me mentally, and all the hair on my arms stood. I had forgotten about the daemon on board the ship. Could he be the reason we're being attacked? Could he be a beacon for these damn things? No, he wasn't here the first time.

I don't know. But—before I could finish my sentence, Rafael practically flew out of the stairwell and straight at a tentacle, severing it completely. *There he is.*

He landed beside her and handed her his sword. She clutched it tightly in her hand before launching herself across the deck in a streak of white flames. Patrick stepped out of her way, mouth agape as he watched her scorch the tentacle that was climbing up the bow of the ship. I watched as she took on several tentacles that were making their way across the deck. Everyone just paused and watched her work.

A costly mistake.

In his awe, Patrick didn't sense the tentacle that was coming up behind him. It snatched him by his leg and began pulling him off the ship. Luna's head snapped in the direction he was being pulled to and just as he went over, she launched herself into the water after him. My heart raced as the tentacles retreated off the ship and back into the water. I went to jump off the side of the ship, but Westley grabbed me.

"You're no help to anyone if you're dead!" He yelled at me, and as much as I struggled to get him off of me, I knew he was right.

"Victoria! Do you see them?" She was already tracking movement under the sea. I watched as she smiled, then looked up at me.

"I feel terrible for the kraken. I wouldn't expect her flames to work underwater, but she's got something protecting them as she's tearing into it. Patrick is trying to pull her away from the thing, but she just keeps going. He's coming up!" She yelled at us. Westley and I quickly threw a line out to him as he broke the surface.

"I need to go back and get her!" he yelled up to us as he broke through the surface, but Rafael jumped into the water and flew him back up. "Get off of me! She's in there because of me!" He struggled against Rafael, but failed miserably to get free.

"She's fine. I can't say the kraken is. But she is coming back up. No sign of life from beneath." Victoria reported.

As if she had commanded it, Luna broke through the surface and grabbed the lifeline. Westley and Patrick began pulling her up as I reached my hands down for her to grab. Her grip was tight as I pulled her over the side of the ship. Patrick moved quickly to her side, Rafael half putting himself in the way.

"Why would you risk your life to save me? You could have died!" Patrick was giving her the business. She didn't stop him from yelling at her or even raise her hand to shut him up. She just let him continue to tell her how he felt. Rafael helped her steady herself from falling as if I weren't within arm's reach of her. Patrick was still scolding her for jumping into the cold sea to save him and for how she was being reckless with her life. I didn't stop him. She needed to hear it from someone who wasn't her mate.

Dark, short red hair bobbed past everyone, catching my attention. Lyra Thilman, wife of Elsa Thilman, was bobbing in between bodies on the deck to reach Luna and Patrick. She stopped just short of the two of them holding out two fluffy white towels at arm's length. Patrick smiled and grabbed them from her, placing one around Luna's shoulders first before tossing the other over his shoulder. They both thanked Lyra as she made her way back through the crew and to her wife. I watched as everyone slowly gathered around Luna, admiring her and gawking. I think they were more surprised that she just jumped in without any hesitation.

I put my arm around Luna, pulling her to my side. "Can you please let me know the next time you plan on jumping off the ship?" I said into her wet hair. She let out the cutest giggle and nuzzled into my side.

"Next time I'll try to think first and not just jump in to save others." She poked me hard in my side, pulling herself out of my arms. She took a step back, looking up at me. "Why didn't you jump in?" Her eyes pierced into my soul in that moment. I tried to jump in, but not for Patrick.

"I wanted to jump in behind you; I tried." I said as Westley stepped up between us.

"I stopped him. He is no good to any of us or you if he jumps after you every chance you put yourself in danger." His words were sharp and blunt. Luna just smiled. Patrick and Rafael took up flank behind her. Fuck, fuck, fuck. I went to step around Westley as Victoria joined in the mess.

"You're right. But if I wasn't here, Valyn would've jumped in to save your brother." Her words were as sharp as blades as she spoke. "But I am here. I jumped overboard after Patrick when even you didn't move to help. Valyn knows he doesn't need to save me. But I figured he would jump in for your brother. I just got there first. I like you, but I think maybe it needs to be reminded that I am not just his wife; I am his mate. The pull to save your mate regardless of the danger level will take precedence over all else. You would do well to remember that."

I wasn't used to seeing her this cold towards anyone. She turned from us and walked back to the cabin, Rafael and Patrick in tow. Westley just stood there, watching her walk away. Victoria let out a low whistle as Luna vanished from sight. I watched as Patrick and Rafael stood guard outside of the door. "Should we be concerned that he is now guarding your wife and following her around like a lost pup?" Victoria leaned into me as she spoke.

"I don't think we should be concerned. I do worry that Luna is now going to protect Patrick no matter the cost since she thinks neither of us would've stepped up to help him." I said, glancing at Westley, who turned and looked at me in defeat. I understand what he was saying, but he needed to understand where she was coming from as well. "I get what you were saying. I think she just wanted to know why I didn't step up first, like I should've. She asked why I hadn't jumped in. She wasn't questioning why I didn't jump in for her."

"I didn't mean to sound so harsh. I'm just in the usual spot of commander. I have never liked it when people question you. I'm sorry." Westley truly was apologetic. He wasn't one to intentionally make someone feel out of place or put down. He just needs to work on his delivery, especially with Luna. Lately, she's been a little colder towards people than she was before. War is slowly taking my bubbly wife away from me. I hate this.

CHAPTER 27
RAFAEL

The wind whipped against me as I leaned against the cabin wall just outside of the door. Patrick's teeth had been chattering loudly for the past few minutes, making it hard to focus on anything but that obnoxious noise. To his credit, though, he stood there sopping wet with a towel draped over his neck as the salty seawater absorbed into his skin. I was cold, but I was also used to frigid waters and torture. I guess that's one benefit of Marcloff's torture of his troops. We can withstand a good deal of punishment before even letting the slightest crack show. I kept my eyes closed as I leaned my head back against the wood. I could hear Luna slamming what sounded like wooden drawers closed. With each step she took, I could feel it through the floorboards. I kept my arms crossed tight over my chest, pulling my right leg up to rest my foot against the wall.

"Should we go in and check on her?" Patrick's voice pulled me from my drifting thoughts. I cracked an eye open to look at him. His messy brown hair, matted against his forehead, looked much darker now that it was soaking wet. But the look in his bright green eyes gave me pause. He wasn't looking at me when he spoke; he was looking at the door, waiting for it to open. Or was he watching it because he could see through it? His eyes were bright, almost as if they were glowing. I saw that same brightness from Victoria's eyes as she was watching Luna under the water. Could he see through walls? I closed my eyes and rested my head back against the wall.

"I think if you bother her right now, you might find yourself at the end of her blade. She sounds absolutely pissed off, and I don't want to be on the receiving end of her wrath." I could feel his energy shift as he relaxed back against the wall.

"I guess you're right. I shouldn't have laid into her the way I did. It wasn't my place to do so." He relented. I could feel him shifting from foot to foot.

"Honestly, I'm surprised she didn't shut you up. She let you air your feelings, which is more than I can say for your brother. Think he's okay?" I asked him. I had watched his brother's reaction when we took our posts. He looked hurt by her words and maybe that he was rethinking his own words to her. I know she's not mad at him; that is for certain. I think she's just hurt that he thinks she wants Valyn to put her first instead of the others.

"You're surprised?" He choked out a deep laugh. "Dude, I wasn't thinking, but I'm damn sure if she wanted me to shut up, she would've made me. As for Westley, he'll be fine. He's blunt, but he's not used to someone not backing down when he speaks."

"Are you worried that they might treat you differently for choosing to stay by her side when she walked off? It's not like she snapped her fingers and made you follow." I said, still trying to keep a calm and collected composure. I wanted a better read on him.

"If they question why I chose her, I will tell them the same thing I'm about to say to you. Fuck you. I am in a life debt to her. She saved me from drowning at the hands of a fucking kraken. She put her life at risk. Goddess or not, she didn't have to jump in after me. She didn't have to rescue me. She could've let me and everyone else on the ship die. Instead, she chose to take your sword and unleash hell on the beast. So, if you or anyone else questions where my loyalty lies, you can all go fuck yourselves." Patrick showed more anger than I would've thought. I guess questioning his character was probably out of line. "What about you, huh? You follow her around the ship like a shadow. She didn't snap her fingers and make you follow. So spill it."

I opened my eyes to size up the rather tall man before me. He had muscles, nowhere near like Valyn, but enough to make him a threat to others. Not knowing his powers or abilities, I wanted to tread lightly. "Her uncle's right hand ordered me to follow and protect her. I didn't argue when he told me to stay with her and keep her safe. She has this gravitational pull that surrounds her, pulling those around her in like the world revolves around her. It probably comes with her powers, but she's interesting." I just shrugged and leaned my head back again.

My answer seemed to be enough for him, as he went quiet again. I could hear her muttering something in the room, but I wanted to give her space. If she wanted someone to talk to, she would open the door. Maybe I could send a shadow in just to be sure she wasn't hurting herself in some random way imaginable. As I took a breath to summon forth a small shadow, the lock on the door clicked and the door opened.

I pushed up from the wall and took that as my invitation to enter. Patrick seemed to think the same way I did and followed suit. I expected Valyn or Westley to come over, but neither did. They just moved around the ship aimlessly, it seemed. Victoria was barking orders at everyone, including them. I think she knew Luna needed the time without being interrogated.

"Close the door behind you." She said as she sat behind the desk, flipping over maps and making notes in a random journal. Part of me wanted to get her away from here. The other part of my brain lingered on how tight and see-through her white top had gotten. I glanced at Patrick and, to his credit, he was keeping his eyes up at her face the entire time. Poor kid, he probably wants to look so bad. The towel she had dried off with had been discarded by the bed.

"Why didn't you get into dry clothes?" I asked her, making it well known that she should probably take the wet shirt into account with her present company. She just shrugged her shoulders and moved another map out of her way. "Okay, then what are you looking for?"

That seemed to catch her attention. Her brown eyes, shimmering with flecks of gold and silver swirls of what I could only describe as stardust, looked up at me. A grin graced her lips. "The kraken isn't the scariest thing in these waters. Noro is a sea wyvern that stalks the shores of Anchora in Floria. We had an encounter with her not too long ago, but the fear everyone had of her was out of place. She was just trying to protect not only her children, but the children of Anchora. They would fall from the cliffs or drown at sea, and she would protect their souls until they found their way in the afterlife. I heard her speak to me, thanking me for stopping the crew of the Selestine from killing her and her newborn."

I watched as she took her finger and traced a line from Anchora in Floria all the way here to where the summer realm thrives. She was marking the water flow and patterns of how the sea would be moving. Patrick practically choked on air at the mention of Noro. I heard about the legends of sea wyverns. They bred in Hellis and were released on the people of Cerulia. It wasn't true, though. Sea wyverns, krakens, merfolk. None of them belonged to any one realm. There wasn't some magical gateway undersea that could stop them from traveling how they pleased.

"You met Noro?" he said, his eyes still wide in his head. She just smirked. I watched Patrick visibly shutter at the thought. "You're either very brave, very lucky, or very stupid."

"She wasn't bad. I don't think any creature is inherently bad. I think something is controlling the sea creatures around Doria. The kraken had no life in its eyes, and all I kept hearing in my head was, make it stop. He sounded sad and utterly defeated." Luna described the kraken's emotions as if it pained her physically to see the creature suffering. Could she hear the thoughts of creatures? If so, that would come in very handy against some of what Marcloff had made. Abominations that should never walk the planet have been made and caged in Minaris. I fear for when he finally releases them from their prisons.

"What do you think is strong enough to control sea creatures?" Patrick asked her as he took a seat across from the desk. She shook her head and looked over a few other maps. I honestly didn't know how she could make out the lines and patterns; looking at it like this was giving me a headache.

"I hate to say it, but Undine." She whispered. She looked utterly gutted when she spoke the name of their Goddess of Waters. I hadn't met any of the gods or goddesses before I met Zekon and Alistar. I didn't get to meet Talissa or the others until recently, and then there's Luna. The only veritable goddess that I have spoken to on more than just a few simple formal words, but I knew their gods and goddesses, mostly. I did my studying after I met Zekon. I wanted to see the life that he pictured as his future. I think once he meets Luna, he'll absolutely love and adore her. They are so similar, except him being a half-daemon and all.

"I don't envy that thought, Luna. Victoria won't enjoy hearing it either." I looked at Patrick as he gazed at the door. His eyes still glowed. I'm trying not to open my big mouth and ask him, but it's getting really fucking hard not to.

"My grandmother and Undine are friends. Maybe I can ask her if she knows how her friend is doing." Luna pulled her phone out of her bag under the desk and quickly typed away. I watched as Patrick got up and hurried to the door.

"We've got company," he said as he opened the door, exposing Valyn, Westley and Victoria standing in the doorway; Valyn's fist was in the air mid-knock. Patrick moved away from the door and closer to Luna. I instinctively moved to the other side of her. It's odd feeling like I need to protect her from her mate, but he's been treating her like a porcelain doll since we got on board.

"May we come in?" Valyn asked before crossing the threshold. We both glanced down at Luna, who had rolled up a map and secured it with a small piece of rope. I looked back at Valyn and shrugged. I could see that it bothered the other two, but they kept their mouths shut.

"I don't care. I'll leave the room." Luna stood up, map in hand, and made her way out of the cabin. Patrick followed closely behind her. I waited, hesitating at the desk. Valyn moved into the room, making his way to the desk. Victoria and Westley moved in behind him. The door shut behind Westley as he made his way inside.

"What was she looking at?" Victoria sifted through the paperwork and maps that were still scattered across the desktop. I slipped the notebook Luna was writing in into my jacket. She didn't want them seeing the map, so I highly doubt she wants them to snoop into her notes.

"She was looking into the sea wyverns. She said something was off with the kraken. Something about dead eyes or some shit." I said nonchalantly. I didn't actually know her plan, but I didn't want to give them too much information. Even if we are on the same side. "She sent her grandmother a text asking about the ongoings of Undine. She's got a working theory of some sort, but I don't know much else. Sorry."

I excused myself from the room, closing the door behind me as they began speaking among themselves. I took the quiet moment to head up to the top deck and check out what Luna had been scribbling in the notebook. I nestled between two barrels, hiding from anyone looking in this direction. Something told me no one would come looking for me, but I could be wrong.

I flipped through the first few pages, making sure it wasn't her private diary or something special like that. I may be snooping, but I'm not a disrespectful snoop. *That's why you watched her getting fucked through shadows. Fucking idiot. What do you think she would say if she found out that you gripped and pleasured yourself to her? Think she would trust you? Or are you hoping she'd fuck you too?* I was really starting to hate that little voice in my fucking head. I didn't need it reminding me I fucked up on a royal level. But, if given the opportunity, I would do it all over again.

The first few pages were just elaborate portraits done in pen and pencil. The first page was a detailed drawing of Valyn's face with his newly acquired scar. The next displayed a gorgeous picture of Victoria, her hair flowing in the wind beneath a heavily shaded bandana. There were sketches of flowers, animals and the stars. A few pages in was a very detailed drawing of Patrick and Westley, standing around a barrel looking as if they were in mid-laugh when she started drawing. I chuckled quietly to myself as I marveled at her talent, but then I flipped the page.

Staring back at me was my own face. Every detail, outlined perfectly. She shaded in my eyes, one with a blue pen, the other with black. She caught the details of my own scar with precision, as if she had traced the scar over my eye right onto the paper. Little freckles and faint scars that I had long since forgotten about, she caught them all in her detailed drawing. If I didn't feel the paper in my hands, I would think I'm looking into a mirror. When did she draw this? I didn't see her at all with this journal in front of her.

My thoughts began to wander as I turned the page and saw more drawings. These of men I don't know. They must be the rest of her mates. Each male had exquisite details drawn into the features, like she was drawing them from memory. I wish my memory was as good as this that I could draw my memories into existence. At least the ones that mattered. I pushed the thoughts that bubbled up deep down inside of me. I flipped a few more pages and halted on a page filled with coordinates and names. Markers most likely for the map that she had taken with her. Maybe she was right and something really was wrong with their water goddess. It would explain the hostility from the sea.

I wonder if Valmor would have any idea about the sea creatures. He was always telling me how I had to see the oceans and the wonders that lived there. Maybe he might know if the Goddess Undine had lost her mind or if Marcloff finally found a way to control an immortal.

CHAPTER 28
RAFAEL

Valmor answered on the first ring. "What's wrong?" His voice sounded cold and off. Maybe I was bothering him. Or maybe something was happening in Hellis that I wasn't aware of. It's not like I had been in contact much since I've been with Luna.

"What's your take on the goddess Undine?" I asked, trying to keep my tone nonchalant. The silence on the other end of the phone was rather deafening.

"What do you want to know?" He asked. The coldness of his voice was gone and replaced with the more casual tone I was accustomed to.

"Do you know anything about her or her doings? Sea creatures around Doria are going crazy; the ship we're on got attacked by a fucking Kraken," I chuckled as I continued flipping through Luna's journal.

"I'm sorry, what? You're on a ship? Captain Motion Sickness is on the choppy seas?" I could hear the disbelief and the laughter that burst out of him at the thought of seeing me on a ship. Something crashed on the other end of the phone. "Shit! I need a fresh coffee now. All jokes aside, there hasn't been a Kraken sighting in a good century. Are you sure that's what you saw?"

"Yes, Luna said it sounded like it was being controlled, lifeless eyes and just wanted it to stop. And before you ask, I had no idea she could talk to creatures. She apparently had a run-in with Noro not that long ago. She said, the creature isn't bad." I let out a soft chuckle at the thought of her saying, not every creature is inherently bad.

"You think there might be something else at play here?" Valmor questioned. His curiosity was piqued at the thought of what the actual answer to my questions was.

"I don't know. I don't think Marcloff has control of any sea creatures, but that doesn't mean he didn't find a way to start. You know just as well as I do what he is capable of. Are we sure he hasn't bred anything new and exciting?" A long pause echoed from the other end. I could tell he was thinking of all the creatures that we already knew about, not even thinking of the ones we didn't know of.

"Let me run this by Zekon and see what he might think. Valdis and the others are still here as well. Maybe we can do some reconnaissance while they are here and try to get a better handle on the situation here. As far as your question about Undine is concerned, I am not the person to ask that question to. I never met her. But maybe talk to her daughter? You might have better luck with her." Valmor was right, but something tells me that is not an option.

"I appreciate you're looking into things. If I find out anything, I'll let you know. How did the reunion go?" I asked, trying to gauge the situation back home.

"It went well. Zekon wants to go public, and I'm trying not to let him do that. You know how dangerous that would be for Hellis and for him." There it is. Valmor is looking out for himself. It wouldn't be dangerous for Zekon; if anything, it would give hope to the people that someone other than those from Hellis actually cared. Announcing Talissa as his mate and wife would be the best thing for himself. Valmor just assumes that he would have no place in the court, no room for his advisor position. I think Talissa would keep him on. He's a good guy when he can get out of his own way.

"My friend, I think you need to let Zekon do what he wants. If you try to stop him, it could be looked at as treason. You know that as well as I do. Treason has always been a crime worthy of death." I reminded him that I am not the only one whom Zekon is harboring. Valmor is a demigod, not a daemon. If he caused problems, it would look bad on Zekon.

"I know, but aren't you as worried as I am that this could have a catastrophic fallout with our people?" Valmor tried to get me to see his side. I took a deep breath and looked down at the deck where Luna was standing. I may not have been with her long, but I can tell she would be just as worth it.

"Valdis is public with Luna. It's no secret how the people of Infernia revere her. I think they would be ecstatic to know that Talissa was on their side, fighting for their freedom from a tyrant." I don't think we are going to have to worry about the people turning their backs on Zekon if they didn't turn their backs on Alastar or Valdis." I had to get him to see it my way. These women are not the problem. They are the solution we all need.

"You may be right, but we don't know for sure. I have to go. Be safe, and watch your back. Can't have you dying on me." Valmor chuckled before the line went dead. I put the phone back in my pocket, casting my gaze to the sky. A star shot across the sky so fast I almost missed it.

Lend me the strength I need to keep her safe. I want a new world for all of our people.

CHAPTER 29
VALYN

"Do you think she will forgive me?" I asked Westley and Victoria as they took the seats across from the desk that Rafael and Patrick had vacated. It was odd to see two other males protect her so vehemently. I didn't think anything would bother me more. I trusted Patrick, but to see him just switch against me like that didn't anger me; it made me sad. Rafael I didn't know well enough to decide how I felt about him having her back like he has. But I get it. He was given orders to protect her; he's a soldier just following orders.

"She's your mate. She will forgive you regardless. I mean, for fuck's sake, didn't she forgive Bastian for the bullshit he pulled?" Victoria reminded me of the time we had found out Niklaus was her mate as well.

"He wasn't the only one she forgave for that. We all laid hands on Niklaus. We almost killed him, not knowing what it would do to her. I guess only time will tell." I said resigning myself to look over the maps on the desk.

"My bigger concern is what she was doing looking through all the maps? Does she know what she is looking at, or do you think she is just trying to figure something out by looking at locations and things like that?" Westley pointed out. I wasn't sure whether or not she actually knew how to read maps. What I did know is that she might be right about Undine playing a bigger part in the chaos from the sea. What if something were here, and we didn't know?"

"Victoria, can you call Jasmine and see if she has heard anything from her mother yet? I know you said she didn't want you on the sea until this craziness was figured out, but if Luna's theory is correct, maybe something happened to Undine and she might need help.

"I can try, but I can't promise you anything. I'm in hot water with her for setting sail back on the Birkenhead after what happened to the Selestine." Victoria excused herself from the room, leaving Westley and me alone.

"Do you think that we have a chance of getting ahead of this? What if Luna is right and Undine is in danger? How the hell are we supposed to help save the Goddess of the Sea if we can't get down there ourselves?" Westley's concerns were ones I had of my own. I would be able to get below sea long enough, but I don't know what it would look like for the others. Luna might be able to join me under the sea, but then again she might not. Granted, she was in fight mode earlier with the Kraken and did a stellar job.

"Wait a second. Where the fuck did a Kraken come from? I thought they went extinct a few centuries ago." Westley seemed to realize it the same moment I did.

"There have been no Kraken sightings in a few centuries. Maybe it went into slumber and not extinct like everyone thought." Westley tried to help me figure it out, but we both were coming up short. I looked at a map of the Kilspur and the Selpie seas. The only creatures we've been hearing rumors of was those like Noro. Sea Wyverns taking out ships and attacking people. But, as Luna pointed out, Noro wasn't bad. She was protecting the souls of the children that the fae of the Autumn realm let fall to their deaths on the cliffs. She only attacked those who entered her waters and threatened her.

"What if we've had it wrong all along and it wasn't sea wyverns attacking ships, but Krakens?" I said, looking over the water patterns that had been marked in on the map. "What if we have both Krakens and Sea Wyverns to worry about?"

The door opened once more, than Victoria sauntered back in. "No luck. Her mother isn't responding to calls. She said she was going to go home and see her mother tonight. Maybe get some eyes on her to put all our minds at ease." She took her seat again, glancing between us. "The fuck did I miss now?"

"Oh, you know, the idea that Krakens aren't extinct and that we probably have Krakens and sea wyverns knocking at the doors of Doria," Westley said nonchalantly. I watched Victoria pale at the mention of sea wyverns and the thought of more krakens.

"You have got to be fucking kidding me? Can your wife figure it out? Can't she talk to them or some shit like that?" Victoria started panicking, and I knew the spiral would only continue.

"We will talk with her later. Right now she needs to relax, and I need not to push her." I said. Westley smiled at her and then looked at me.

"I'll go talk to her. Let's face it, she's not just mad at you," Westley reminded me. Maybe he was right. She needed someone besides me to talk to. Patrick and Rafael are her confidants on this voyage and I have to understand that.

"Fine, you do that while Victoria and I mark out where the attacks occurred. The last thing we need is merchants following our routes and getting attacked and worse, killed. We can't shut down trades with the surrounding realms, but we may have to find a different means to get the products back and forth. And before you even say it, the realm portals are not feasible.

Imagine carrying boxes and crates through the portal one by one. Ships are our fastest options." I said, cutting them both off before they could argue with me.

Westley got up and excused himself from the room as Victoria and I set about mapping out our next course of action.

CHAPTER 30
LUNA

Doria's nightlife awaited us just off the coast. Many of the crew barely made it home alive after the giant kraken attacked us in the middle of the sea. The Birkenhead took severe damage, but we made it here alive. Valyn, Westley and Victoria had holed up inside the captain's quarters after I walked out, going over the maps and marking where we got attacked, and where they got attacked previously. They had been coming up with a plan to keep others away from the path that could potentially harm others. I couldn't sit in there with them as they set about their plans and ideas. I needed to be as far away from them as I could be. I knew what they were talking about only because Valyn had opened his thoughts to me.

The night sky was calm now. Stars twinkling in the dark blue sky, barely any clouds in sight. The cool breeze coming off of the Selpie Sea chilled me to the bone. I guess it's to be expected when you're out at sea at night, regardless of the season. Not to mention that I didn't fully dry off after jumping in to save

Patrick. A sudden brush against my shoulders had me tensing up tightly.

"Sorry, I just thought you could use a sweater." Patrick Moore let the sweater hang loosely on my shoulders. "I didn't mean to scare you. I'm sorry." He looked out at the city and smiled.

"It's okay, just maybe a little warning next time so I don't stab you or swing on you." He chuckled, but nodded. "Thank you. I was just thinking that it was getting chilly."

"My brothers and father had taught me how to be a gentleman. It's a big deal within our family, actually. I know Prince Valyn is your mate and should be the one looking after you, but you're giving off the vibes that their bickering from before was stressing you out, and that you rather not be around them right now." Patrick said as he leaned up against the side of the ship. I nodded slightly. All the arguing was giving me a headache, and I really didn't want that to happen. "I should have said this to you sooner, but thank you for saving me. I'm sorry I yelled at you back there. I was just worried about your safety, and I don't want you putting yourself at risk for me."

"What are you thanking me for? Also, don't mention it. I'm not as fragile as people make me seem. I can take a scolding from a friend." I teased as I joined him. He looked over at me;

his bright green eyes felt like they were looking straight into my soul.

"You saved my life not once, but twice. The sea has been my home since I was a child. My brothers and I would always be out here. Either with our father on his fishing boat, or with Valyn and his brothers. We all have a bond to the sea. Or so we thought. My father always warned us that the sea was a fickle mistress who would lure us into a false sense of security just to take our lives. I never believed him until now." He looked back out at the shore. Night merchants were setting up shop for the night market, fewer than I remember from my last visits. It was looking like Mistveil's docks here. Tents lined up on the beach, some with purple tops, others with black. Torches danced to life as the fire from the owners of the stands signaled they were open for business.

"Do you think they are right in keeping people away from the sea?" I asked him as I watched children run along the beach ahead of their parents to the market stalls. He watched them too, a smile tugging at his lips.

"I think they will do the right thing for all of those involved. The safety of our people means more to them than their own lives. I'm sure you have noticed this by now. They put their loved ones first before themselves, not realizing that losing them would hurt their loved ones the most." He spoke so softly. I could hear the admiration and worry in his voice. He didn't want to lose any of them, and neither did I.

"Then I guess it's our job to remind them that they are just as important as the rest of us." I replied with a smile. Patrick smiled back at me. Our attention turned back to the market, vendors shouting out to passersby as they perused the stalls. The rest of the ship had gone quiet, the crew resting up before we made port. I can only imagine that they want to get off this ship and back to their families as fast as they can.

"I wonder if the others made it back to Doria yet," Patrick said, more to himself than to me. But it caught my attention. I thought everyone who was on board was the entire crew.

"There were others?" I asked. His eyes darted to me and then back to the shoreline. He let out a deep sigh.

"Yeah, a few refused to come back on board. I don't envy Vic, or Valyn, or even my brother. They have to go to the homes and let the families know they are no longer in the Royal naval per desertion. They refused to go back to sea. Honestly, if they were here, you would have people to save because they were useless during the first attack. Hiding in barrels and lying low, leaving the rest of us to pick up the slack." I could feel some rage radiating from Patrick as he talked about the others.

"That's enough, Patrick." Westley's voice cut through our conversation, ripping our attention to the second in command. Westley walked up to where we were standing, giving his brother a stern look. "Go get your stuff ready. We will be off boarding shortly." Patrick gave him a look before turning his attention back to me.

"It was nice chatting with you, Princess. I hope we can speak again soon." Patrick bowed before he left us. I watched as Westley looked out over the shore. He smiled as he watched the children dragging their parents along to the different stalls.

"What was that all about?" I questioned. Westley took a moment before looking at me.

"People are afraid, Princess Luna. They fear for their lives daily. Being out at sea used to be a comfort for us, something we took for granted. The sea never turned on us until now. I don't blame those who chose not to return after the first attack. But they are not civilians; they knew the dangers of being in the navy. They chose that danger, time and time again, when things were safe. Now, at the first sign of genuine danger, they run like cowards. So yes, I understand my brother's rage at them. I also understand why they chose not to return. I hope you don't think less of them; they put themselves and their families first. I can't fault them for that." Westley's words reminded me of what Patrick and I had just talked about.

"I can't blame people for not wanting to put their lives at risk if there is another way back. Another attack came on the way here. At the end of the day, you can only expect so much from people. Wouldn't you put yourself first if you had family at home waiting on you to return safely?" I asked him. I didn't know whether or not he did, and I really shouldn't have assumed. He let out a low chuckle.

"I do. My wife is seven months pregnant. I choose myself first most times so I can make it home to her and our unborn child." He paused as footsteps came from behind us. Rafael leaned up against the railing beside us. "I signed up to be in the navy. I followed my older brother's footsteps, and I know the damage that can be caused when you don't think about yourself first. I'm no good to anyone if I am dead."

Rafael sucked in a deep breath, and for a moment I wondered what was running through his mind. "You just gained yourself a guardian daemon, Westley. Like it or not. As long as Luna is with you, I will be with you as well. You will make it home to your wife and unborn child. I promise you that." Westley paused as he took in Rafael, and I mean really took him in. I don't think he's actually looked at him at all since we boarded the Birkenhead.

"Why would you make that promise to me? You barely know me." Westley was suspicious of him. And I guess I couldn't really blame him. Daemons are supposed to be the enemy, yet here I am mated to one, and apparently have one as a personal bodyguard. Not like it's needed, I huffed to myself.

"I wasn't there to save my wife or my unborn son. I know the pain of that loss; it's not a pain I would wish on even my worst enemy. Well, maybe one person. You seem like a good person, so I will do my best to protect you and keep you alive to see the birth of your child. What are you having?" Rafael smiled widely, small canines caught my attention. Were those always there?

"Not yet. Alyssa doesn't want to know the gender yet. She's thinking it'll be a girl. Part of me hopes she's wrong, but a big part of me hopes she's right." Westley gushed over his wife and the pregnancy to Rafael, who looked interested in the conversation. Smiling and nodding and adding in his own little advice. I quietly excused myself from their conversation and made my way to the back of the ship.

Would I want to bring a child into this world right now? I can only imagine what's going through his wife's head every time he leaves. The thought of children made me smile, but what world would we be bringing them into right now if we willingly decided that now was the time to get pregnant? It's irresponsible of me to even be thinking about that right now. The world is on fire, and that needs to be fixed before I even consider having a child.

Even though my mind is made up, it doesn't stop my heart from thinking about the possibility of children with my mates and how wonderful of fathers they would all be. While also imagining what those little ones might look like. Maybe one day we will have a family with children and live in a much quieter place than we do now.

CHAPTER 31
LUNA

Westley had apologized once more for his blatant disrespect earlier, and I had to do the same. I was just as much in the wrong to snap at him like I did. I really need to get a handle on my attitude before I end up chopping off someone's head for questioning why my hair is blue, or why my eyes sparkle like the galaxy above. My patience has been wearing thin lately, and my urge to lock everyone I care about up in a dungeon and go off by myself to murder Marcloff in the most gruesome way imaginable has been very strong. I don't know if it's because I haven't seen my other mates recently, the lack of sex with them all, or just hormones running amok inside my body as all of these damn changes have been happening.

Finally alone with Rafael, I looked up at him as he reached into his jacket. "I grabbed your notebook off of the desk after you left. You took the map, so I figured you needed that, or at least would want it. Victoria immediately started going through the maps and most of what you were touching after you left the room. I gave them the theory you have, but not all of it. Let them do some figuring things out on their own." I took the journal, running my hand over the deerskin cover that bound the pressed pages together. It was one of the few things I had left of Gunther. He wasn't always that great to me, and knowing everything he did to my mother enrages me. But, for years he raised me when he could've cast me out the front door with nothing more than the clothes I had on my back. I should toss it into the sea and let it drown. But part of me can't let go of the last encounter we had before he died. Drake is my father, but Gunther had kept me safe in times when I couldn't take care of myself.

"Thank you. I didn't mean to leave it in there. I'm assuming you looked inside?" It was a question, but also an assumption I had made. He could deny it, but ever since becoming a goddess my senses have become so keen, I'll be able to smell him on every page that he touched. This was one of my ways of gauging the level of trust I can give him.

"Yes. I wanted to make sure it wasn't a personal diary or anything that you had left behind." He didn't deny it. Honestly, I was surprised. I opened the book and flipped through the pages until I found the drawing of him. He found it on his own.

"Sorry. I probably shouldn't have looked. You did a great job catching some features that even I forgot about."

"I've always been able to draw, but ever since my final changing, I see details that I never saw before. Ones I didn't even know existed. Drawing centers me and keeps me focused when I'm having a spiraling anxiety attack." I confessed as I turned back to the shoreline. "Celvenia had night markets, but nothing like the one out there. You didn't let children run free in the streets, and if you were a woman capable of bearing children, you didn't go there alone unless you had knife skills and an uncanny ability to kill someone."

"Celvenia is a human city. Why on earth were you there?" he questioned, and then it hit me. He knew nothing about my past. Nothing about what happened to me with either of my changings or the fact that until about a year ago, I didn't even know who I really was. Time has gone by in the blink of an eye now that I think about it. If you would've told me five years ago that I would have the life I have now, I would've asked how drunk you were or what drugs you were partaking. Now, this feels like I'm living in one of my fantasy books from back home.

"I lived there." I watched as shock rippled across his face. "There is so much you don't know, and so much that I am still learning myself. I went through two changings. The first when

I got here a little over a year ago that took me from a powerless human into the true fae that I was. Then, my death, which was actually my final changing, where I gained my goddess powers. That was more recently."

I watched him take a deep breath, contemplating his next words carefully. "I have questions. A few, but I don't want to just assume if I ask you will be comfortable answering them." He paused, waiting for my acknowledgement to move forward. I nodded my head and kept quiet, giving him the floor to ask what he wanted. "You lived as a human, how? Your features are those of the fae. Were you treated fairly there or more like an outcast? And finally, what do you mean you died?"

There was a lot to unpack here. Every question he asked had a lot more than just a simple answer. I guess I can start with the most recent event. "I was technically murdered by one of my mother-in-laws. She's dead now, but I was killed in the middle of my final changing into goddesshood. It was a bit of an interesting time. That's how I met Talissa and the others. That's also when we found out that they were being poisoned and essentially held hostage in Celestia. As for how I lived as a human, well, it was apparently magic. It held off my fae changing, kept most of my fae features at bay, and what it didn't hide I was able to conceal with some hair dye and bleach.

People could tell I was different. I didn't fit the normal mold of those in Celvenia. However, I made friends who accepted my uniqueness. They have never treated me any differently because of who I was. They saw me for who I was on the inside. We were our own little brand of misfits."

I smiled warmly, thinking about everything we dealt with and how far each of us has come. I was lucky to have them with me in this life. "My life as a human is over, but I brought those friends with me. Well, the twins at least. Virgil was kind of brought to the fae realm against his own will, but to be fair it was my brother Nox who brought him here after my half-brother stabbed Virgil in the chest."

"Your half-brother is the one possessed and working under Marcloff's control, correct?" Rafael looked at me with hesitation. I couldn't tell whether it was worry or concern. I would not break at the mention of Luther, though. I have many things I want to say to that man when we can finally get the Hilmer out of him. Not to mention I want to beat his ass for everything he said, before and after his possession.

"Yes. He is my mother's son, but his father was my false father. The one who gave me this journal. He wasn't always the best to me, but in the end he did apologize for his actions. Well, in part, of his actions. There was still much he was taking to his grave.

Thankfully, my mother and real father were able to explain to me why I was treated the way I was. It made a lot of sense. Do you know the Hilmer possessing my brother?"

Rafael nodded. "His name is Ishtar. He is one of Marcloff's right-hand men and also his most loyal Hilmer. He was someone I worked with closely, but we are worlds apart. For starters, he is a Hilmer, and I am not. I have a conscience, and he doesn't. But most importantly, I have values that I hold to a higher standard."

"Do Hilmers have a body of their own?" I questioned, it had been a thought on my mind since this whole war had started.

"Not really. They have vessels. Some are daemons who want to become strong and are willing to sacrifice who they are for Marcloff's version of the greater good. However, most Hilmers take vessels who are prisoners, draining them of their souls and life forces until they are no longer necessary." Rafael's words echoed the hollowness in my heart. "The stronger the vessel, the longer they can use it. If a Hilmer possessed a god or goddess, they could use their life force for eternity." Something registered with him the moment he made the connection between gods and Hilmers. "Your brother is a god."

"No, he is only a halfling. One who hasn't completed the changing, that I know of. He still has the weakness of a human body." I corrected him. A wave of relief washed over his face, but only for a moment. "Do we need to worry that a Hilmer might've possessed Undine?"

"I wouldn't think so, but you never know. If so, that makes our job so much harder." Rafael sighed as he looked over his shoulder at the shore. The Birkenhead was coming to a halt at the dock. Soon we would make landfall and would have to figure things out much quicker than I anticipated. If Undine had been compromised, we might be fucked.

CHAPTER 32
VALYN

Joyous laughter and conversation filled the air as we departed from the Birkenhead. Children shouted and waved at us as we made our way from the dock and onto the beach. The night market was in full swing; merchants of all sorts were touting their wares for the people of Doria. Westley had parted ways with us once we hit the beach. He wanted to get home to his wife to let her know he was safe. Victoria began browsing the stalls as she waited for Jasmine to join her. I just stood back and watched as Luna was joined by Patrick and Rafael as she made her way through the crowd of people. Most smiled at her and waved; some bowed, knowing who she was to me and, in turn, to them. Children offered her shells and little trinkets they had found on the shore. Luna graciously accepted every little gift with a smile and a gentle nod of thanks. Rafael and Patrick looked like they were her body guards the way they put themselves around her.

The night air wasn't as thick as it normally would be during the day. The humidity level was relatively low for this time of year. I made my way through the throng of people to reach Luna. I gently wrapped my arms around her waist, pulling her closer to my side. Rafael and Patrick seemed to take the hint and made their way through the crowd to the closest armory stall. Doria has some of the best steel for making weapons. Taiga was second best in comparison.

"Enjoying being back on land?" I whispered in her ear as I placed little kisses on her check. Her giggle sent chills through me.

"It took a few minutes to get adjusted to not rocking, but the sands helping with that." She pressed into my side as we made our way through the market, looking at stalls filled with jewelry, clothes, everything one could possibly want. Luna caught the scent of a stall filled with pastries and steered right to it. I couldn't help but chuckle a little at the though that even after being at sea, she still wanted something to satisfy her sweet tooth.

"Prince Valyn, good evening. What can I get you?" A young woman with long blonde curly hair smiled at us from behind the counter. Her eyes shifted to Luna as she looked at all the pastries and cookies that were on display. "Princess Luna! It's an honor. My name is Lena. Let me know what I can get you."

Luna looked up from a strawberry croissant and smiled. "Can I have this one, please? It smells so good." Lena smiled at us as she put on gloves and went about wrapping up the strawberry croissant in a pink wrapping paper for Luna.

"Would you like it boxed up, or would you prefer to eat it as you go?" She asked with a wide smile. Luna was practically drooling looking at the pastry. Sometimes I forget just how much she likes sweet treats and sugary goodies and drinks.

"I think she'll eat it as we go. Is that a strawberry lemonade you've got there?" I asked, looking at a glass container that was mixing a red and pink liquid. Lena smiled and poured some in a plastic cup with a lid and straw before handing both items over to Luna, who smiled widely before thanking her repeatedly. I pulled out my wallet and went to pay, but Lena put her hand up.

"We don't take money for our treats at the night market. We just like to give back to the community that has helped us build up to be the best cafe in the city. Oh, the lemonade is more on the sweeter side, it has a slight bitter bite on the back end once you get to the bottom though." She smiled at us. I noticed her tip jar sitting on the counter and pulled out the largest bill I had in my wallet and stuffed it inside. She looked at me with wide eyes and smiled. "Thank you."

"Have a good night, Miss Lena. I hope the rest of the evening stays as good as it's looking like right now." I said as Luna nodded again in thanks before we left the stall. Luna was humming at the taste of the pastry, making the cutest of sounds as she ate and drank happily. We looked at a few other stalls before reaching the end of the market. It was getting late, and soon each stall would close up for the evening. My eyes landed on Rafael and Patrick, both eating and laughing as if they were good friends who had just recently seen each other after years apart. I still didn't know what to make of Rafael. Something about him was off. Then again, I knew nothing about him. Westley had filled me in a little bit on the ship. Losing his wife and unborn child is what had him flipping sides. It explained a lot of the scars and the super-protective nature of Luna. Surprisingly, he didn't set me off nearly as badly as Virgil still did. I've just gotten used to him being around and knowing that I could kill him in a heartbeat if he fucked up. Either that or Nox would kill him. Tensions have been high throughout Cerulia lately. The human lands have been plagued with the greying, and nothing seemed to get better.

Luna was still smiling away at the people. Giving high fives to the little ones who wanted one, hugging the others who asked. She made the perfect princess, even with no formal training. Nox had all the training to be a prince since birth, yet he was rougher around the edges around people. They were both shaped differently. Both were raised completely different. Where Luna struggled with people and being accepted, Nox didn't have that. The people accepted him, not needing to earn their approval or respect. Luna's had to do everything from the ground up. Maybe the struggles she went through, we all should've gone through before having the right to be called princes. She makes interacting with the people less like a chore and more like an honor. She refuses to let people treat her any different. I've learned so much from her, and yet, I still feel like I know nothing.

Nox and Virgil were helping Undas and Drake look for Otius's blade before it could be used against any of them. Vanalli and Vanessa have been working with Allura and the demigods to find Melody with Damian. So far no news has come my way about any of it. Bastian has been holed up in Taiga with Holly and Sirius, trying to get a read on the daemons that Holly wanted to autopsy for fun. Niklaus has been training day and night with Nora just to make sure that when the time came, they could protect everyone when the war finally kicked into full gear.

My mind raced on and on about where everyone was and what they were doing, that I wasn't paying much attention to Luna and what she was doing. I finally spun on my heels looking around the stalls for her bright blue hair. I finally laid eyes on her in front of a fortuneteller's stall. She was speaking with the woman behind the counter, a somber look on her face. Worry and dread filled me as I made my way to her. She was thanking the woman and turning away as I reached her.

"Is everything okay?" I asked her, letting her decide what she wanted to tell me about the interaction. I watched something flash across her face, a hollowness fill her eyes like she was about to cry. I hugged her closer to me without another word between us. Whatever she was told, she was keeping it close to her chest. I knew better than to pry. For her mental health and my sanity, we made our way straight out of the market and onto the path home. I noticed footsteps behind us, chancing a glance back to see Rafael and Patrick following us up the path. A noticeable shift in everyone's behavior and attitude. Victoria was behind them, with Jasmine in hand. I hadn't even looked for my cousin all night, but I could see the worry and concern on her face.

Luna was strong, but whatever the fortuneteller had told her, had her shaking in my arms.

We made it to the house after about a ten-minute walk from the beach. The lights were on inside; the smell of a pineapple cake lingered in the air as we opened the door. My mother was humming in the kitchen as we crossed the threshold. Victoria and Patrick made their way into the kitchen to let my mother know of our arrival. Rafael and Jasmine stood in the foyer waiting for instructions on where to go.

"The living room is down the hall on the right. Make yourself at home. I'm going to take Luna up to bed. It's been a long day." Jasmine knew where the room was and took Rafael down the hall as I took Luna upstairs. I opened the door to our room, the wide space was dimly lit by sconces on the wall on either side of the bed. The shadows danced across the floor as the midnight air trickled in from the open window, moving the curtains around the window and the bed gently. I pulled the cotton sheets back for her to take a seat on the bed, but she didn't. She looked so lost, like her mind was a million miles away from here.

"Come on, let's get you out of those clothes and into something more comfortable to sleep in." Luna just nodded at me. Letting me guide her into the attached bathroom to get her cleaned up. I knew better than to start something with her, even if it was all meant just to get her distracted. I grabbed a thin, light-grey tank top and a pair of soft blue shorts. I waited patiently as she took off her clothes. I examined every inch of her body, committing it to memory. I felt so bad for her. I worried about what was going on in her head, but I can't force her to talk about it. She went to grab the clothes from me, but I stopped her. "I got you, my love."

I slowly helped her put her top on, then her shorts. I went to step back, but she grabbed me, pulling me by my waist close to her. She buried her head in my chest and began sobbing. Letting everything that was in her slip away. The composure that she had been carrying with her this whole time. The thoughts that I knew she was having issues with all came to the surface. I just didn't know how much more she was holding in.

"I miss them all." She sobbed into my chest. And I felt it then, the weight of the world that she has been carrying. Even with all of us checking in mentally with her when we are apart, we haven't been together as a whole for what feels like forever. She hasn't felt the energy boost that she needs from us all. Even if only in a small amount. None of us considered what being apart would do to her mentally. I can do only so much for her by myself.

"I know you miss them. I'll see what I can do right now, my love. You need to sleep. Hopefully, this time you can get some sleep with no nightmares." I placed a kiss on the top of her head and guided her out of the bathroom and back into the bedroom, covering her up in the sheets before turning off the lights. I left the window open so the cool air could soothe her to sleep. The sound of the waves off in the distance should do the trick to help her.

She was lightly snoring before I even closed the door. I took a deep breath before tapping out a quick message to my brothers and Valdis.

She needs everyone. Even if it's only for one night, she needs a physical recharge, *and I can't do it alone. If you can step away for a night, get to Doria. ASAP.*

I put the phone back in my pocket and headed back down the stairs to join the others. I just hope she can sleep tonight with no issues, and that the others can come to see her before she spirals.

CHAPTER 33
NOX

Virgil's constant chattering teeth were getting on my last nerve. I told him to bundle up and pack extra clothes before we left, but no, he insisted he was used to the frigid cold. Bastard had no idea what he was in for. Thankfully, Undas had also had enough of his incessant teeth chattering and lit a fire for us in a nearby cave. Virgil and my father had decided that they couldn't go on any further and that we needed to rest. They insisted Yida would still be there in the morning, and I knew they were right; I just didn't know what kind of condition we would find it in. I wish we had gotten Bastian involved in this little hellscape mission. At least he would know more about the territory and the people who lived there.

"You're worried." Undas stated. The man had an uncanny ability to sense when I was on edge, and it unnerved me most of the time. He leaned up against the mountain next to me in a dark black t-shirt and long denim jeans. His bright red hair seemed dim in the coldness of the mountain pass. I also think it had something to do with the unusual lack of sun this time of year around here.

"I'm not worried; I'm annoyed. Why did we bring my father and the human with us?" I questioned Undas's reasoning behind bringing them along. I get my father, but why Virgil? He wasn't immortal, granted, but he was great with a sword and has had my back in almost every fight that we've encountered, and he's grown on me. But this was different. He could die out here, and even though he had a zero chance with my sister now that she is mated and married, she would still obliterate us if anything happened to him.

"Harold isn't the only one who can grant fae life." Undas said bluntly. I paused. That thought had never crossed my mind that maybe he wanted to become a fae.

"Has he expressed wanting that as an option?" I asked. He and I had never discussed it before, hell I don't even think I told him that there was an option like that. Would he really want to give up being human to become fae and live a lifetime knowing that the woman he loved he can never have because she is taken? Wouldn't that be fucking cruel? I think it would, but that's just a personal decision.

"He has. Not to you because he thinks you will talk him out of it and not want him to go through with it." Undas was blunt with me and it kind of hurt. He has become a good friend to me. I might've told him to weigh his options because there is no going back, but I would've been supportive. "Before you question me. Yes, he knows the risks of turning fae. That there is no going back once he changes, and that he risks Luna's fury when she finds out that he didn't consult with her first. We all risk her fury. But, he rather not be the reason something happens to someone else because they have to keep an eye on him so that he doesn't die every time he's in a fight with us."

"Who will do it?" I simply asked. I wouldn't want to be the one holding someone's life in my hands.

"I will. Harold's done it a handful of times, but your father has never done it once. He doesn't want to be the one to risk Virgil's life if something goes wrong. None of us wants to risk Luna's wrath if something happens to him. Virgil also doesn't want to feel like a burden on us when we go into battle. We always have to make sure that he is safe and that he is still breathing. How many times during this mission have we had to stop so he could rest? He hates it, but he's here. He sticks by all of our sides. This mission means more to him than I think you realize. It's not just a way to prove his worthiness, which he has already proved a hundred times over, but it's to find something that can kill not only Luna, but his new family."

Undas's words struck a chord with me. *New family.* We have become his family since he's come here. His own family had disowned him and refused to acknowledge that their son still lived. They rather look at him like he is dead instead of the possibility that he "defected" to the enemy. I didn't think about that at all in the time we had been together. I was only thinking of myself and not of him and what he was going through. I've been a dick and a shitty friend.

I glanced back inside the cave. My father was huddled around the fire with Virgil sitting next to him. As cold as it was, my father wasn't actually feeling any of it. He might feel a little bit of a sting because he's nothing like me or my grandfather, but he doesn't need the fire... yet. Virgil was putting his jacket near the fire, close enough to warm up the inside, but not too close enough for it to catch a blaze.

"Why didn't we just call Bastian? He could've helped us with recon." I finally said it out loud. The thought that had been swirling in my mind since the moment we set out on this mission.

"Because if Luna needs him, which she will. He would have to choose between going to her or staying with us. He would choose her every time and we would have to accept the fact that he would leave us. Just like if something happened to your mother, you father would take off in a heartbeat. Same with me and your grandmother. It's a thing that comes with being mated. Eventually, you will find that out." Undas was right. If Bastian was here and something happened to Luna, he would feel torn, but would pick her. Then he would come back to help us out of guilt. I will say that much about him. He was one who hated choosing sides and would always feel guilty about choosing something over another. But he was loyal. That meant more to me than anything.

"Fine. How much longer are we going to be resting before we finish up and get to Yida? I don't want to be caught like a sitting duck waiting to be fried." I pushed off the wall and looked at Virgil as he repacked his pack and put his jacket back on. "How much longer until you plan on changing him?"

Undas took a moment as the snow began to fall again. The fresh scent filling the air. The wind picked up, moving the pine trees back and forth. "I think we might want to get inside with them. It looks like a storm is coming, and we probably should rest up. Not knowing what the situation in Yida is right now, we are going to need our strength. As for Virgil," Undas paused as he looked at Virgil and my father. "I think sooner is better than later."

"So, this is his test?" I asked. Undas nodded. "Then let's make our boy immortal." Undas glanced back into the cave where Virgil and my father were chatting, then back to me.

"Aren't you worried something might go wrong?" He asked, his brow raised.

"Of course I am. But like you said, it's not your first time. Just," I paused as I watched him laugh with my father over something that was said. "Try not to kill him. I've grown to like the human."

Undas smiled and entered the cave. His body taking up the far wall of the cave. Virgil looked up from the fire and waved for me to come join them. To think this whole friendship spawned from my little sister, making me promise to keep this man alive. Her feelings may not be the same as when she asked that of me, but they still love each other regardless of the form.

I entered the cave with a smile. Tomorrow we will be in Yida, and hopefully on our way home with the only weapon that could kill a god.

CHAPTER 34
LUNA

The salty sea air caressed my skin, washing away the sweat from the evening. The words of the fortuneteller still circled in my head.

You will be their undoing. But you will be the world's rebirth. You will lose many. But you will save many more. Your choices will dictate the outcome of the war. But you may not see the other side. Pick your battles carefully. Pick your allies even more so.

I didn't think Valyn needed to hear those words. I don't think any of them need to know what she told me. I didn't think anything bad of the older woman. She was kind and felt bad, hesitating before telling me what she saw. She only relented when I asked her to tell me. I needed to know what I could do to change the tides of war. I grabbed my journal; I needed something to write all of my thoughts down on. My head was swimming with the thought of one of my mates or my family dying at the hands of Marcloff. What if it's a friend instead? I don't want to lose anyone. I wrote out each sentence on a separate piece of paper. This way I could use the whole sheet to tear apart the meanings of the whole thing. She said I might not make it to the other side. Does that mean I will die? Only one blade out there can kill me for good, and that's fucking missing. What if there was another way to kill a god that we aren't aware of?

My head was spiraling, trying to think of what that could mean. What other type of threat could take me out? I started letting the pen glide across the paper, carving out a random object in ink. I had no clue where my mind or hand were taking me, but I had no choice but to continue letting it go. An arch here, a few straight lines there, more arches and a pillar. When my hand finally stopped moving, I blinked at the page. It wasn't a weapon. It wasn't some random common tool that could take me out.

It was a cage.

A jolt shook me awake from a near slumber as I felt like I was falling. The room was empty. No sign of Valyn or any other life, for that matter. How long had I been sleeping? Slipping out from under the covers, I made my way to the balcony. I noticed my bag, with my journal in it, was sitting on the little table by the door. I grabbed it and thumbed through the pages. Didn't I write something in this?

I decided to take it out onto the balcony with me. There was a cute little iron table that Valyn had bought for me a little while ago. It had the cutest two little chairs on either side, so we could dine outside if we wanted to with the beautiful view of the city and the sea in the distance. Doria was one of the first cities I had seen since coming to the fae kingdom. It's hard to imagine that in each realm there was a human city or two that weren't afraid of the fae, but instead embraced them. I wish Celvenia would've embraced the fae instead of listening to someone's fears.

All fear comes from some small kernel of truth.

I sighed. That little voice was right. All fear sparked from something. Even if it was just one interaction, all it takes is one rumor and one person to believe it. Then it all spreads like wildfire and there's no containing it. Fennik had explained that his father was worried the greying would infect his people. Not realizing that his people were also the humans that he chose to abandon. I never really confronted my father-in-law about his part in the suffering of my sister and others. It's not like he created the greying, so it wasn't fully his fault. But he held some responsibility for not helping the humans. I think when we return home that I will talk to him about it. He's always been kind to me, so maybe he will understand where my feelings are. There are children that are getting sick and dying. Gods forbid a Hilmer tries to possess a child. They would die instantly.

I shook off the thoughts of death and thumbed through the pages of my journal. Did I really only dream of writing in my journal? I retraced my steps, writing out the words the fortuneteller had foretold. One sentence on each page. I let my hand glide across the page once more, praying that the image was different this time around. It wasn't. A gilded cage decorated with vines sprawled out on the page before me. A bed lay in the center of the cage, a shadowy image in the center of it. Nothing else was around the bed.

What could this mean? I was deep in thought when a thud sounded across the balcony. I quickly jumped to my feet, holding my pen as if it were a deadly knife to plunge into my invader's eye. "Woah! Don't stab me. That would be really messy, and I wouldn't want to have to be the one to clean that mess up." Rafael was standing before me, arms up in surrender. I let out the breath that I held, placing my pen back on the journal.

"You are going to get yourself stabbed one of these days. You know that, right?" I said as I closed the journal up so he couldn't see what I was writing. "What's up?"

"I got word from Valmor about Undine. I wasn't sure if you heard from your grandmother yet. Jasmine hasn't heard anything, but I didn't want to give a report to anyone else before speaking with you first." Rafael stood at attention. A perfect soldier waiting to be given an order.

"Alright, what's going on?" I wanted him to just spit it out. I needed some good news, but the look on his face told me it was anything but good.

"Marcloff released one of his abominations into the seas. I've got an idea of which creature it is, but it's one of his creations and if I'm right, it went after Undine to take power of the seas." He said as I watched him visibly shudder.

"Get Jasmine. I want her in here when you tell me about the creature. She needs to know what the possibility is of her mom's safety." Rafael nodded and took off the same way he came. He wasn't gone for more than a few moments before he came crashing back onto the balcony with a loud thud, Jasmine in his arms. "You know doors exist, right?"

Jasmine took a few steps away from him and got closer to me. "I like my feet on land or in the water, not the air." Jasmine quipped. I laughed a little at the look she was giving him.

"I think he has an aversion to everything but the air." I laughed. "Please have a seat. I didn't want Rafael giving me his intel without you. It has to do with your mother." Jasmine's eyes flared as she looked between us. Her turquoise and black braided hair jingled with the charms in them as she took her seat. We both turned our attention to Rafael, who was taking the jokes very well.

"If the intel is correct, and the creature is the one I am thinking of, it's not something I would want to be caught in dark waters with. Marcloff has the sirens, merfolk, and most of the dangerous sea creatures that want war and destruction willing to sacrifice themselves to take back the seas. He captured what can only be described as a legendary sea dragon, not a wyvern, and merged it forcefully with a siren. Beauty above the water, death below. I don't know if it was born or magically joined together. But the last time I laid eyes on the creature, it was toying with me. Taunting me with a hauntingly beautiful song that had me ready to jump into the tank with it to my death. I had no control over my body or my surroundings. Luckily for me at the time, Marcloff didn't want me dead. If he did in fact release it into the seas like it's believed, it would've gone after the most powerful being in the sea to take reign of the waters." Rafael paled at the memory of his encounter. I felt bad for him.

"You think it was released and got to my mother? She's been around sirens, merfolk, sea wyverns and sea dragons her whole life. Not to mention krakens, whales, sharks, jellyfish. You name it. What makes you think this is what got her?" Jasmine retorted at the accusation.

"Look, I'm saying that she wouldn't have seen it coming. I don't believe that your mother would've fallen prey so easily. But you can't deny that things in the sea have been off. Unless you have a better theory." Rafael opened the floor for her to speak her mind, but she didn't. No one could argue that the sea had become volatile. "I hope your mother is safe. I hope she didn't meet the creature, but we need to assume the worst."

"It can't kill Undine. She's a goddess and a very powerful one at that. There is only one blade that can kill a god or goddess and that blade, although stolen, wouldn't be at the depths of the sea. Maybe it captured her. You said it's a siren, sea dragon hybrid. I didn't know there was a difference between the species, but maybe we can get lucky and get her out of there safe and alive." I offered, looking at Jasmine, trying to console her while the world around her began burning. The fear I could sense from her was palpable. A fear I knew all too well. "We will go check it out. We just need to let the others know what our theory is."

"I'll take you to my home. Just promise me you will help save my mom and not try to kill her." Jasmine looked me dead in the eye. I could feel the fear and the promise of death behind her words if something happens to her mother by my hands or anyone who I trust.

"I promise you, as long as she doesn't try to kill me, I have no intention of killing her, only saving her." I said, keeping eye contact with her the entire time. "You have my word."

That seemed to be enough for her. We stood from the table and made our way into the room. "We'll leave tomorrow. I haven't seen Victoria in a bit and I would prefer some alone time with her before we all go risking our lives... again." Jasmine said with a wink. I couldn't help the chuckle that escaped my lips.

"I completely understand where you're coming from. Enjoy the evening. I'll see you in the morning." I smiled. Rafael and her left me alone with my thoughts.

Tomorrow is going to come fast and hard. We all need to be ready for the worst.

CHAPTER 35
LUNA

I headed back out onto the balcony as I awaited Valyn's arrival in the bedroom. I had watched Victoria and Jasmine head off down the path to wherever they were staying this evening. Hand in hand, they laughed and stole kisses as if nothing was going wrong in the world. I envied them for that.

I wasn't looking forward to dealing with the chaos of the morning. Things wouldn't be easy, and truthfully I would rather Valyn not come with us. Someone needed to stay above the sea, on land to help those who might need them more. Westley was a good choice as the peacekeeper, but we all knew that could be very limited. People needed to see the royal family, and although I am part of it, Valyn and his mother were the better-suited options to stay and help. Neither of them will like this decision, but I can handle it. I had to do this by myself. I couldn't risk losing Valyn if something had me sidelined.

The door creaked open as Valyn entered the room. He looked so tired. His appearance, which was usually put together, was now disheveled. The deep purple bags under his eyes were showing hints of blue and red. He needed sleep. I can't even remember the last time he actually slept. He tossed his shirt to the floor and flopped onto the bed, searching with his hands to find me. I came back into the room and lay on the bed next to him, putting my hand within arm's reach. He wasn't searching for my hand, however, instead grabbing for my breast.

"There are my comfy pillows." He exclaimed as he pulled himself up to rest his head on my chest. I could feel the weight of the world slowly slip away from his shoulders as he relaxed against my skin. "Can we just hide in here for the next few days?"

I let out a low chuckle. "No. You know we have things to do tomorrow. Things that are going to be tough for the two of us. Not to mention our friends and family. Did Jasmine tell you the plan?"

"Oh, you mean the one where you and she run off to play hero underwater and expect us to stay here and wait for you both to return?" He lifted his head, and I could hear every drop of sarcasm that dripped from his tongue. "I don't think it's a good idea for the two of you to be going there alone. I can be of use. So can Vic."

"I never said you both couldn't be, but you can also both be stubborn and hardheaded and a giant distraction for the both of us. What if something happens to you? Do you think I could forgive myself? What if I lost you? You might be immortal, but there are more things out there that can kill you than there are that can kill me." I felt him shudder at the reminder of how technically fragile he was compared to me.

I knew it was hard to hear. It was hard enough for me to say. I didn't want there to be this feeling of inferiority between us, but I wouldn't be able to go on if something happened to him and I wasn't there to make sure he was safe. Or worse, I was there, but was unable to save him. Almost losing him once was enough. He took a deep breath and buried himself back in my breasts and hummed. Something tells me this was his way of relenting.

We laid there in quiet bliss for a few moments, listening to the soft howling of the wind coming in from the sea. The smell of pineapples and something sweet filled my nose. Something smelled absolutely heavenly. It reminded me of the pastries from Lena's shop. Maybe she was already baking some for tomorrow. I wonder if she had breakfast food at her cafe or just pastries. My mind slowly wandered off until Valyn's fingers slowly ran up underneath my shirt, gently grazing the underside of my breast. A shiver went down my body at the touch. I was fully focused on the man laying on top of me instead of the sweet smells from outside.

He lifted his head, smirking at me as he gripped my breast hard, eliciting a soft moan from my lips. He pulled up the shirt, exposing my bare skin to him and the wind. My nipples peaked as the icy breeze caressed my skin. He rose to his knees, glancing down at my partially covered body, and grinned. His jeans were still hugging his hips, exposing the deep v cut below his abs. Noticing where my gaze went, he stood up and dropped his pants in a playful little dance. I could watch this man all day. The way his hips swayed as he slowly inched them down. It took me a moment to realize he had no boxers on to speak of. I watched as he pulled his pants painfully slow down the shaft of his cock, stopping just above the head. "Like what you see, princess?"

I let out a low growl at the pause in my pleasure. He chuckled and grabbed my ankles, pulling me to the edge of the bed. The feel of him grabbing me and moving me around was primal, the need in me rising with every teasing kiss he was placing up my thighs. His fingers hooked the bottom of the shorts and ripped them down my legs and onto the floor so fast. Before I could regain composure, he was spreading my legs wide, licking his lips in anticipation before devouring me. He gripped my thighs as he lapped up every drop of wetness that dripped from me. The growl of primal satisfaction rippled through me. I grabbed him by the hair and pulled him up my body.

"My turn." I growled as I flipped him onto his back and straddled his face. "Tap out when you've had enough." I teased as I rode his tongue into a wave of ecstasy and pleasure. Wave after wave of orgasms rocked me as I put more of my weight down on his face. The moans of absolute pleasure from him vibrated throughout my whole being. I felt a hand rest on my spine as the scent of lemons filled the surrounding air. Valyn gripped my thighs tight as I turned to see Niklaus next to the bed. It threw me off my rhythm and gave Valyn the chance to flip me onto my back.

My head hung at the edge of the bed as I looked around the room at Bastian, Damian, Fennik, and Valdis, who were leaning up against the wall. "That was a beautiful view, Valyn. Why did you have to go and ruin it?" Bastian teased, his smile near feral.

"Because I wanted her to see you all. Now fuck off. We're not sharing her tonight. It's one on one." Valyn growled as he kicked his pants off, releasing his cock. It bounced twice before it landed inside me. Thrust after thrust, pulling me through orgasm after orgasm. I could tell they all wanted to join in.

Their gazes leaving their imprint on my skin. Valyn knew it as well. "My turn." He growled as he buried his seed deep inside me. I couldn't help but release with him a wave of pure bliss and pleasure. He gently pulled back and kissed me. "I guess I have to share you now." He teased, pulling me up into his arms. "Let's get you cleaned up first."

And with that, he took me into the bathroom and showered me off, making sure I could still stand. I heard the commotion outside of the bathroom. The others must be getting the room cleaned up and themselves ready. "Why didn't you tell me they were here?" I asked, sex brain making it a little harder for me to focus.

"I didn't know they arrived. I could tell you needed them. You needed more than I could give you. So I sent them a message and told them to get their asses here. Even if only for a brief moment in time." He washed away the strawberry soap from my skin before turning off the water.

"Thank you." I whispered as I pulled him into a hug. I kissed him deeply as he attempted to dry me off. "I don't think I should bother with clothes, do you?"

"I guess not. One on one or?" He questioned, giving me a moment to decide what I wanted. One on one would be the most effective method, but I knew they all had to get back. We all had a duty to our people, and running around having hours of sex probably would be frowned upon if anyone were to find out. My frustration at this situation was growing by the day.

"All at once. This way, no one will know they're gone." I smiled at him. He just shook his head and laughed.

"I'll let them know. I'll sit this one out though since I was able to have you to myself before we left and, you know, in front of them all just now." He teased and smiled at me before heading out to tell them what I wanted.

My cheeks flushed a bright red as I thought about the last time we were all together. It was necessary, not just for me but for them as well. Things were about to get tough for all of us, and a sexual recharge was just what the priestess ordered.

CHAPTER 36
RAFAEL

Holy fucking shit! I really need to stop fucking drinking when I am around her and she decides it's fuck-a-thon time. My shadows alerted me the moment she had her panties dropped in front of Valyn. I don't know why I needed to know, or why my shadows were obsessed with her, but I don't need this fucking torture. Slipping into the shadows like it was nothing new for me, I watched like the creep that apparently; I was now. I had never met the other males in the room, only recognizing the faces from her drawings. She didn't skip any details.

The black-haired male had her legs spread wide for him. I heard his growl as he took her scent in. A scent that flooded the shadows, swirling around my head, ingraining itself on my brain. I heard her whimpering as he toyed with her while the others watched, cocks in hand just waiting their turn. I seriously wonder how they all manage to wait their turn and the vast amount of self control they all—Before my thoughts could finish she had the copper-haired male in her mouth, the blondes cock in one hand and, the only male I recognized; Valdis's cock in the other. The crimson-haired male waited patiently as the black-haired male positioned her on top of him, lining her ass up for the last one to find purchase in her.

Holy. Fuck.

The room was charged with sexual energy, pulling my thoughts in so many directions. I never thought the innocent-looking princess would be so filthy, so kinky. It's kind of hot. Her lewd sounds filled the room, the moans and growls as each male met her rhythm, not missing a beat or fucking up the rhythm for her or the others. This isn't the first time they've all taken her like this. She was glowing, silver and gold illuminated the room, forcing my shadows to recede closer to the walls. If this kept up, I would be forced back into the room Valyn had so graciously given me.

I wasn't drunk this time. I should go back to my room and mind my own fucking business. But I couldn't. My shadows wouldn't allow me to move away from this spot. I watched as, one by one, each male pumped her full of their cum. The copper-haired one came first, removing himself to sit back with Valyn and take in the show. Valdis took that opportunity to replace his cock in her mouth. Watching her swallow him was beautiful. She slowed her pace to savor him, to bring him to the edge before picking up the speed and forcing a release from him. I watched as it rocked him in place. The blonde took Valdis's place shortly after and had zero luck in holding off. She had him finished in seconds the moment he entered her mouth.

With three down, there was only the last two left. The crimson one plunged himself into her ass, gripping her hips tightly. He wrapped her hair around his fist, pulling her hair gently so that she was looking down at the male beneath her as he dug his canines into her shoulder. The scream that tore from her throat set my shadows off to try to protect her. I had to forceable pull them back so as not to be detected. The scream calmed to a moan of pleasure as she worked both of their cocks like a pro. I watched as the male beneath her guided her hips hard down on him as he flooded her with his cum. The male behind her following suit. I watched as she came with them, her eyes rolling back in her head as pure bliss took over her.

She collapsed onto the one beneath her as he chuckled, moving her hair from her face and placing kisses all over her face. The crimson-haired male pulled himself free and went to the bathroom, fetching a warm wet towel and a dry one. He cleaned her up as thoroughly as he could before taking care of himself. Each one of them put their boxers back on. Well, all the ones who weren't trapped by a now sleeping Luna. Valyn finally moved from the seat, helping the one on the bed move her and get her covered by the sheets.

"I'm really glad you guys could make it here. She was spiraling after talking to a fortuneteller. I don't even know what was said." Valyn said to the others. The blonde stood up and opened the curtains to the balcony to let the air flood the room.

"I'll take coming to my mate's aid over sitting through another night shift with my mother at the Mor. Maggie runs a tough ship and where I'm blessed that I am able to learn from her and my mother, Luna, needs me more. They both told me to take the night." The blonde sat on the bed, stroking Luna's hair as she nuzzled up to him. I felt wrong staying here and listening, but my shadows had me rooted in place, not letting me move.

"You're doing what you have to do so you can protect her, Niklaus. You're skilled in battle, but out of all of us, if she goes down, you're the one who can heal her." The crimson-haired one said as he put the towels back in the bathroom.

"Thanks Damian. Things have been chaos. We had a call to Daglidell the other day. The daemons are trying to set up camps outside of the city. We had to help restock the hospital there. You don't realize how many people aren't as lucky as us to have the money and powers that are suffering until you're there."

The blonde—Niklaus—just shook his head as if trying to wash away an image that was haunting him.

"Solaria is no different. Vanalli and Vanessa took Elucia with them to find Melody. They think they have a lead on her whereabouts, but they're unsure if she's a vessel or if she's running for her life. Allura has been insufferable, trying to get involved at every turn. Bastian, what's Holly and Sirius's take on the reaper that Luna pissed off?" Damian had looked at the black-haired male—Bastian—while he was talking. So, these were her mates. Each a prince of their respective realms. That leaves the copper-haired one. That must be the last mate, Fennik. I tuned out most of what they continued talking about. These seemed to be matters for their respective realms and not something I should be prying into.

My shadows finally released me after they recognized that the men in the room with Luna wouldn't hurt her. I needed to go find a damn drink after that.

Fuck. Fae. Wine.

You would think fae wine wouldn't affect a daemon the way it does a fae or human. Oh, you'd be wrong. I have been flying high mentally since polishing off a bottle that Valyn's mother had given me when I went downstairs after spying. Cassandra was a lovely woman who moved with grace and beauty. She didn't treat me like I was a burden or a problem when I had gone downstairs and asked if I could trouble her for a beer or something. She handed me a bottle of some type of fruity fae wine and left it up to me if I'd like a glass or just to drink from the bottle. My dumbass picked, chugging from the bottle.

Not surprising that I now find myself naked in the shower trying to sober the fuck up before dawn breaks. I let the warm water trickle down my body, my cock throbbing at the drunken reminder of what I had watched a few hours ago. Why the fuck do I keep torturing myself by watching her get fucked? What sick level of twisted am I that I can't force myself to look away, even when my shadows won't let me leave? It's been a fucking nightmare being around them, and I should just leave. I should get as far away from them at night so my shadows can't intrude on their most intimate moments.

You can't do it though, and your shadows know it. You're weak. There it was, the annoying, pesky voice in my head that loved to berate me and tell me what a piece of shit I really was. *Why don't you just take her for a night? Show her what a more experienced daemon could do for her. Oh, that's right, you're fine with being the creeper in the shadows who jerks off to the princess getting roughly fucked. Go on then, masturbate to the thoughts of what you just watched. Who am I to judge* you?

I shook my head, trying to get the damn voice to shut up and stop giving my overly drunk brain ideas. I need to sleep! Fuck! The warm water wasn't helping me at all. Fae wine was a dangerous fucking thing, and you'd think by now I would fucking know better. I slammed the shower knob off a little harder than I expected, ripped the towel off of the bar and lazily draped it around my waist. The bed looked soft and inviting, beckoning me to come to lie on it. To hell with drying off, to hell with putting clothes on. I dropped the towel to the floor, plunging into the softness of the bed and sheets. I'll give the summer realm some credit; their bedding was nice and light, perfect for a night like tonight.

I didn't know when or how, but the darkness of slumber took me far away from here.

Moans and whimpers filled my ears as I plunged hard and fast into the tightest pussy I'd ever felt. Over and over, the wetness made my cock so slippery that I'd almost slipped out a few times. I had no idea who the woman was beneath me; the darkness surrounding me kept most of her features from my sight. Her hands gripped the bedsheets at her thighs tight with every thrust. She felt amazing, her pussy throbbing around my cock as I plummeted to my death inside of her.

"Harder." Escaped from the lips forming in the darkness, as if the beast inside me was slowly revealing this beauty to me one body part at a time. Her breasts were large, the perfect rosebud nipples pebbled under the cool air, giving me the most nefarious of ideas.

"As you wish." I said as I thrust hard into her, making her scream out in pleasure. I leaned my head down to her nipples and gently blew on them, watching them harden before I bit hard on her left one, pulling roughly with my canines. She arched her back, pushing her body closer to mine, wrapping her legs around my waist, pulling me harder into her. A little chuckle left my lips. I let go of one and went hard for the other, kneading her other breast in my hand. I could feel her shaking, trying so hard to rotate her hips against me. A feeling of need and want. Something I hadn't felt in so long.

I wrapped my arm under her waist, hoisting her up so her breasts pressed firmly against my chest. Her lips met mine as she kissed me greedily. I rolled us onto my back so she could take the top, giving her the control she was so desperately seeking. As if realizing it, she pushed her hands firmly on my chest and dug her sharp nails in as she rode my dick like there was a gun to her head and she had no choice but to cum or she would die.

Her breathing picked up heavier as she rode me hard, slowly sliding her way up to the tip of my dick before dropping hard and fast. She rotated her hips as she did it, creating a whole new sensational pleasure that I'd never experienced before. I was in pure bliss, my mind completely numb to who this was or why I couldn't see anything more than her body and lips. Part of my mind was screaming for me to focus, but I couldn't, not with this goddess of a woman riding my dick. I was close to coming, close to releasing myself into a woman that I knew nothing about, and I didn't care.

I held her by her hips on my cock as I felt the swelling of my balls. I could tell she was so close to coming, but I wanted to taste that release. Lifting her up from my cock, which was throbbing at the emptiness it was now feeling, I gently laid her down on the bed. Her little whines of protest were so cute. They sounded so familiar though, like a voice I had heard before. I shook my head, stopping my mind from ruining the moment for me. I spread her legs, taking in the beautiful sight of her soaking wet pussy. The scent of her arousal was maddening. I no longer thought about who she was or why this was happening. All I cared about now was tasting her juices and making her feel the best pleasure in the world. The world had stopped the moment my tongue touched her clit. The taste of euphoria and the universe crashed into me as I devoured her like I was now the one with the gun to my head. Eat her pussy like it was my last meal or die. I'd gladly feast until my jaw gave out.

My hands gripped her thighs hard as I lapped up every glorious fucking drop, my cock aching beneath me as I tasted the best nectar on the planet. I could lose myself in this taste, letting it keep me in this darkness forever. I could taste her getting wetter, feeling her body tense up under my hands. It was time to let her know what I was capable of. Swirling my tongue around her swollen clit made her twitch under me, trying so hard to grind her pussy into my face. It was cute, but I would not let her have control of this. Her hand found purchase in my hair as she guiding my head for a moment before I bit her clit hard, eliciting a screaming moan that could wake up the dead. I felt her shake and tense as I bit harder. The moans and begging filled the air, making my head spin.

"Fuck me!" She cried out, right as I was about to plunge my tongue back into her to finish her off. Fuck it, she wants me to fuck her until she cums all over my cock. So be it. I pulled myself up over her and smiled.

"As you wish." I said once more, and I went full hilt into her. Thrusting hard and fast into her soaking wet pussy. The screams of pleasure ripping from her with every thrust had my cock aching to release. "Come for me." I whispered in her ear. As if on command she came hard, her pussy gripping my cock so tight that I had no choice but to flood her with all I had pent up. "Fuck!" I moaned out as I released inside of her warm pussy.

Heavy breathing filled the room, but I wasn't done with her just yet. "Clean me up." I demanded as I pulled my cock from her. I grabbed her by the hair and guided her lips to the tip of my dick. She gladly parted her lips for me as she took my cock all the way to the back of her throat, sucking up every drop of her and I mixed together. My eyes closed as the warmth of her mouth sucked me off, my hand still wrapped in her hair, guiding her up and down my cock. She made the cutest of sounds as the back of her throat touched the tip of my cock, but she didn't choke, she just took it. She ran her fingernails gently over my balls, eliciting an electricity over my whole body. As if she knew what she was doing, she popped my cock from her mouth and began sliding her hand up and down my cock, twisting her hand as she moved. What she did next was a whole new level of pleasure that I didn't know existed as she licked my balls, gently sucking on them. My cock hardened, threatening to release all over the face that I couldn't see. As if she could sense it, she popped the tip of my dick back into her mouth and sucked me and stroked me into oblivion. My hot, thick load sliding down the back of her throat as she swallowed every fucking drop. Fuck me.

Collapsing onto the bed, she curled up to my chest. The light from the dawn slowly trickled into the room, chasing away the darkness from my mind. Finally, I could see what beauty had come for me in the night. I glanced down at my chest as the orangish pink glow from the sun began illuminating her hair. Bright blue curls washed over her back like the waves of the sea outside. She looked up at me with a grin on her face, her chocolate brown eyes swirling bright with silver and gold, stared back at me. The pure terror that filled me in that moment froze me in place.

In my arms, smiling up at me, was the Goddess of All, the princess I swore to protect. The obsession of my darkness. I had fucked the one I was supposed to protect.

Darkness flooded me once more as I tore up from the bed in a cold sweat, covered in my own semen. I was alone, the night sky still twinkling with stars. My breath was heavy and labored from the panic that I had just endured in that last moment. Then I heard it, that dark distorted voice in my mind, the bastard of showing me what I truly was.

Gotcha.

CHAPTER 37
LUNA

Panic and fear set in the moment I laid eyes on Rafael. I couldn't make out the body beneath me, but the scent reminded me of Valdis; I didn't think it was anyone else. His features were blurred in a cloud of darkness. The panic in his eyes said it all. He didn't know it was me, either. I lay here in bed, surrounded by my mates, when I awoke. With their limbs a mess around me, Valdis held me the tightest. Was he the reason I couldn't scent anything but him in my dream? Was his scent so powerful that it tricked my mind?

Slowly, I untangled myself from the mess of body parts and went to the bathroom. I needed to shower and get rid of the feeling of betrayal. I turned the water on and stepped in before it could warm all the way up. I needed a cold shower of reality to remind me I wasn't dreaming anymore. Why did my mind do this to me? Why did I get pulled into such a vivid dream? My head spun over and over at the thoughts running through it, that I didn't hear the bathroom door open. Bastian poked his head behind the curtains and let out a low whistle, startling me from my thoughts.

"I didn't mean to scare you, baby girl. What's with the shower?" He asked as he looked me up and down, trying to see if there was some visible reason I was in a cold shower in the early morning hours. I tried to come up with a reason worthy of telling him, but I couldn't tell him or any of them what had just happened in my mind.

"I had a bad dream. I just needed to wake myself up. I'm sorry if I woke you up." I said, offering him a small bit of the truth without fulling laying out the disaster that happened. He smiled and stepped into the shower with me. His cock throbbing hard from morning wood. I couldn't take my eyes off it. You would think that, with the way my mind was right now that sex would be the last thing on my mind. But he was my mate, and maybe just the distraction that I really needed.

I pulled him into a hug, his body pressed hard against mine as he adjusted his cock between my thighs, stroking it against my slit. "Can I help wake you up or should I go back to bed?" He teased me. I kissed him, gently nudging my tongue against his lips awaiting permission. He gladly took me in, his tongue swirling around mine. His kiss was as cold as the snow in Taiga. The scent of pine and snow filled the bathroom, swirling around me and pulling me in. I knew this wouldn't last long because morning quickies never did, but I would gladly take this moment with him.

He hoisted me up, wrapping my legs around his waist as he cocked a grin at me. "Fuck me, Bastian." I said as I thrust my hands into his hair, pulling him back into our kiss. He gladly obliged, sheathing himself fully in me. His cock was so thick and so big that it filled me to the brink. I loved the way he was with me—gentle but not too gentle. He waited for me to adjust to him before thrusting in and out of me at a deadly slow pace. I knew why; it had been so long since we had one-on-one time with each other that he wanted to savor it and not rush. He also wasn't going to last long, and he was always about me getting off first. I was still sensitive from my group session and my dream romp that I wasn't far off from coming undone on him.

He pulled away from our kiss, burying his face in my neck. I felt it the moment he opened his mouth and closed his canines on the base of my throat. A sharp pain followed by unlimited pleasure poured out of me as my blood filled his mouth. I returned the favor, marking him again as I pulled from him. His blood was sweet, yet earthy. It was a blissful feeling binding that if you had told me this years ago, I would've called you disgusting. Now, it was my happiest moment. He let go reluctantly as he thrusted hard up into me. "Baby girl, you need to come. I can't last much longer." He said, his voice rough and heavy. I nodded for him to go hard, and he absolutely understood the assignment as he fucked me thoroughly up against the shower wall until he spilled into me as I flooded all over him. He kissed me deeply through our orgasms, pulling me tighter.

"I love you." I whispered into his lips as he pressed his forehead against mine, reluctantly pulling out of me.

"I love you more, baby girl."

Bastian had cleaned us both up and grabbed my clothes. Neither of us was going back to sleep, so instead he suggested we take a run and get our heads on straight. I wanted to protest the early morning torture, but I needed to clear my mind more than he knew. From everything. We jogged together down to the beach, where we parked our asses on the rocky shore, watching the sunrise over the sea. The sky filtered from the dark purples and blues of the night into the bright hues of pinks, oranges and yellows of the dawn.

Bastian had been filling me in on everything going on in Taiga. From Sirius and Holly essentially shacking up together, to the reaper that was trying to kill me because I stole souls from her, to Holly autopsying every daemon she could get her hands on. Which, apparently, was a ton since Yida was currently at war with the daemons. A force had come in over the last week, and he and Bertrum had been spearheading the missions to get the beast legion there without alerting the surrounding towns of the chaos. So far, we had limited casualties, but the daemons just kept coming. He said he was going to have to leave soon to head back.

"Then why did you leave them? Where is Hector?" I asked, horrified that he had come all the way to Doria just to help me deal with my internal spiraling.

"Valyn said you needed us. And as much as you needed me, I needed you too. I needed to feel you in my arms and know that you were safe. I needed to see you, kiss you and recharge my energy by being with you. Hector and Kieran are with Bertrum. Kira is with Harper in Mistveil with your mother and Lilly. Everyone is safe. I just needed to be with you." Bastian pulled me into his side, placing kisses to my cheek and the top of my head.

"I need you safe. I need to know that I am not a distraction to you while you are dealing with this. Is there anything I can do to help? I can see if Nox can spare some troops to help; maybe he can come and bring Virgil. They would have your back, and at least then I know Nox could get you out of there safely." I said, thinking about how I can demand my brother to help.

"That's unnecessary. Your brother and Virgil, as far as I know, are helping your father and grandfather find that damn blade. I swear, your grandfather is a fucking piece of work." He paused before continuing and looked down at me. "I'm sorry I shouldn't have said that."

"If you were wrong, I'd say to apologize. You're not, so no need. I know Talissa was saying he was a decent man, but the way my grandmother speaks about him and my great-grandmother speaks of him, I don't think he was ever truly a good person. Power corrupts people; gods are no exception. If anything, I think it might be worse for them." I said as I thought about everything the man did. He had a blade forged that could kill his own kind. Was that out of paranoia, or did he have a plan of who he was going to use that blade on?

"I think when you live that long, anything can corrupt you. Not you, but you know what I mean." He laughed.

"I get it. I couldn't imagine living that long. The way his mind must've warped. Illisandra seems to be nothing like him though. I wonder if I could actually get to know her and trust her?" I had been thinking about what she had said to me. I need to talk to her again, but something tells me that would be very hard right now with the world plunging into chaos. Otius probably has her locked up in some tower like a stolen bride.

Bastian groaned as he looked up at the sky. "The morning is upon us, and if we don't head back now, Valyn will have a search party out looking for us. He's not thrilled with your plan, but he gets your desire to help. Something tells me it's more than desire. I just hope that you're wrong and Undine isn't compromised. I don't think anyone could take her down that easily." He helped me up from the rocks, and we made our way back home.

Everything that I was worried about still plagued me, but now there was a whole new thing to worry about with him and the army in Yida. I can't be in multiple places at once to keep everyone safe. But I can't lose any of them either. I wouldn't be able to forgive myself if anything happened to them.

CHAPTER 38
LUNA

Damian and Niklaus were already outside as if they were waiting for us to return before leaving me again. I really hate these goodbyes. I know they will not last forever, but they are still too long. Bastian put his hand on my lower back as I slowed my pace. Fennik and Valyn slipped out of the house smiling and chatting with one another. The only one missing was Valdis. I hope I hadn't missed him! Panic took hold, making it harder to breathe.

Calm down, little one. I'll be out in a second.

Valdis's voice washed over me, calming my heart so I didn't spiral more. I noticed everyone around me paused, watching me as I slowed my pace to a stop right before reaching them. I could see the sadness on their faces as we all knew this was yet again another bullshit goodbye. "One of these days, we will stop saying goodbye to each other for long periods of time." I whispered more to myself than to the group. But they got it.

They knew my pain because it was a pain that we all felt. Pain that we all wish would just go away.

Valdis emerged from the house with Rafael in tow. I couldn't even look at that man without thinking about that dream. How horrible is it that I dreamed of him and me in that position? I shook off the thoughts before they could take hold again and make me spiral. Valdis took one look at me and was by my side in an instant, gripping my chin to look up at him. As if putting on a very public display of affection, he drew me into a slow but deep kiss. Damian cleared his throat once he deemed the kiss was long enough. Valdis pulled back and chuckled to himself. "I guess I took too long." He smiled as he pushed a rogue strand of hair from my face.

"You're not the only one who doesn't want to leave her, you know." Damian huffed as he pulled me into his chest, inhaling my scent deep into his lungs. I nuzzled my face in his chest as the smell of cinnamon bourbon wafted around me. I need them all. I need every scent draped around me to get me through this time apart. Lemon swirled around me as Niklaus pulled me from Damian, placing kisses all over my face from cheeks, to nose, to my lips. I couldn't help the giggle that escaped as he stopped and brushed his fingers against my cheek.

"Find me in your sleep if you need me. I promise I'll be awake. Night shifts have been a bit of a bitch lately." Damian and Niklaus stepped to the side, letting Fennik wrap me up in his arms. He lifted me up, and spun with me in the air. When he finally put me back on the ground, I turned to look at everyone. Bastian was the last one waiting. His smile was wider than it had been this morning. I could see the clarity in his grey eyes as he walked up to me. Fennik placed a quick kiss on my lips as he moved out of the way.

"I hate goodbyes, my love." He lifted my chin with his fingers, catching my lower lip between his teeth. I could taste the snow from his lips, the cool air that swirled in my mouth as his tongue made its way into a slow, elegant dance with mine. Bastian took his time, no rushing, just the two of us against the world. It was an odd feeling knowing all eyes were on us. We all needed this time together, and I wish it were longer. I wrapped my arms around his neck, holding him a little longer before we inevitably had to let go of each other and go on with our duties.

No one rushed us, which I thought was odd as well. Maybe they all knew that Bastian was dealing with the most right now. Maybe they realized he needed this more than I could tell. Bastian's arms wrapped tightly around me. I could feel his breathing as if it were one with my own. After a few moments, he finally broke the kiss. I could see his eyes swelling up with tears he wouldn't let fall, at least not in front of his brothers.

"None of us wants to leave you, little one. But we have little choice in the matter. I'd rather throw you over my shoulder, go back inside and lock myself in that room with you and tell everyone to go fuck themselves. But I've been told that it's selfish of me to think that way. So, until the day I can do that, I will just continue to burn the world for you." Bastian confessed, and it ripped at my heart. I felt a part of me break knowing this time would be the longest. With no accurate way of killing Marcloff, there was only the hope that I was strong enough to take him down myself. What if I wasn't though? What if I couldn't kill him or, worse, what if I had to die to kill him?

I would have to keep that thought to myself because that could be a very plausible option if we can't find a way to put him down for good. Talissa and Zekon hopefully can find something that can do the job. Maybe Rafael might have some better options on what he thinks would work. But how do I look him in the eyes and talk to him after that? Why is this shit so tough?!

"We all have a job to do. Let's get it done and over with so we can be together again. I'm tired of saying goodbye. Let's cut their heads off and burn everything they know to the fucking ground." I announced to the group. They all gave me a wide-eyed look as if I had just said something bad. I mean; to be fair, I am ready to go on a bloodbath killing spree. I'm tired of this asshole thinking he can take control of the world and not get pushback.

"That's one way to put it, princess." Bastian said as he placed a kiss on my cheek. "I think as long as we are all able, we need to get together like this once a week. It would be best for all of us involved. This way, none of us goes crazy." I give him a long side-eyed look. It will not be feasible, and we both know that. Hell, we all know that. Bastian gives a look once more. "We can try, princess. We all need to try; there is too much at stake."

I relented, knowing that there is nothing I wouldn't do to be right there by each of their sides, helping them with the issues in their realms. Valyn stepped out onto the porch, looking over at me as Victoria and Jasmine came up the walkway behind me. I guess this was goodbye for now. Time feels like it's slipping through my fingers, and I would give anything to bring it to a full stop.

"Hey guys, why's everyone looking so sad?" Victoria asked, her arm still draped over Jasmine's shoulders as they walked up to us. Jasmine looked around at us and then slipped out from under Victoria to give me a quick hug.

"I'm sorry if we're interrupting. I can drag her off into the house. We didn't realize you were all saying goodbye," Jasmine whispered into my ear as she hugged me tighter.

"It's okay; the sooner we can get this done and over with, the sooner I won't have to say goodbye anymore." I whispered back as I let her go and smiled. She nodded in acknowledgement, moving back next to a very confused Victoria. "As much as I want to drag this on, we have to get on with this." I gave each of my mates a soft smile as they made their way to the gates that would take them back to Mistveil, then back to their realms. I hated watching them leave me. A piece of my heart breaking at the sight.

Valyn moved from the porch, making his way to me. "Soon this will all be in our past. I know it doesn't seem like it right now, but we will outlast this," he said as he wrapped me up in his arms and held me there while silent tears dropped from my eyes. Jasmine did well at keeping Victoria preoccupied so that she didn't interrupt. I could thank that woman for the gift she just gave me. I pulled back from Valyn, took a deep breath, and wiped my eyes. I couldn't let this get to me. We didn't have long before we had to leave, and I needed to get my shit together before I was the reason things didn't go to plan.

"When are we leaving and how are we getting there?" I turned from Valyn to ask Jasmine. She was the one who had figured out when was best to go and how we would get there. She smiled at me widely and Victoria and Valyn groaned.

"How do you feel about whales?"

When Jasmine asked me how I felt about whales, I thought she just meant, like, do I like them, have I ever seen one? Things along those lines. Not that we'd be fucking riding whales to the depths of the Selpie! Valyn and Victoria had apparently protested this form of transportation, saying it was unsafe and that they would rather take one of the navy's submarines. But nope, Jasmine won out saying that the submarines would cause harm to the aquatic life that lived down there and that how can the most powerful person walking Cerulia save people from death while being trapped in a sinking can. I couldn't help but burst out giggling at their expressions when she called the submarine a tin can. Neither of them thought my outburst was funny or cute. Despite my smiling at them and trying to apologize, Valyn made threats to take it out on my ass when we got back. I acted as if I were zipping my lips and tossing the key into the sea.

"Valyn's powers and my own can help you breathe underwater with a bubble that will act like normal air. Water will go into the bubble and act as oxygen. You just can't panic; that would probably cause water to actually bypass the magic and drown you." Jasmine said with a not so comforting smile. This woman was very lucky that I trusted her with my life because of Victoria's blind faith and trust in her.

"So, water equals oxygen, and don't breathe too fast or I'll drown. Gotcha, sounds easy enough." I tried to say without wincing at the thought of dying in the water. Flashbacks of the drunken night with the mermaids flooded my brain, and I quickly shook them off. I was drunk and did not know what I truly was. This is different; I am a goddess. I can do this. I will not allow myself to let my anxiety cause me to drown. I wonder if I could die by drowning? Like, would that be a thing? I wonder.

"Stop it!" Valyn shouted, drawing my attention, and theirs as well, to him. He walked over, gripping the back of my neck and forcing me to look up at him. "You are not about to let that little intrusive thought have you fucking experimenting down there. Are we clear?" Jasmine and Victoria looked at him with the look of utter confusion on their faces, then at me. Victoria just shook her head and got back to paying attention to the large black whales waiting patiently for us in the water.

"Crystal." I said back with a smile. Valyn flicked my nose but didn't bring up my thoughts to the others. "Wait, are we leaving Patrick and Westly behind?" I looked around and it was just the four of us. Rafael wasn't even with us, which I wasn't fully opposed to. I barely said two words to him before we left. Then again, he didn't say much to me either.

"They're staying here with Rafael to help secure the borders. Rafael is going to be doing some scouting since he can get in and out of places with his wings and his shadows." Valyn said with a twinge of jealousy in his voice.

"Do you wish you had wings, my love?" I teased as we made our way over to the edge of the beach. The whales were huge, terrifyingly so. The closest thing to its size that I had been near has been Nox in his dragon form. By the looks of it, these things are bigger by a long shot. I'll have to tease him about that next time I talk to him. Whenever that is. The realization that I haven't checked in with my family recently hit me suddenly. I haven't spoken to anyone since we left. Not even so much as a text message. I'm a shitty sister and daughter. I let my thoughts wander to happier times that I swear are all manufactured since we've been in the grips of war since I came to Mistveil. I wonder if I had stayed in Celvenia, would the war be as bad as it is, or would we not have even known how truly fucked the world really is. What about Luther? If I had stayed, maybe he wouldn't be soul backpacking a fucking Hilmer. A cold tingle makes its way across my skin at the thought that this might all be my fault.

I must be screaming internally because Valyn rests his hand on my lower back, running it slowly up and down my spine as if I weren't just having a meltdown of cosmic proportions. This man is both a blessing and a curse. I look up to see his turquoise eyes looking down on me. The scar still fresh on his eye reminds me why we are doing this. I found love when I came to Mistveil, truth, and most importantly I found my family. Although right now we are all scattered across the world, we are doing it for the people who can't defend themselves. The humans, who only have minor weapons who would be killed for fun by the daemons. It's bad enough Marcloff is using them as fodder for Hilmers to control. We have to defend those who can't defend themselves.

"Alright, let's go. We need to check on your mom and make sure she's good, and if she's not, well, we will just have to figure out how to save her without her killing one of us or us killing her." I said. Jasmine shuddered, but nodded nonetheless. She knew the importance of what we had to do. If her mom was behind the attacks on the ships, we have to save her, and we have to do it quickly.

CHAPTER 39
LUNA

Riding on a whale was not on my bucket list of things to be doing this year, but here I am riding the waves of the deep blue sea on the back of one of the largest mammals on the planet. Jasmine wasn't kidding when she said that her magic and Valyns would create a bubble-like helmet to help me breathe underwater. Not going to lie and say I didn't have a slight panic attack when we dove under the water, but it's so beautiful. Not only does it help me breathe, but it also helps me see underwater clearly. Victoria, Valyn and Jasmine didn't need these helmets, they had the luxury of having water powers ruining naturally through their veins. Valyn said I could probably form one myself, but I didn't have time to figure that out before we needed to head out.

I watched as we all moved through the water. Bright colors flashed by in swarms. Pinks, greens, blues mixed with yellows and oranges. Fish of all shapes and sizes filtered into my vision. The sea seems so at peace right now. Gentle and calm. Something I rarely think it has felt like since the war begun again. I felt Valyn pulled me tighter against his chest as my ass lined up on his cock. If I didn't think it would be super inappropriate to grind into him while riding this majestically beautiful creature, I would be doing everything I could be turn him on. But I let the non-horny aspect of my brain take over and continue to enjoy the beauty of the underwater world I've found myself in.

Honestly, it was so serene that I almost forgot about how deadly the sea really is. The kraken, Noro and her babies, mer-folk and other sea wyverns and who else knows that creatures lurk in these waters further down. I try not to let the thought of them linger in my brain for too long. Which luckily for me, I don't have to. Jasmine waves, catching my attention, then points in front of her. A sprawling coral mansion was coming into view in front of us. It looked just like our castle back in Mistviel, just made out of beige, pink and blue coral and shells. It looked like a sandcastle that a child would make, only much larger and seemingly sturdier. It was gorgeous, so much so that I almost missed the barrier that was surrounding it. It was more transparent, but the swirl of water around the base of what I would call the lawn gave it away. Victoria and Jasmine slid gracefully off of the whale they were attached to, Jasmine petting it like it was the best little pet as it waited for its partner.

Valyn gently moved me first, helping me slide off the back of the one we were riding. He followed close behind me as Jasmine did the same to thing to the whale that we were riding. I watched them both in awe as they turned from us and gently swam away. I treaded water, keeping my arms moving in tiny circles, my feet kicking softly to keep me in place. Jasmine took what I could only describe as a collective breath before swimming to the main gate of the home. Victoria and Valyn followed her with no signs of concern, but something felt off to me. Like a darkness hovering around the place that no one could see but was palpable to me. Even underwater.

I followed hesitantly as they swam through the barrier and landed on their feet on the sandy lawn. My hand reached out to touch the barrier and something about the feel of it had my body wanting to recoil away. I did not like the feeling it gave off, but Valyn was now inside of this damn thing; I had no choice but to go in with him. I steadied myself, touching it once more as it rippled away from me as I entered. The darkness swarming inside the barrier itself had sent goosebumps down my arms. None of the others had given any indication that they felt it. Which made me all the more worried about what is hiding in here.

"My mother should be awake by now. She loves her beauty rest." Jasmine joked as she made her way up to the large sandstone looking door. The knobs were made of seashells, light beige with brown stripes, mirroring on either side. Vanalli never got back to me about Undine. Nothing about what to expect or what I could possibly be walking into. Victoria shared a quick glance with Valyn before following Jasmine inside. Okay, so maybe they did feel something. Valyn rested his hand on my lower back and ushered me in along with him.

"I'm assuming you felt it?" He whispered into my hair as he pressed a kiss to the top of my head. He easily could've said this mentally, but I think this is more for Victoria to hear. I nod, making eye contact with Victoria. Jasmine didn't feel it. She would've felt it the moment we hit it, but she's been here multiple times. It had me spiraling a little at the thought that she could be compromised and that we were just led into a trap by someone we trusted. "Keep your guard up, first sign of trouble you get the fuck out of here. Understood?" I nodded again, not trusting my voice to betray me. I liked Jasmine. She was kind to me and super sweet, there is no way that she is sleeping with the enemy.

"Mom! Where are you?" Jasmine trilled as she walked through the front of the house towards the living room. Everything looked like it was made out of the same material as the house. Turquoise seemed to be the favored color here. Curtains and a large circular rug were both a turquoise in base with while embroidery and accents on them. The couch was beige, with a dark blue blanket draped across the top of it. A large wooden table sat in the middle of the room in front of the couch, flanked with two beige chairs with dark blue throw pillows on each. Plants were lined in pots around the room. Walking ivy and what looked like underwater hyacinths decorated the room with a bright green and pop of purples. Bobbles and trinkets lined the shelves with sea glass bottles dangling from ropes above the windows. The room looked inviting, but shadows lurked in the corners, as if watching us.

Jasmine left us in the living room as she fluttered through the house calling out for her mom. I looked at Victoria who was bouncing on her heels, she was uneasy here and by the looks of the pictures on the shelf on the far wall, she was here before and looked all the world comfortable. Valyn stepped over to Victoria to whisper something between them, her nodding response was all I needed to know that she was feeling it as well. Something was off, and I hope for her sake that Jasmine isn't in the middle of this.

After a few minutes, Jasmine reemerged from the hallway with a defeated look on her face. "Her room is locked; she's not answering to my knocks or my calls." Jasmine slumped onto the couch and put her face in her hands. Victoria sat on the couch next to her, running her hand idly down her back as she looked at us. "Short of breaking down her door, I don't know what else to do."

"We kick in the door and if she complains, Valyn can fix it. Let's just hope that she's okay." I wasn't one to play around. A door could be fixed, a life taken by a daemon would be something completely different. Victoria went to open her mouth but immediately closed it. Valyn stepped closer to me, giving Jasmine a wide berth to take into consideration what we were saying.

"Last door at the end of the hallway with the conch shell engraved in it." She relented. I couldn't tell if she was relenting to us so Valyn and I wouldn't be in the room or if she was truly okay with our plan. Victoria stood up from the couch to join us when Jasmine grabbed her hand. "Can you stay here with me?"

"I'll be right back, I want to go with them to make sure they get the right door. Plus, I don't know about you, but I have to pee really bad." Victoria was giving an excuse to leave the room.

She was doubting her lover; this could end very badly for them if Jasmine has turned.

"Okay. I'm not following. My mother would wreck me if she saw me kick in her door." Jasmine said shaking her head. "I'm sorry, I feel like I should be doing more." I shook my head and offered her a veiled smiled.

"We got it. You just sit back and wait for our call. I promise we won't make a mess." My reassurance must've been enough. Victoria and Valyn slipped from the room as I took in Jasmine one more time searching for any sign of deception or hint of darkness. Either she was masking it really well, or she wasn't part of the problem. I just hope we aren't about to make the biggest mistake of our lives but pissing off the Goddess of the Waters.

CHAPTER 40
BASTIAN

I just wanted to come back to Taiga and enjoy the glowing bliss after having my time with Luna, but no! Why the fuck can't people just keep themselves out of trouble for at least one goddamn day. Bertrum was already waiting in the foyer of the manor by the time I returned to Moonward Manor. Scouts had reported suspicious activity in the mountains while I was gone, and he decided I needed to check it out personally. Of course, this couldn't have been handled by him or the scouts. So now I have to trudge through a snowstorm up into the mountains to see the suspicious activity for myself.

Snow blanketed the surrounding forest floor, crunching beneath my paws as I thundered through the snow towards the mountains. It was eerily quiet aside from my own steps. The normal chatter of animals and chirping of the birds was nonexistent right now. The clouds were darkening more as the snowfall thickened around me. For any normal person, fae-alike, this would be a complete whiteout; then again, any sane person wouldn't be out in this.

The smell of smoke wafting down the mountain through the trees is what caught my attention, shifting me from my current path up to the mountain pass. There were disturbances in the snow as if a group had been traveling through here. Maybe a day or two ago at the most. Again, no sane person would be out in this kind of weather. I glanced at the sky, taking notice of the black clouds in the distance. Something sent my fur on edge, coming from the ominous clouds. Bright flashes danced across the sky, bringing the clouds closer to where I was heading. The mountains were dangerous along on a good day, add in heavy snowfall and thunder snow? That's a recipe for death and disaster.

An eerie silence cut through my thoughts as the scent of something ethereal caught my attention. It was potent enough to make me concerned about who might be out here. I noticed the scent continued in the direction I was already heading, so I kicked it into high gear. Pushing hard through the thick snow was becoming even harder for me. I grew up out here, racing Damian through the snow when we were kids. We were always racing to see who was the best and who was the fastest. Naturally, I beat him every time, but that was only because I actually liked the snow. He hated the cold, and he hated the snow. My mother said he was just like my aunt Scarlett when it came to her dislike of the snow. Scarlett and Allura moved to Solaria when Damian was about a hundred. Melody was only fifty when they moved, leaving me and Holly here. Melody tried to get her sister to come with them, but Holly was like me, drawn to the cold here. Later, I actually found out that it was because the snow reminded her of death. She would always tell me, "Winter is the death of the year, Bastian. It's the quietest time for all of the world to reflect on its life for the year." She wasn't wrong. Not much thrived here, but it was still beautiful.

The scent of smoke and the ethereal being grew stronger as I approached a cave opening. Warmth flooded the area around the opening, forcing me to halt short of it, so I didn't slip across the exposed stone that was normally covered with snow. I quickly shifted back, manifesting jeans and a t-shirt, with a nice pair of black boots. I've looked gods in the eyes before and stood my ground. Hell, my wife is the most amazing goddess I've ever met. If I can handle her, I can handle whoever this is. I moved onto the stone and peered inside the cave.

"What the hell?" I shook my head as I thrust my hands into my pockets. No wonder Bertrum wanted me to come check it out. I entered the cave, and as I expected, weapons were drawn on me. I wouldn't expect anything less. I raised my hands and smiled. "If you guys wanted a winter tour of the mountains, something could've been arranged." I smirked as my father-in-law quickly put his sword down and shook his head. Nox and Virgil both sheathed their swords as well, but Undas hadn't moved except to glance over his shoulder. He probably scented me before I even made it to the entrance. I made my way further in, closer to the fire, and took up a seat next to Nox. "Seriously though, what are you guys doing out here? This storm is shit and won't be lightening up anytime soon."

"How did you know we were out here?" Virgil chimed in. Not so much an answer to my question, but by the look of him, he wasn't faring well out here in this weather, even with the fire. Nox gently nudged him in the ribs. Virgil just gave him a look.

"Well, this is my realm, and people traveling in such horrible conditions have a tendency to set off my scouts as suspicious activity, and with what is going on right now, everyone is on high alert." Undas and Harold both looked at me with confusion on their faces. "I'm assuming you don't know what's been happening." I sighed once more, taking a deep breath before continuing. "How about this? You tell me why you're sneaking around in the middle of a blizzard, and I'll fill you in on everything that I know."

"There is a rumor floating around that Otius's blade is in Yida. We were heading there when the storm struck. We didn't tell you because, gods forbid, something happened to Luna while you were with us. We didn't want you to feel obligated to help us if she needed you." I could honestly respect Drake's bluntness. He was always kind and respectful, but was blunt when things came down to it. I didn't like the frills that most of the politicians and leaders added onto things to make it feel like they were kissing my father's ass. Drake also didn't like that sort of thing either. It made things easier when people just said what they wanted.

"I hadn't heard such rumors. Yida is full of monks and religious fae who believe the gods will fight their battles, and if they die, then it will be in the name of the gods and also the will of the gods. I highly doubt that they would hoard Otius's blade. I also would've heard something from their general. They use their magic more to protect the land and themselves. Mainly with shields and using the elements to their advantage. A weapon wouldn't be their choice of retaliation. Plus, it's a sacred artifact, they would've sent it directly back to Solaria." Something didn't seem right about this. "Where is Vanalli?"

"She is with Vanessa and Elucia, looking for Melody. They think she has the blade and is either possessed by a Hilmer or that she is taking it to ground. Where we aren't sure, but Vanalli sent Alric to Floria after the last attack to help Fennik and the Crimson Army," Undas said, looking slightly annoyed for some reason. I wonder if Undas still doesn't trust the demi-god? Personally, I don't trust the man as far as I could throw him. I'm still slightly alarmed that she sent him there, splitting up the two demi-gods.

"You don't think they went to Umbra, do you?" one of the few places that you can enter but cannot escape. Not without Damian, at least. Hell, myself, our mothers and cousins, cannot enter without the risk of being trapped there. Undas raised a brow at me as he shook his head.

"I hope you are wrong. For her sake and for the others' sake." Undas glanced between the men in the cave before speaking again. "We answered your question. Now you answer ours. What's going on?" Fair enough.

"The Selestine was attacked and sunk off the coast of Mistveil, and we almost lost Valyn." The cave went completely silent; the howling from the wind outside was all that could be heard. "Luna brought him back, but she also brought back a little boy who was knocking on death's door and three people who had already died. All the while trying to keep Valyn alive, or so I've gathered. She also healed everyone in the Mor without knowing what she was doing. Long story short, she pissed off a demi-death god, Sirus had to step in and get the bitch to back off, Luna fought a kraken, has apparently gained bodyguards of her own, and is about to go check on Undine in her home at the bottom of the Selpie Sea. So, excuse me if I seem a little uptight."

"Back up. Did you just say my little sister raised the fucking dead?!" Nox's shock was all over his face. Virgil was green as if he was about to puke, but it was the look of pure horror on Undas and Drake's faces that had me worried.

"Unintentionally. Like I said, it's dealt with, but yeah. She gave a little boy back his life." I replied dryly. Honestly, I don't know why he seems so shocked at what his sister can do. She might be even more powerful than Otius himself. My bigger concern was the look on Undas's face. Drake began to speak, but Undas stopped him.

"She is coming into her powers, which is a good thing and a bad thing. If she continues to gain new abilities at the rate that she is, it might be too much for her. Has anyone checked in on those whom she brought back to life? Do they have full autonomy? Can they make decisions for themselves? Or are they mindlessly wandering and waiting? If she can control the dead, then she can create an unkillable, or more so, a disposable army." A chill ran up my spine at his words.

"Luna wouldn't use people, alive or dead, like that. This is the same girl who refused to kill a spider when she was a kid because she believed it was the guiding eyes of some god and was a good sign and not a creepy crawly like the other girls in Celvenia. I know that I've seen her kill Hilmers. I know that she is already different from the girl I grew up with, but Luna wouldn't hurt people who don't deserve it. Dead or not." It always hurt me to hear Virgil talk about her. I know he's known her longer than all of us in this cave, but him knowing details about her as a child, a preteen, and a teenager rubs me the wrong way sometimes. Also, knowing that he's the one who deflowered her pisses me off to no end, but I have to respect it. It is difficult, and I can tell it bothers the others as well.

"Sadly, the girl she was before the war is no longer the same girl that she is now. She has grown and is taking control of life. Even though the life she is controlling right now is like entering a whole new world entirely for her." Drake finally spoke. I could see how much it hurt him to talk about the time he lost with her when Gunther banned Erina from returning to him with Luna. I know Gunther is already dead, and honestly, I'm glad

I never had to meet the man who put them through pain and agony. "Maybe you could tell us a story about Luna as a kid. I don't think we are going anywhere, anytime soon." He looked out towards the entrance of the cave where snow was whipping by faster than even our eyes could catch.

Virgil looked around at her brother, her father and her grandfather, but when his eyes landed on me, I could see the sadness there. "Only if you're alright with it." He said it to me. I was actually shocked that he cared about my feelings, but I nodded, allowing him to speak. "When Luna was about twelve, shortly after Erina had left, Gunther had sent her out into Mistward by herself to prove that she could provide for herself and that she could find her way home without Luther's help. Luther and I were livid when we found out, but Luther was banned from going and helping her. Luther had begged me to go find her because she was shit with directions, didn't do well with hiking, and was clumsy. He was worried that she would fall and drown it the small stream." He paused and chuckled to himself. "Clearly, I went out because I also knew that she was stubborn and would stay out there just to prove the old man wrong about her. But this was also a time when we were told that the fae wanted to kidnap and kill us if we were in their woods for over three days. Now I realize how stupid we were, but back then it felt real to us. I was expecting to get out there and find her sitting there by the river, crying. Instead, I saw her, her blonde hair a mess like she had just wrestled a bear, with the shittiest of grins on her face. Luna had a fire going, a small makeshift tent made of leaves and sticks, and at least four cooked fish next to her as she was eating a fifth. She was humming as she ate and was doing the smallest little dance of victory. She went out with just the clothes on her back and a canteen for water, and that was it. When I found her, she had made a bow from spider silk and sticks, with arrows made of sticks and stones that she had hand-sharpened. When I approached her, she had the bow drawn on me before I made it within two feet of her little camp. She threatened to shoot me if I didn't leave her alone to finish out her little adventure."

Nox broke the story with a snort. "So you're telling me she's always been a shoot first as questions later kind of girl?" I pictured her exactly as he described her, all but the blonde hair. Granted, when we met her, she had blondish-blue hair, but she had already told us why that was. I could see the grin he had talked about. She still gives it when she is happy.

"Oh yeah. I did as she said, too, because I knew damn right well that she would've at least taken me out at the knees for interfering." He paused, and I watched his face drop. He almost didn't continue, but Drake rested his hand on his shoulder, assuring him he was safe to continue. A knot formed in my stomach. "She came home two days later, just before the three-day mark. Gunther didn't see the pride in her for staying out there late; he didn't see the success she had by feeding herself, making it home safe, and not dying. No, he saw her not coming home faster as a weakness. That she wasn't fit to take care of herself and that she needed Luther to take care of her and train her more. It pissed me off because the adventures became more frequent until she made it out and back in a timely manner. *His* timely manner. She became more and more stubborn with him as time went on. Lilly was sick and Gunther was fading; he didn't tell anyone until he was sidelined. She took her training seriously enough that even though the people of the town treated her differently, they paid attention to her. Once she was sixteen, General Rothsberg tried to convince Gunther to let her become a dragon rider since her skills with a bow and arrow were better than half the people we had. Gunther refused and threatened Vikrum with a sword at his throat. Luther was his successor, not Luna. Granted, Gunther apparently knew the truth about her and just kept it a secret from everyone. I had a plan to get her out of there and away from Gunther, giving her the life she should've had and deserved. I was just afraid she would say no. At least you guys saved her when I couldn't."

Virgil's hands curled up into fists, and for once I felt bad for him. I know everyone else has slowly accepted him in their own ways, but hearing him talk about her and the plans he had and what he would do for her, kind of killed me. She had told me she loved someone and belonged to someone else, more so that she wanted to belong to that someone before she met me and my brothers. To know that if fate hadn't destined us to be together that she might've chosen him, well, I guess he would've deserved her. Nox patted him on his shoulder but looked at me.

"My sister is blessed. And apparently has been blessed for longer than we knew. I'm glad she had you looking out for her when none of us could." Drake and Undas muttered their agreements, but Virgil was looking at me. No hate anymore, no rage, just sadness and defeat. That might actually kill me more. The acceptance. "Undas, plan still the same even without the trip to Yida?"

"Yes, clearly he had earned it long before we met him." Undas replied. Drake just nodded, and Virgil closed his eyes. What the hell was I missing? Before I could ask, Fennik was screaming in my head.

Bastian! I need your help! It's urgent and I don't have much time!

Fuck.

Undas said that he would guide them all back to Taiga and then to Mistveil before my feet hit the ground in Floria. Virgil asked how he could help, but Nox and Drake told him he was best to stay put with them. They were right, honestly. I tore from the cave fast and heavily, talking to Fennik and trying to get Damian's attention to help as well. But then it hit us: Luna needed our help, and we were needed in Mistveil.

Why the hell was all of Cerulia falling apart at the same time?! How many ways in does this asshole have? Taiga was safely sealed off from Hellis; we ensured it when the whole reaper debacle happened. Winter would not fall to the likes of Hellis. As I ran through the snow, back as my wolf, I could hear the thunder rolling in with the snow. A dangerous omen that death was upon us. The wind howled as I raced back to Taiga, slipping between trees and shrubs. Bertrum and Kira were outside talking when I blasted by them, pulling a curse from Bertrum's lips as he excused himself from Kira to follow me.

I had managed to get a message out to Valdis to send him to help Fennik since Luna gave him orders to stay put in Hellis. She didn't know that Fennik was in danger and needed help. Thankfully, Valdis was already trying to figure out what he could do to help when I got to him.

"What is it?" He asked as I changed and got dressed. His eyes darted all over me to check for injuries or blood. "I didn't think seeing Luna's family in the mountains would cause you such distress."

"I wish you would've just told me who was out there and saved me the awkwardness." I replied as I shoved a soft grey t-shirt over my head.

"Sorry, I figured you'd find it interesting." He shrugged. "What's got you panicking?"

"Floria and Doria are under attack, and I have to go to Mistveil to help with an evacuation of Doria." I said as I forced my feet into the closest pair of actual boots I could find. "Oh, and my wife doesn't know about the attack on Floria because she's in the middle of the fight in Doria. So there's that."

"How can I help?" Bertrum was immediately offering his assistance, not just because Luna is my wife, but because the woman who he swears is his mate is my wife's best friend and would cause bodily harm if he didn't help her.

"Call Hector and see where he is. If he is still in Taiga, send him to Daglidell. There is plenty of room there for refugees to go. Tell him to meet up with Jared. They can figure out where to put everyone. I doubt Damian would object." I said as I grabbed my sword from its resting place by the front door. The fireplace was still roaring, the smell of firewood wafting around me. "Have Kira, Holly and Sirius stay here at the Manor. I want everyone together right now. Once that's done, get to Dagelidell yourself and help. We're going to need everyone."

"Sirius and Holly will want to help." Bertrum said as he stepped to the side of the door. "Harper is also in town. If either of the sisters finds out that Luna needed help and they were sidelined, they will be pissed."

"Then give them something here to do. Taiga can't be without a leader, especially right now." I said as I took one more look around for anything I might need. Bertrum nodded, and just like that, we were both on our separate ways.

CHAPTER 41
FENNIK

Fire rained from the sky, lighting up the darkness of the night. The Crimson Army was already outside the walls, fighting off the hordes of grimlocks that were surrounding the city. Daemons on winged beasts flew high above the city, shooting arrows on fire down on the citizens who were just trying to enjoy an evening of festivities. Screams could be heard throughout the streets; calls to arms rang out through the chaos.

Moments ago I was in the arms of my wife, sensually pleasuring her the best way I could without us physically being together. Now, I was throwing my clothes on and ripping through my home looking for weapons and Elijah. He was most likely already outside with the army. I grabbed two swords and sprinted down the gravel pathway that led up to my home from the city. Daemons didn't seem like they could set foot inside the city without burning up in ghost flames. My home was no different. Valdis and his family were probably the only ones who could right now.

Alric was standing at the edge of the path, a grin on his blood-covered face. "What the fuck?" I stammered as I approached him. His opal eyes wide with insanity. Blood droplets slipped from his dark blue hair onto the ground as he heaved air into his lungs.

"They started attacking out of nowhere. Elucia is with Elijah. They sent me to come get you." He had finally caught his breath before glancing down at the swords in my hands. "Think that'll do, prince?"

"They'll have to." I replied. "Let's get to your wife and my brother." I took a step forward, but Alric grabbed my arm. I looked down at where he was gripping me and then slowly glared up at him. "Let. Me. Go." I growled.

"It will not be that damn simple. The fucking city is on fire and they're on the other side of the wall. You got a better fucking way out of here?" He said, pointing at the vast, ever-growing fire in front of us.

"There is one, but Luna half collapsed it when she met face to face with Marcloff recently. We may be able to get through there and make it work, but I don't know if workers started fixing the tunnel or not." I said as I looked at the prison off in the distance. "We have to traverse a prison that's essentially a maze.

I'm pretty sure you would actually love it in there. You might even get some ideas."

His wide grin grew wider. A laugh escaped his lips. "Elucia and I built the labyrinth ourselves for Otius's blade. It was impenetrable. Maybe when this chaos is over, we can take a look at your prison and give you some ideas." He quipped as I led him toward the prison. I hadn't been in there since Luna and Marcloff's decimation of the halls in the castle. I almost guarantee that Tanis helped Marcloff escape through the old tunnels. It's the only way he would've gotten out unseen.

The grass outside the prison still showed scorch marks from the first battle. Alric stood in the doorway admiring the iron gate and the inscriptions carved into the stone. My uncle had helped build this prison with my mother when they were in their first two decades of life. They said it was a necessary evil that every realm should have in cases of emergencies. My mother wasn't always psychotic. At least not that I can remember, but that doesn't matter now. She made her bed and lied in it. I shook the last memory of my mother from my head.

"Do you have a map of this place?" Alric questioned as I passed him to enter the stone structure.

"I don't need one. I got lost in here as a child and my mother refused to let my uncle help me out. She said that I needed to learn how to get myself out of here and out of trouble." I paused for a moment. "I guess she really did teach me something." I let out a soft chuckle as I started down the hallway, Alric practically on my heels. When he and Elucia showed up at Vanalli's request, I was hesitant, but I'm glad to have them here.

I forgot how empty this place was after Drake and my father were held here. Daemon bodies still littered the floor from where the Crimson Rebellion tore through this place to get to them. They fought through this place to find Erina. I can only imagine the carnage we'll find at the end. Alric let out a low whistle as we passed through a crossroads in the prison.

"Someone went insane down here." He noted as we stepped over daemon corpses. He was examining them as we moved, for what I wasn't sure. Blood had dried on the floor; no weapons were in sight. I'm assuming the rebellion cleared this place of all weaponry during their attempt to take over. We moved further through the prison until we reached a long tunnel.

"This is the original way out into the forest right outside the city. I can't guarantee it hasn't been sealed off." I slowly made my way through the tunnel, trying not to trip over loose stones and rubble. There were no lights down this far. Runoff water from the ground above the tunnel seeped through the stones, dripping softly into small puddles as we passed. If Alric weren't breathing so loudly, I would swear I was in here alone. Moss covered the stones the further we got; our steps quieted by the moss. Normally, I would find this relaxing: the loudness of the world hushed by the stones and foliage. It was so quiet that if danger lurked ahead, we wouldn't know.

Chittering sounded ahead of us; the rotting smell of decaying flesh became stronger the closer we got to the end of the tunnel. I glanced over my shoulder to check on Alric. His blade already in hand as he moved stealthily behind me. I clutched the leather handles of my own blades tightly. We would be ready for anything that comes our way. Slowly we made our way towards the noises from what I could only assume to be daemons.

"I smell fae, my lord," a raspy, half-broken voice called out through the tunnel, sending chills down my spine. An enormous shadow was cast along the wall ahead of us. An enormous beast on two legs was all I could make out from where we stood. Alric grabbed my shoulder and pulled me back before I could go any further.

"They smell you, but not me. Maybe you can distract them while I circle around and get the jump on them from behind." Alric whispered his plan as if it were one that was simple enough.

"What about the lord it speaks of? What if they can scent you but haven't noticed you yet?" I retorted in the same whisper. He was right, they hadn't scented him... yet. I knew better than to believe that they didn't scent him. Demi-god or not, he gave off a distinct scent. He took a brief moment to think about what I pointed out. "There is no way they can't scent you. I'm sorry."

He shrugged his shoulders as his eyes followed the shadow of the beast along the wall. "We don't have much time to come up with a plan then, Prince." He was absolutely right. We had only a few minutes before we'd be able to see the full extent of the creature lurking in the tunnel. I wish I had someone I trusted with me. Bastian would really come in handy right now. At least with his beast legion he might have an idea of what the hell we were up against. That's it!

Bastian! I need your help! I shouted through the bond towards my brother. *It's urgent and I don't have much time!* It had taken him a few moments, but he reached back to me.

What's wrong? Bastian didn't sound as worried as Luna would've if I hadn't blocked her from hearing my thoughts.

Floria is under siege again. No daemons can be inside the city without lighting on fire, but they are flying over it and raining fire on the city. Alric and I are in the tunnels trying to get out to help the Crimson Army, but there is a large shadow of a beast that has us stuck where we are.

Two legs or four? He asked simply.

Two, from what I can tell. It's fucking huge, Bastian. I thought quickly, my gaze darting between Alric and the shadow as it got closer to where we were. *It said it could smell the fae in the tunnel but hadn't caught wind of Alric yet.*

Get out of there! Run! Do not try to fight it. Damian and I can be there shortly. Get. Out. Now! Bastian was screaming in my head to run. Normally I wouldn't be afraid of a fight, but the fear in his voice had me terrified. I glanced between the shadow and Alric once more.

"We've gotta go now!" I said as I gripped Alric by his shirt and tossed him back down the tunnel. We took off, running back the way we came. That's when I heard it. A disembodied laugh that had me losing my balance and slipping on the moss-covered stones. Alric spun on his heels trying to help me back to my feet. "Just go! My brothers are on their way! Get them!"

Alric wanted to fight me, but whatever look he saw on my face had him second-guessing that. He nodded, redirecting himself back towards the entrance, and took off. I couldn't make out his body as he moved, just a quick burst of blue light. I watched as the blue light vanished around the corner. I just only hope he can get them back here fast enough.

"Little fae, little fae. How delicious you smell. Come out, come out, wherever you are." The raspy voice croaked out, echoing off of the surrounding walls. I forced myself back to my feet and took off running again, trying to avoid the moss the best I could. Thunderous pounding filled the tunnel behind me. "Little fae! Come out to play!" It echoed again. Fuck! It's getting closer.

I dug in deep and ran as fast as my legs would take me. I didn't want to risk shifting into my wolf, not knowing what I was up against and in doing so, losing the only weapons I had on me. Light filtered into the tunnel from the prison. I was so close to being free of the darkness. "There you are, pretty little fae." The creature's voice broke through the sense of safety I had found.

I was fucked.

CHAPTER 42
NIKLAUS

Baked pastries filled the morning air, keeping me in the memory of bliss from hours ago. I already miss her. Watching her fall asleep in a pile of limbs, her body touching each of us, was perfect. I walked back to my house with a grin that shone bright as the sun. Nothing and no one was going to take that from me. It was early enough that the children were bustling about, heading off to lessons for the day as their parents stopped at the market to get their groceries.

The walk home was anything but silent, but it was normal. The most normal, mundane type of morning. Their everyday lives are playing out just as they do every day. I notice the flowers blooming in the gardens around the little preschool just above the small stone wall. Some of these children were beyond gifted, flourishing all different flowers and fruits and vegetables. The spring realm always birthed gifted healers and farmers. We are very lucky to be able to provide to the rest of the realms. The wind blew softly through my hair, dancing around me as I drew closer to the house. Normally, I wouldn't have paid attention to the little things around here. I'd normally be stumbling home drunk right about now, showing my people that their heir was nothing more than a childish drunk. But that's all changed since Luna came around. No one looks at me with pity in their eyes, or crosses the street far ahead of me just so they didn't have to cross paths with me.

Now everyone waved and smiled. Parents let their kids run up with excitement in greeting instead of keeping them away from the smelly drunk prince. It was a refreshing feeling, like I wasn't a major disappointment. I finally made it back to the house, ready to climb into bed where my wife's scent was heaviest, but something was wrong when I opened the door. It wasn't very often that my mother was in my house. It also wasn't often that she looked so panicked.

"What's wrong?" I said, by way of greeting. My mother wrapped her arms around me, pulling me close to her chest. Her heart was racing, and I could hear her sobs. I rustled out of her arms and looked at her. "What is happening, Mom?" She grabbed my hands and squeezed them tight.

"Doria is under attack. Where are your brothers and Luna?" She frantically looked out the window, hoping to see the rest of our little group standing about outside. My heart sank as she looked back at me. "Where is everyone, Niklaus?" Her accent thickened as she said my name. I hadn't heard her accent in decades; it only came out when she was worried or scared.

"Everyone went back to their realms. We all have things we need to take care of in our homelands. Luna and Valyn were heading out to meet Jasmine to go check on Undine. Things haven't been that great. You already know what happened at the Mor with Luna. Something has them concerned about her safety." My hands shook uncontrollably. I wanted to reach through the bond to Luna to make sure she was safe, but I wasn't sure what was happening, and a single moment of distraction could be life or death. Well, for those she's trying to protect. "What can we do? Do we head to Doria and help there?"

I was tired, but when it came down to it, I've stayed up later. My mother finally let go of me as she began to pace throughout the living room. "I don't know. There is a good chance that they will need our help getting out and somewhere safe. Just where do we send everyone?"

"Daglidell had space when we needed them before. Maybe they could find it in their hearts to help out again?" I offered a small solution; we would have to set up medical tents and take healers just in case. I can't think straight right now. All I want to do is reach out to Luna and make sure she is safe.

My mother had finally composed herself long enough to pull her phone from her pocket and make a call. She walked out of the room and into the kitchen. I just wanted to run back the way I came and head straight to Doria and help them.

What is stopping me? Why am I just standing here? Wrestling with the thoughts in my head was its own nightmare. I could be of help, I know how to fight. I can also assess people on the ground and heal up those who need it faster if I'm there.

Fuck this, I'm going back to help. It's the least I can do. I reached for the door but stopped short. My mother had come back into the room. "Where do you think you're going?" Her voice was stern and with complete resolve. She wasn't the mess of a woman who met me when I came home. This was the high priestess that my mother truly was.

"I'm going to Doria. I can do more on the front lines there than I can anywhere else." The knob twisted in my hand as I pushed my way out of the house.

I could feel my mothers anger from behind me as I took of through the streets. News must not have reached here yet. Everyone was still going about their daily business as if the world wasn't on fire across the world.

Then again, most people always think it can't happen where they live. What's happening over seas can't touch them here. They're wrong. They're very wrong.

The portal to Doria was located inside the grand library in the center of the city. It was designed that way so every realm had access to the knowledge there and a way to meet with apprentice healers. It made scenes to me.

My legs burned as I pushed myself faster. The grand library was finally within sight. Like most of the important buildings here, the grand library was built into one of the oldest oak trees in the city. Lights were hung stringed together through the branches and leaves creating a beautiful ambiance. I ran up the steps that lead to the large round green door. Golden leaves were etched and hand painted along the center of the door, stars lining the top.

I knew better than to run inside the building. Claudia might be older, but she would tear into me if I caused a ruckus inside the library.

Gently I pushed open the door and entered the quiet space. People were already in the stacks reading quietly or perusing the selection looking for their next read. Most were priestesses who were doing their studies, you could tell by the white robes with the teal accents, the purple accents and the yellow accents. Each accent showed how far along in their training they were.

Claudia was watching me from her enormous desk, her blonde hair pulled up tight on the top of her head. How she didn't have a headache from having hair that tight was beyond me. Her slate eyes followed my every move as I made my way to the back of the library where the portal doors were.

Each door was made of oak, beautifully etched with a symbol of the realm that lie beyond. My eyes landed on Doris's door. I was just coming through that same door not that long ago.

I reached my hand out for the knob as Lunas voice cut through my thoughts.

Get to Mistveil!

My hand halted at the knob. She was safe, and clearly calling the shots. That's all I needed to know. I pulled my phone from my pocket and called my mother.

"Luna called the shots. I'm needed in Mistveil. Call Maggie and see if they can get tents up. I'm heading there now."

There was no need to say anything else, my mother didn't bother saying anything either, she just hung up. As much as I wish I could've said something more, now isn't the time.

I moved my hand from the knob that would've taken me to Doria and grabbed the one that would take me home. I'll follow her orders to the end of my days and forever beyond that.

CHAPTER 43
DAMIAN

Something wasn't sitting right with me. Chaos was dancing around in my brain when I got back to Solaria. The halls were empty of the normal chatter I had grown accustomed to. Everything was silent.

I made my way back into the house, my footsteps echoing off the marble floors. I stuck out like a sore thumb here. I wasn't meant for the bright white of Solaria. I missed my home in Daglidell. I missed the night sky littered with stars everywhere I looked. The calmness of the air as the stars twinkled and shot across the sky.

We haven't had any of our celebrations this year. Not the Rites of Ulnar, not a single birthday, none of the solstices, not even the Celebration of Vanalli. I guess it's different now that we actually know Vanalli personally.

We need to celebrate something, some type of victory. Everyone needs something to celebrate to boost morale. Wait, when the hell was Lunas birthday? How the hell do I not know this?!

I tapped out a message to Erina, shame filling me as I asked when Lunas birthday was. I don't think anyone knew, she never really talked about it. Hell, when is Valdis's birthday? We suck as a mate group when we don't even bother to know when everyone's birthdays are.

Lost in thought I don't realize where my feet had ushered me to. The walls were lined with bookshelves from the floor to the ceiling. A plush white armchair was snug against the window that overlooked the whole city. Lunas favorite fluffy pink blanket was still draped across it as if she had just stepped away.

Vanilla and citrus filled this room. The scent dragging my thoughts back to last night. I wanted to just take her away and bring her back here with me. Our time has been limited. I don't like it. My father hasn't spent this much time away from any of our mothers. Yet here we are, constantly separated from our mate. Only one of us lucky enough to have her for a long period of time. I hate this.

I sat in the chair and pulled the blanket up to my face, breathing in her scent deeply. My heart ached from missing her and it's only been an hour. Her last book was still sitting on the small book table in front of the chair. It had a red cover with yellow lettering on it, a wolf design etched under the letters. It was some type of romance book, usually she grinned ear to ear when she was reading, but this book made her cheek redden.

My phone buzzed in my pocket, I just assumed Erina was finally texting me back. I wasn't expecting Vanalli's name to pop up on the screen.

"We haven't found Melody yet. But we need safe passage onto Umbra." Her text sent a cold chill down my spine. Why the hell do they need to go to Umbra?

"Can I ask why?"

"There's a gate to Hellis in Umbra. We think Melody might've been taken there. If she's possessed, the Hilmer would go to the closest and fastest way back home." Vanalli made a point, but it wasn't one I liked.

"I'll head to Daglidell and meet you there. It's easier to get into Umbra from there."

Get to Mistveil! Lunas voice screamed in my head, echoing off the inside of my skull. *Doria is under attack and we're going to need your help in Mistveil.*

"Vanalli, change of plans. Luna needs me in Mistveil. Doria is under siege." I tapped out the message quick and pocketed my phone before running out of the little library and back to the portal. I didn't wait for her reply.

Someone please call my mom and tell her what's happening. I don't have much longer. I love you guys! I pulled out my phone and called Erina. Her phone went to voicemail, "Doria is under attack. Luna is there helping the people of Doria get to safety. She's telling us all to get to Mistveil to help. If you can, please come help." I ended the phone call right as I made it to the door. My hand gripped the metal knob as I pushed the door open with such force that I thought it would rip it off the hinges. If she needed me in Mistveil, that's where I would be.

My feet hit the stone walkway behind the house and I took off, not even bothering to gently close the door. I'm pretty sure it slammed behind me, but that was the least of my concerns right now. I could see the old tower by the sea was opened up as if it were a portal directly to Doria. People were flooding through to a massive sea of tents. It took me only a few moments to sense Niklaus was inside the tents. Bastian was on my heels following me through the woods to the shore. We need someone with the ability to teleport close to the tents just in case people were badly injured.

"Why aren't you running off to Doria yourself to save her?" Bastian asked as we slowed our pace as we got closer to the tents. I looked at him.

"Same reason you didn't run there either. An order from our mate isn't something we can ignore, and it will root us in place. Did you even try to go there or did you just come here on instinct?" I asked him as we turned the corner to see all the tents filled with people.

"No, I came here on instinct. I thought maybe it was just me and I wasn't thinking straight. There are a lot of people here. There is no way that Mistveil has the space for everyone." Bastian was right, there are plenty of hotels that they can be placed in, but that will only work for so long.

"Daglidell has room, so does Solaria. We can always move people there temporarily. Those who aren't injured can be moved immediately, and we should probably focus on that." I replied as I noticed a group of children wandering around. I moved my way over to the group and tried to look friendly. Niklaus and Fennik were the two who looked the friendliest, sometimes Valyn, but Bastian and I always looked like we were going to rip someone's head off for looking in our direction. "Hi there little ones. Where are your parents?"

A tiny little girl huddled into the arms of an older girl, stared up at me like I was the enemy. The older girl pulled the little one into her arms tighter as she answered me. "We don't know. We were pushed through here and told to head to the tents, but there's too many people here."

"We can take you there. My name is Damian and this is my brother Bastian. And you are?" I tried to smile as I pointed to Bastian who was looking around the field for something.

"I'm Ellie, this is Leesa, and that is Bernard and Tommy. We are all siblings." Ellie said as she pulled her brothers out from behind her. "You are Prince Valyn's brothers, right?" I nodded. I guess knowing who we are is a start to prove that we won't hurt them. She turned to her siblings and gave them a smile that did not meet her little green eyes. "You heard them, stay close, hold hands. Bernard hold Leesa's other hand, Tommy, you have mine." And just like that she was leading her siblings between Bastian and myself.

We made our way through the crowd of people as took the children to the medical tents. Athena was outside of the tents helping sort patients and getting people to their families. If anyone could help us, she could. Her eyes lit up the moment we made it to the front of the line moments later. "I'm so glad you boys are safe and here." Her eyes fluttered down to the tiny little group of children huddled between us. "And who do we have here?"

"This is Ellie, Lessa, Bernard and Tommy. We're hoping their parents are here." I said as Bastian excused himself to go help out an elderly couple that was trying to make their way over. Athen smiled at the children and checked her list.

"Are your parents Marina and Tholin Harring?" The children lit up beside me, each chanting yes, yes, yes. Athen pulled back the curtain and pointed over at the bed in the corner of the large room where a slender blonde woman was pacing next to a burly brunette man who was laying on the cot with a bandage wrapped around his head. The young children ran through the tent to greet their parents. All but one.

"Thank you Prince Damian. You didn't have to help us, but you did. You have my gratitude." Ellie couldn't be any older than maybe fifteen, her red ringlet curls were plastered to the side of her face and her green eyes shone bright. She has seen the worst of things, yet I can still see hope in her eyes.

"You don't have to thank me. Getting you and your siblings back to your parents is going to be the highlight of my day. I can't wait to tell my wife about the brave little girl that I met today." I smiled at her as she looked back at her parents.

"Princess Luna is the reason we made it through the portal thing safely. She is also the reason we are all alive. Please tell her my family and I say thank you. I know you don't want to hear it, but we want her to know that we are grateful." With that, Ellie took off into the tent, running into her crying mother's arms. That is something that I can't wait to tell Luna. I don't know what she is doing in Doria, but I trust her, I just need her to come home safely.

CHAPTER 44
LUNA

The stairs leading to the top floor matched the same sandy marble as the rest of the house. A plush carpet that reminded me of the royal navy blue of the sea draped the stairs and the hall before us. Something putrid hit my nose as soon as our feet hit the top of the stairs. Valyn's nose twitched at the stench, but it was Victoria who stepped back down the stairs that caught my attention. It's normal to feel disgusted by this stench, but knowing what that stench is, I don't blame her for stepping back.

"How did Jasmine not smell this stench? It smells of rotten meat up here." She said, covering her nose with her sleeve. I don't think any of us expected this. I could see her hesitation about joining us again. If the smell of decay meant anything to us, it's that Undine is deceased, or something up here is causing it.

"Would you rather not go in there? We can handle it for you. You don't need to see what might be in that room." I offered her. Valyn ran his hand idly up my spine as he nodded at his cousin. We could handle this if she couldn't. She hesitated for a moment but shook her head. We should've known better; she would want to know for Jasmine's sake. "Alright. Then we are going to do this my way." The two of them looked at me, their twin turquoise eyes staring into my soul as I smiled. I closed my eyes and searched for my little shadow darling. Ophelia sat there, coiled tightly with her head peeking out at me. She perked right up as I called her forth, letting her shine brightly in her smallest form. "I need your help; let me see through your eyes once more."

Victoria and Valyn both sucked in a breath as Ophelia leaped from my hand and slithered under the door like nothing more than a light breeze. I ignored the way they looked at her. I knew she wouldn't hurt anyone unless I told her to. I had to remind myself that Valyn had only seen her once, and I don't think Victoria had ever seen Ophelia or any of my little pets. I closed my eyes, focusing on what Ophelia was seeing, and I didn't like it.

Undine was lying in her bed, with shadows looming around her. Each shadow seemed darker than the next. Undine looked so much like Jasmine. Her skin looked ashen, not at all like the warm mahogany of Jasmine's skin. Her teal and black braids lay dull and limp on the bed around her face. Ophelia got close enough to her that I could sense she was still breathing, but only faintly. Her eyes were closed, but I could see them rapidly moving beneath her eyelids. She looked as if she hadn't seen the light of day in months. A darker shadow moved around her bed, gracefully touching her cheek as it whispered something in her ear. Her soft groans from the bed were the only thing keeping me from busting that door down and destroying the shadows in there right now. Ophelia slipped from the bed, heading back for me, when Undine sat up in bed, her eyes flashing a bright white. Water began flooding the room as Ophelia quickly slipped through the crack and back out to me.

"We're about to have company!" I shouted as I thought long and hard about the way I could make a scythe out of some elemental power I possess. The only things that came to mind were starlight and earth, and I grabbed hold. I pulled the earth from beneath my feet and wrapped it in starlight to bind a large scythe. Victoria let out a small gasp, while Valyn gripped the hilt of his sword, dragging it from its sheath.

"What—" Before he could finish asking his question, the doors before us flung open as water cascaded from the room and into the hall. "Shit" I could hear him say as the water knocked him off his feet and to the floor. Victoria had grabbed the door frame, as I dug the tip of the scythe into the floor and held my ground as the water rushed by me and cascaded down the stairs. I heard a welp come from the floor below, but I knew it was only Jasmine's surprise at the waterfall.

A deep, throaty laugh echoed through the hall as a dark figure trudged through the water. The putrid smell of decay hit my nose like the smell of rotten eggs left outside in the sun. I tried so hard to hold back the bile burning up the back of my throat. Valyn was back on his feet, stomping through the water to put himself between me and the figure. It took me a minute to to realize that Victoria was at my back. Both had swords that I hadn't noticed before now. How the hell didn't I see them?

"You three weren't invited here. Why are you in my home?" The voice sounded broken, disembodied even, like it didn't belong to the goddess whose mouth it was coming from. My grip on the scythe tightened at the sound. Shadows danced behind Undine, each dancing with her long ebony and teal braids. She looked too thin as the white sheer fabric clung to her body exposing ribs and boney arms. The way Undine was described to me was of a vuloptous goddess with curves like the hills of Eldory. The goddess before us was anything but that. Her frail body limped from the room, the crushing waves still rushing through the halls trying to take us out at the ankles.

Valyn's eyes lit up bright white as he forced a break in the waves. It took me a moment to realize Victoria was doing the same thing. Both pushing the waves away from me and back towards Undine.

A brittle laugh escaped from her. "You really think you can take me down, Prince of Summer?" She snapped her fingers, waves rushing faster and harder from all around her. I took a deep breath, searching for my little water snake. It took me only a moment as she poked her head up from the depths of my soul to realize that she was being summoned. Her body, a fluid liquid, poured from my left hand, dripping to the floor until her body became complete. She looked at the goddess at the end of the hall; a shiver racing down her spine. Not in fear, but anticipation of a fight. I never named my elemental snakes, but she reminded me of a Aurora. Magestic, elegant and free-spirited. She slithered from me, through the water edging closer to Undine.

Aurora was a very fitting name for her, slithering through the water like the aurora borealis in the darkest night sky that can only been seen up in Taiga. She was beautiful. I focused on her movements, catching her sight with my own. Her eyes saw the shadows for what they really were. Daemons, puppeteering Undine with smoke and poison. A glimmer of silver caught my attention through the shadows, drawing Aurora's sight to a long blade hiding itself in a shadow. She inched closer through the water to get a better look at the blade itself. Shining silver with what looked like twin dragons on the hilt, a sapphire in one dragon's eye, a ruby in the other. Fuck.

"She's got Otius's blade!" I shouted, causing Valyn to lose his balance as he glanced between Undine and myself. I saw the terror in his eyes, the command to run on his lips. "I'm not leaving!" I could see through Aurora's eyes as Undine grasped the blade behind her back. Bad timing for Jasmine to come running up the stairs.

"There's water everywhere. What the hel—" Her gaze looked straight past us and directly at her mother. "Mom, what the hell is going on?!" Jasmine went to go to her mother, but Victoria stepped in her way. "Vic, move. That's my mom." Jasmine looked at her with pleading eyes, but to Victoria's credit, she didn't falter.

"She's not your mom, Jas. At least not the mom you know." Victoria tilted her head in the direction of Undine. I watched as the realization of Undine's condition hit Jasmine fully. Her eyes widened, tears filled them as she finally looked at her mother. Jasmine dropped to her knees with a splash, and I made the worst mistake I could've done.

I took my eyes off the blade.

CHAPTER 45
LUNA

Undine was fragile, but the shadows puppeting her were anything but. Her movements weren't fluid like the water she commanded. They were clunky, like a baby deer just learning to walk for the first time. Even with her uneven movements, she was fast. Before I could hear the scream rip from Victoria's throat, a searing pain cut through the back of my leg. I heard clashing of metal on metal, and grunts coming from behind me. But all I could do was register the fire burning through my leg, trying to make its way further into my body.

I can't tell if I was screaming from the pain or if it was one of the others, but it hurt like hell. I reached for the cut, but my body instantly recoiled from the wound. My body refused to let me touch it. I could make out the sounds of more clashing of steel, grunts and screams. I just couldn't take my eyes off of the black wound that now graced my leg. Rage slowly filled my bones as I recalled what the blade's true purpose was.

Kill daemons.

The side effect being that it could kill any god or goddess that got cut by the blade. It was described to me as an instant death, not a burning pain. This was more of an irritation than a feeling of death. I should know; I died once after all. I forced my hand down to the cut, ignoring every warning bell screaming in my head and focused on Niklaus.

I need you to heal me. Think you can do it through our mental link? I reached out to him, trying not to sound urgent as the battle around me raged on.

What the fuck, Luna?! What happened? I ignored his demands and tried to sound a little more urgent in my request.

There is no damn time! Can you do it or not? Okay, that sounded way harsher than intended.

I can try. Follow my directions and don't lose focus. I can't guarantee this will work. I could hear him sighing as if this was going to be a big discussion later. *Press your hand to the wound and try to stop the bleeding. Just let me know when you have the wound covered.*

Already did that. I snapped at him. *Nik, I love* you, *but I need you to hurry the fuck up. I don't know how much Valyn and Victoria can keep Undine from trying to kill me again.*

What the fuck did you do to piss off Undine?!

NIK! Focus!

Alright, alright! Sending what I can your way, focus on my powers like you have before. It should amplify what you can use. I felt a warmth flood my veins as I followed the bright green light that I have come to know as Nik. I put all my focus on my hand and watched as the light engulfed my entire leg in a bright green glow. My attention was pulled away before I could admire our handiwork.

A scream ripped from Undine's throat. "NO! You should be dead!" My attention snapped from my leg and up at Undine as she lunged for me again, tossing Valyn to the side like he was nothing. I quickly grabbed my scythe and blocked her advance. I drew the blade up, the beautiful sound of steel singing as Otius's blade flung from her hands and across the room. A growl tore from her throat, shaking the entire home at the core. I'm going to taunt either her or the shadows. One way or another, we are walking free. With or without her being alive.

"Victoria, grab Valyn and get him and Jasmine out of here. I got her!" I shouted as Jasmine stayed locked onto the floor, not moving, and Valyn slowly got up from the ground.

"I'm not leaving you!" he shouted at me. I could see the anger in his eyes at my clear dismissal of him. It's not me being heartless, I just can't have him here with what I have to do.

"You don't have a choice. Jasmine isn't going to leave her mother willingly, and you know I can handle myself. Now go!" Undine was up and back on her feet, the blade back in her hand as if it hadn't been thrown a good twelve feet from where she was. These fucking shadows are going to be a big problem for me if I can't isolate her.

Begrudgingly Valyn moved past me and scooped up Jasmine as Victoria ran down the stairs in front of them. *We will talk about this when you are done.* I knew it wasn't hate that laced his words. But it sure felt that way. I kept my eyes locked on Undine as she charged at me again. The way she held the blade was off, holding it high by her face in a reverse grip. The only issue with holding the blade that was is that it's too long for her to get the quick stabbing motions. Bad thing for me about her holding it that way is its long enough that it will get me quicker than if it were a dagger. I watched the shadows duck around the sconces on the wall, keeping to the darkness as they pulled on the strings of shadows that kept Undine on her feet.

I had an idea, one that could either hurt me or kill Undine. I'm hoping it will keep us both alive. She stabbed at me wildly with the blade, going for my face, my arms and my stomach. Missing each blow by about an inch. My scythe deflected her blows, but it was getting dicey. A shadow zipped across the hall behind her, creeping slowly down the hall, staying in the edges of the shadows. Aurora was watching it ready to attack the little dark figure, but I knew she would just bite through it, no damage done to it. Lyria is the next best option, and she was itching to get out.

I knocked Undine back on her ass a little harder than I had intended. I let a little smirk grace my lips as Lyria dropped from my hand, her golden heart-shaped head pushed against my palm as a thank you. "You know what I need you to do, little one."

Just like that, the whole hallway became illuminated, not a shadow insight. Undine went to move, but collapsed onto her knees, barely being able to hold herself up. I could hear the labored breathing from here. Watching her try to fight to stand told me all I needed to know. The shadows held her together. I walked over, kicking the blade back to where Aurora and Lyria sat coiled up waiting patiently for me to praise them. Lyria wrapped herself around the blade so it would be safe. It was the cutest thing ever.

Undine was coughing up black blood as I approached her. I knelt down to look her in the eye. "It's over, creature. Leave her, or I will make you leave." Undine looked up at me with hate in her eyes, but it wasn't the goddess I was looking at. It was the

Hilmer that took over the goddess. Fuck. My. Life. I can't get away from these fuckers, can I?

"You are in no position to demand me to leave my vessel, child." The Hilmer spat as it tried once more to get Undine off of the floor.

"From where I am standing, I am in *the* position. You, however, let your vessel fall into a dismal state. You ended up killing yourself by not keeping up appearances and using so much of her powers without knowing what could happen." I looked at the blade of my scythe, checking my reflection in a taunting manner to the being. "You could always leave her body and fight me one on one. Or is it true that Hilmers have no form without a vessel?"

It snarled once more at me. "You are a disrespectful little shit! You should be dead! Why are you still alive, little goddess?" The Hilmer was trying to regain control of it's vessel, only Undine's body was frail at this point. She was undeniably a powerful goddess, but we don't know how long this creature has been sucking her life force from her.

"Because I'm not some minor goddess like you seem to have confused me for." My smirk widened as I watched Undine's eyes widen as she took me in. I let the facade down just a bit, allowing the full celestial glow to radiate from me. I didn't know Undine. She did not know me. Therefore, her unwanted body snatcher was unaware of my existence in this world. I guess it's been here longer than I've been at full power. Guess news doesn't travel well after all.

"You aren't!" It shouted, recoiling from me. I watched it try to force Undine to move away, to escape from my presence. It was a wonderful feeling knowing that I could strike fear into the eyes of something that is feared by many. It's like an adrenaline rush to the brain. "You can't be her! She died!"

"I'm not my aunt if that's what you're assuming? Talissa isn't dead, though. She was just resting." I smirked, but it just shook Undine's head as if trying to shake away a memory. Undine's eyes hardened as she looked at me. I could see a little light struggling to come to the surface of her eyes. She was still in there, and she was fighting like hell to take control.

"I'm not talking about the Goddess of Destruction and Renewal. She was always bound to come back. There is no life balance without her walking the planet. No, I'm talking about the Goddess of All. The Goddess who destroyed our ancestors long before this meaningless war. I am much older than those you have met. I remember her. She was loving, and kind. But, when the God of Darkness swooped in, she had to destroy all most everything to protect those of this land. She walked amongst all the creatures that roamed this place, never looking down on anyone for their true natures. She never judged even when she had the authority and ability to do so. This war is nothing. Marcloff is nothing but a foot soldier trying to capture the darkness while he slumbers. When the God of Darkness awakens again, you will have to decide what you're willing to do to save the ones you love." The snarling stopped; the Hilmer realizing it was doomed. I watched as it took one last sigh before speaking again. "I am not what you think I am. Do I thrive in chaos like a Hilmer? Yes. Am I a filthy Hilmer? No. Like I said, I am older than them all. I have a true body, but I like to test out the elders of this planet every now and then. She was a treat. I'll leave her. But, you will see me again. Only next time, I will be in my body and you will need my help. Even if you rather not have it."

"What is your name?" I called out as I watched Undine's eyes slowly begin to close. Her eye peeked open and a smile crept upon her face.

"Kaos."

CHAPTER 46
LUNA

When her eyes fluttered open, I could see the Goddess of the Water was back in control of her body once more. I reached down to help her to her feet, knowing that she wasn't going to be able to move on her own. Lyria stayed on top of Otius's blade as we neared her. Aurora slithered between Undine and me to make sure I was alright as I reached for the blade. Lyria moved, but slowly. She didn't trust Undine near the blade, and I couldn't blame her.

"They are protective." She said, her voice as weak as the rest of her body. I nodded my head as I helped guide her down the stairs and into the sitting room. I helped her as she took her seat on the couch. I grabbed the blanket that was draped over the back of the couch and helped her put it on her lap. I didn't know how far away Valyn and the others were. Quite frankly, I'm glad it's just her and I here right now because I had a lot of questions for her. "Ask them. I'll answer what I can."

"Mind reader?" I asked, tilting my head to the side as I took the seat opposite her, placing Otius's blade beside me. She shook her head and smiled briefly.

"I can only imagine what you must be thinking." She paused and glanced between the blade and my leg. "I have questions as well. I feel like I owe you answers before I have any right to ask them though."

I watched as she fidgeted with the strings on the blanket. "I'm not going to judge you. I don't believe that you intended on becoming a vessel for whatever that thing was." She looked at me, her eyes distant for a moment. "Or did you?"

"Not in the sense that you might think." Shock rippled through me as I let her words sink in. Did she really let that thing, Kaos, take over her? "Let me explain. I was researching a way to fortify the against seas the dangers of the ongoing war. I knew that even when things seemed calm, they weren't. About a century ago, Noro, Abrixo, and Jiltara all were acting differently, and that had me worried that the seas were no longer safe. So, naturally, I began doing some research. I came across a book that talked about the primordial gods and goddesses. We were told growing up that Otius was one of the first gods to walk these lands. I don't know if you know anything about him, but he's a narcissistic piece of shit who treated everyone in his family like they were the problem and that he was infallible. He wasn't one to mince words. He was *the* god, and everyone else he just allowed to exist. The other gods put him on a pedestal and treated him as if he were above them all and the law of the land. I brought my findings up to his daughter Vanalli, but she was just as shocked as I was to find out that we weren't the first gods to roam this planet." Undine paused and took a deep breath, visibly still shaken by the entire ordeal.

"Wait. You said a century ago. How long has Kaos been with you?" I gulped as I looked her over. The frailness, the color drained almost completely from her skin. "How long has it been since you've been out in the sea herself or in the sun?"

Undine didn't answer me immediately. She looked at her hands, turning them over as if finally seeing what I've been seeing since I first saw her. "Since the moment I read that book. Kaos was attached to it, or so I thought until she told you that she was taking me for a joyride. At first, it was just a little voice in my head, warning me about a bigger enemy that would eventually wake up. I ignored it for a good long while, thinking it was just my brain thinking about the book and going through all the information that I read there. But now, I can't recall when I stopped leaving the house. Hell, I can't recall anything over the last five years." By the time her eyes met mine, tears filled them. She lost five years. Five years of memories, time with Jasmine, self-control.

"I'm sorry." I whispered out as the sadness deepened in my soul. The reminder of what it's like to have time stolen from me made this whole situation hurt more than I think I realized. I lost ten years with my mother. My whole life was a lie from the moment I was born, a hidden little secret that I don't know if I ever would've found out if Gunther hadn't sent me to Mistveil. I still had issues grappling with how I should feel about Gunther and the lies and secrets. He raised me; he wasn't always cruel to me. Sometimes he treated me like his child. I sat there in silence with her for a few moments longer.

"You have nothing to be sorry for. It wasn't your fault that I got hijacked. Things have been foggy for me, but the only reason I'm telling you anything is because of the fear I felt in Kaos the moment she saw you and the immediate threat you possessed. And for the fact that you saved me. Is Jasmine the reason you came here?" Undines eyes focused on me. The goddess was slowly coming back to life before my eyes. I nodded, keeping quiet and letting her ask the questions she wants to ask me. "Who are you? Why is a primordial goddess afraid of you? Why did you help my daughter and how do you know her?"

Each question had a slightly long explanation, but the last one was simple. "I met Jasmine through Victoria. Prince Valyn is one of my mates. Your daughter helped us not that long ago with safe passage to Anchora. You talked about Noro. She was just a grieving mother, not for her own child but for that of the children of Floria who fell to their deaths. She protected their souls when their parents didn't. I don't think she was particularly dangerous, just heartbroken by the heavy weight of loss on her." I watched Undine closely as I spoke of Noro. Something tells me the sea wyverns aren't truly what people believe. I think Undine knows that too. "As for who I am, I could give you three guesses." I smiled at her. I don't know how much she knows about my family or if I even have any of the markings of my grandmother, but I know from stories that my mother had told me that she knows Undas.

Undine cocked her head to the side like a dog examining something with such intensity. "You are new to your role as a Goddess which is practically unheard of. You're also a little more savage and hands on then most of the goddesses I've grown up with or raised Jasmine around." All truths. I'm pretty sure it was obvious by the way I handled things upstairs. "I also noticed that you are skilled with weapons. Most goddesses had to learn from their brothers how to fight. Or their husbands.

Most didn't learn from their fathers. You clearly have been well train. You also noticed the best way to quiet the shadows. Yet, I have no idea who you are. I've never seen someone control water that wasn't my own flesh and blood, yet also control light."

I held my hand out, my palm facing the ceiling and focused until a small flame flicked to life, then before it could dance I froze it in time, ice engulfing the flame. Undine's eyes widened as she took in the fire from my grandfather, but the ice from my mother. She let out a low whistle. "Well shit. I know who you belong to now. Do they know you can use their powers?"

"Undas does. My mother doesn't as far as I know. Then again, we haven't been able to be around each other much since this whole debacle started. I'm honestly surprised Valyn hasn't stormed back in here with Jasmine, Victoria and half the naval unit. I should probably get them back in here." Undine nodded. I could see all the questions that she wanted to ask still lingering on the edge of her mind, but I think seeing Jasmine might take more priority over asking them right now.

Valyn, she's safe. We have a much bigger problem on our hands. A few minutes went by as I waited for him to respond. I panicked as it took so much longer than usual.

Good, I need you in Doria. If Undine can, see if she can get you back to land quick. We have big problems here too. Valyns voice was abrupt. Not cold, just commanding. Something turned in my gut at the thought of something happening in Doria.

"Somethings happening in Doria and I need to get back. Think you can help at all?" I asked Undine. Her skin was finally turning back to normal. Her eyes not as hazy as they were only minutes ago. Even her hair came back to life. "Did Kaos use your life force?"

"Kaos used more than just my body. She used my powers enough to see how long it would take for me to burn out and how long it would take for me to recuperate." She glanced out the window to the ocean beyond and sighed. "The time it took to recuperate is taking less and less. Kaos said it would, she said our kind is weak by design. Primordial Gods take about a minute to recoup what takes us days, sometimes weeks or months. Death can come quick to our kind with the right weapon, but Kaos kept repeating that even that was a lie. Your family knows about death far too well." I watched a tear slip from Undine's eye.

Oh shit, she doesn't know. How do I go about telling her the truth? How do I tell her Kaos was telling her the truth? I took a deep breath, relaxed my shoulders and sighed. Undine looked at me as she wiped her eyes feverishly trying to get the tears to stop from falling. "I need to get to Doria, but I can't do it without your help. So, in good faith that I can trust you, I'll tell you two things. Talissa is alive, so are all of her mates." I watched as Undine's eyes widened but continued to speak as she opened her mouth. "As far as death coming for our kind, you struck me with Otius's blade. It burned like hell, but I didn't die. Talissa and the others would've been back to life if Otius didn't poison the waters on Celestia to keep them in his mind, safe. I was stabbed my one of my mother-in-laws and I came back. Death for us doesn't seem to stick."

Undine moved the blanket from her lap and stood, smoothing out the wrinkles in her deep blue dress. It was clearly torn and frayed from our battle earlier. Before I could examine it more, she spoke. "You have Otius's blade. Use it and keep it from Marcloff. If Kaos is right, you might need it for the King of Darkness, whoever that might be. Let me get changed and I will help you get back to Doria. If what you said is true, then I need to do my part and be a better friend."

I nodded as she left the room. I had no choice but to wait for her, but I pulled out my phone a tapped out two quick texts. One to Jasmine and one to my grandmother. Both saying the same thing.

She's alive and she is safe. But we have bigger problems now.

CHAPTER 47
LUNA

It didn't take Undine long before she descended the stairs in black leather pants, a tight navy-blue shirt that clung to her breasts and waist, and what looked like riding boots. No jewelry to be found, aside from a small golden hoop that adorned her right nostril and the charms in her beautifully braided hair, which was pulled up into a bun atop her head. She was no nonsense from the moment her feet hit the floor. She grabbed a trident from the hall closet that rivaled the size of the scythe I had made earlier. It was beautiful, golden with etched carvings down the handle. A sapphire adorned the handle at the center where the hilt met the blade.

"This isn't the first war that I've fought in, but I hope it's my last." She smirked as we stepped out of the house. The ocean seemed at peace; schools of colorful fish floated around the barrier of her home. A gigantic shadow cast across the sandy lawn, causing me to look up. My heart leaped into my throat as an enormous sea serpent glided across what I would only consider the sky above me. A chuckle escaped Udine as she took in my reaction. "You think after meeting Noro, and having your own beautiful little pet snakes that you could handle a little sea serpent."

"Little! That thing looks like it's larger than the whales Jasmine brought me here on!" I gaped. Undine's laugh was harder this time. Musical, but filled with amusement. She was clearly loving every moment of my panic. I took a deep breath as the serpent wrapped itself around the barrier, awaiting its master. "It won't eat me, will it?"

"What is she telling you? You said you heard Noro, listen for her voice." Undine walked up to the large creature and ran her fingers over its snout like it was just any ordinary pet. I guess she could be a pet, honestly. It wouldn't surprise me at this point. I closed my eyes, taking in a deep breath with the surrounding sounds of the ocean. I couldn't tell if there was whispers around me or just flooding into my mind directly, but I could hear something. I focused on the voice, a soft whisper like the wind dancing through the leaves back home.

Hello little goddess. The words played in my mind, a hissing sound around each word. *I won't eat you, savior of Noro. Your deeds for her and her young have been called across the seas. Putting down the Kraken was a mercy, one that we all know he was thankful for. Thank you for saving Undine. She is the mother of the sea, and she was hurting. Everyone should be better now. We can leave when you are ready.*

I looked at the sea serpent long and hard. Its dark black scales shimmered with a deep blue hue, with large sapphire eyes to match. *What is your name?* I thought, hoping that I was getting it right and talking to the creature and not sound blasting my mates.

My name is Jiltara. You are the goddess, Luna. Word of you has spread far and deep. It is my honor to assist you. She tilted her head at me as if in an acknowledging bow. I took that as my sign and bowed back before approaching her. Wearily, I climbed onto her immense body and sat tight behind Undine as a bubble formed over my nose and my mouth to help me breathe. Undine's eyes widened as she took it in. "What?"

"If you could do that—"she pointed at the small watery bubble that made this entire conversation possible—"why did you need my help?"

"I thought you did this."

"Nope." She shook her head before refocusing on the vast nothingness of the sea. "You're either hiding something, or you are more powerful than even you realize." Before I could even respond, Jiltara was on the move, heading for Doria.

I was not expecting chaos to be reigning down on us as we breached the surface. Jiltara expertly weaved around the flaming arrows that were coming our way. Undine was quick to jump off of Jiltara and dive into the sea, her trident at her side as she sliced through creatures that were coming up from the sea. Jiltara got me close to shore before I could jump in myself and get safely to the sandy shore. I turned to see her racing her way toward Undine, ripping creatures apart with her giant maw. Dark blood muddied the water in her wake. Shouts and screams could be heard all around me, but it was the sudden vibration in my chest that had me whirling on my heels to come face to face with Valyn.

"You're alright?" He asked quickly, looking over my body for scratches or bruises. "Things broke out into chaos the moment we got Jasmine out of the house. Westley had called and said that forces were trying to storm Doria from all sides. I didn't want to leave you, but I had no choice, I—" I placed my finger to his lips.

"I'm here. I'm not mad. Let's get these people somewhere safe." I said, moving my finger so he could speak. Instead, he kissed me, a quick but passionate kiss. A promise that he would never leave me again.

"There's nowhere near Doria we can take them. The small towns have been attacked, and their citizens have come to Doria for refuge. At least, those who could make it." Before we could come up with an actual plan, two daemons rushed us from the streets and onto the sand. I had all but forgotten Otius's blade was now strapped to my back thanks to Undine and her quick thinking. The weight was the only reminder that I had it. Valyn was already thrusting his sword at the daemons to give me time to get my weapon ready, but I don't even think he was ready for what I had.

I reached back and pulled the silver beast of a blade from the cloth that it was wrapped in. The blade seemed to sing as it glistened in the sunlight. A vibrational pulse shot out from the blade as I swung it right into the abdomen of the daemon in front of me. What I thought was just a clean sweep, lit the daemon ablaze. It screamed and clawed at its stomach until the fire ignited its whole body. A smile graced my lips as I turned my attention to the stunned partner. Valyn had jumped back, dodging the wild swings from the daemon in front of him, and I took the opportunity to take out the other from behind.

Another scream occurred before the scent of rotten cooked flesh filled the air. It was a repulsive smell that made my stomach turn, but at least they were down. Valyn looked at me and then at the blade in my hand. "What the hell is that?"

I glanced down at my great-grandfather's blade before looking at Valyn. "The only thing Otius did right." Another small wave of daemons came rushing at us from over the dunes. I didn't hesitate and charged at them, slicing and igniting them all. A low whistle came from behind me as I turned from the fire before me.

"Remind me never to piss you off." Rafael and Patrick were a few feet away from me at this point and I don't know if I should be offended that I didn't realize it sooner or that they think I would hurt either of them. Valyn looked over at them both with a puzzled look on their face. "Westley sent us over here when he saw fire coming from the shores and wanted us to make sure it wasn't boats being lit up. We have to get people somewhere safe."

"There's a portal around here somewhere, right? Like the ones that help us travel between realms. If there's one on the shore and we can get it to open in Mistveil, we can send them there for now. I highly doubt your father would turn away people in need." I said, locking eyes with Valyn. Harold was rumored to be a brutal fae man in Celvenia, but the man they all fear is not the same man that I know. Patrick glanced over at a tall tower at the far end of the beach. The stones looked like they were minutes from collapsing, the sea taking back what belonged to it. "Is that it?"

Valyn looked over at the tower and sighed, running his hand through his hair. "It might not work, Luna. The number of people that would need to get through safely could collapse the tower. I don't see how that would work. Plus, there hasn't been any magic running through it since the olden days." I didn't wait for him to finish explaining all the reasons it wouldn't work. We had to see if we could get as many as possible through that gate before it could collapse; it was worth a shot. I heard wings flapping behind me and footsteps running alongside me. It wasn't Valyn. Patrick and Rafael had aligned with me long before this moment. I guess I have my little royal guard.

"What's your plan, princess?" Rafael asked as we reached the tower. Valyn was right; it wasn't in the best of shape, but I could make it work. Patrick knocked his knuckles against the stone, testing out the strength before I did anything.

"Well, for starters, reinforcing it with glass or molten rock. It won't be the best fix, but it will at least keep it standing, hopefully. Then, recharging it. It shouldn't be hard for me to siphon some of my powers and feed it to the portal to keep it open until the last person makes it through. I just need help to get the sand in place." Rafael moved quickly, grabbing stones and piling them up around the base of the tower. Patrick smiled as his eyes flashed bright white. Sand and shells began floating around the tower's base, forming a small wall. I followed their lead and focused my flames to lick up the sand and form tight to the stones of the tower.

"The hell are you all doing?!" Westley shouted at us as he ran over the dunes and towards us. Valyn was talking to Victoria and Jasmine down the beach. Undine had finally joined them after her victory at sea.

"Zip it, Wes. Luna has a plan, and unless you are gonna help, piss off." Patrick quipped to his brother, not missing a beat with the sand. Rafael ignored the two of them and just kept piling rocks up against the tower base. I followed his lead, reinforcing the base in the best way I could think of.

"What is your plan?" He demanded. I could sense the anger simmering in Rafael and Patrick at the lack of respect, but frankly, we didn't have time for that bullshit.

"Get the portal charged up and get enough people through to Mistveil. We can figure out the rest of the logistics once everyone is safe." I shouted back at him over the sound of the flames merging the sand together to create beautiful glass that looked like the waters of the Selpie splashing high on the tower. "How long do we have before the next wave of daemons comes through?"

"Minutes maybe. I'll get those closest to the manor through the gates there. You guys just focus on what you can do here." Before I could say another word, he was off running towards Valyn and the others. We had managed to reinforce the base the best we could. Now it was up to me to let a part of me fuel the portal home. But first things first.

I need you all to listen to me carefully. Doria is on fire. We have to send as many people that we can to Mistveil. I need all of you home to make sure everyone gets through the portal safely and that nothing follows them through. Call your father and tell him I'm making this call. If he wants to be mad at someone, he can raise hell with me once we are all safe. I love you all.

I'm coming to you, Princess. The citizens of Doria might not find Mistveil safe if they see me there. Valdis's voice rang through my head with the painful reminder that we have a long way to go before people see that not all daemons want this chaos.

No, stay in Infernia and help from there. Maybe you can find some place we can take the refugees. Niklaus, I'm going to need you to set up a medical tent when you get home. We can't have the Mor getting overrun with people who have minor injuries.

On it baby girl. I'll fill my mom and Maggie in on everything. Niklaus sounded so confident, so alive. I'm glad he is finally finding his place with his powers. I miss the sarcasm and dominance though.

Someone call my mom and tell her what's going on. I don't have much longer. I love you guys. With that, I cut off my focus on the bond that links us all and focused back on the task in front of me. How the hell and I going to give my power to the portal? A twinkle sounded in my ears as a light pulsed from my chest. No, not my chest, the necklace that Illisandra had put on me. Wait, I can use her power to pause time! I would say now is as good a time as any to try it out. Gripping the silver chain, I pulled the necklace from under my shirt, holding the pendant tight in my hand. I hope this works. I closed my eyes, focusing on the light inside me as the world around me washed away.

"I thought you would never use it." Illisandra said as she appeared before me. The rest of the world on pause once more. "What do you need?"

"A way to kick-start this portal back into existing and save people from certain death. Think you can tell me how to get it working again?" My gaze shifted from her to the tall tower behind her slim frame. She turned to follow my gaze, awe settling in her eyes as she took in our handiwork.

"This is beautiful. Undine must be proud that you're fixing her watchtower." Illisandra glanced past me to where Undine was standing with her trident in hand. "Vanalli would be so upset that she missed this opportunity. They are close, you know. As for the portal, all you have to do is focus your life force into the tower itself. Truthfully, it would be best if Undine helped you since it's an extension of herself."

"Okay, then I'll make that happen. How are you even here?" I asked, realizing I am still clutching the pendant tightly in my hands.

"You willed me here. Granted, I am not here in the physical sense of the meaning, but more of the corporeal sense. I probably look like I am sleeping back home. Either way, you do not have much longer my dear. The sooner you get the portal up and moving, the better it will be for the entire city. The necklace can only hold time sparingly. It's a fraction of my power in there. Continue to use it wisely." Illisandra slowly faded away into the recesses of my memory as the sound of the world came crashing down on me.

Valyn, I need Undine to help me with the portal. It's her tower. I need her help. Nothing else was said, but Undine had turned away from them and headed our way. Valyn headed for the city with Victoria and Jasmine in tow. "Where are they going?"

"Valyn and Victoria are going to round up as many people as they can and start sending them through to Mistveil. His mother has already gotten those closest to their home out already. He said you needed me. What can I do?" Undine was a strong woman, and I absolutely see why Vanalli and she are friends.

"Truth be told, I don't know. Illisandra told me that this watchtower is yours and, truthfully, only you can help activate the portal again. Can you do it or is she blowing smoke up my ass?" Rafael and Patrick looked at me with the oddest of expressions on their faces. Undine just raised her eyebrow at me.

"I don't know how I feel about you listening to a thing that woman has to say. But—" she let out a sigh—"she most likely isn't wrong. All watchtowers along the sea coasts are considered minor temples to me and Jasmine for safe passage through the rough seas. It was considered a way to ensure safety to leave an offering of wine or quartz. Jasmine stopped coming to collect the offerings when the people of Doria stopped asking for safety and just went into the sea as if they owned it. I can't control how people get treated in the sea if they don't respect it. Anyway, I can try to revive this one. It might just take me a moment."

Undine stepped up to the tower and tapped the stones with her trident in a pattern. Two taps north, one tap south, three taps east, two taps west. Each tap illuminated the stones with a bright white light. Patrick stood there, his mouth wide open, as if he were trying to catch flies. Rafael had to grab him and move him away from the tower so Undine could continue her work. Two more rounds of stone tapping with the same pattern had the door to the tower illuminating a whitish-blue glow. "I think we've got it working again. Just tell anyone going through to think of Mistveil as the location they want to be sent to. It will most likely spit them out nearest the closest tower there or the main portal through the castle. Jasmine and I are going to head out to sea. We can stop any aquatic assaults from happening more easily in the sea than on land. It was nice meeting you, Luna. I hope to see you again soon." Undine spun on her heels abruptly, leaving us as she made her way back down to the beach where Jasmine was waiting for her.

"That was *the* Goddess of Water, Undine!?" Patrick exclaimed now that she was out of earshot. Rafael just shook his head as he let go of Patrick's shirt. For what it's worth, I don't blame him for being so star-struck by her. She is the goddess he believes is the reason the sea has blessed him and his family. He whiffled his head and looked at me with a sort of apologetic expression. "What now?"

"Now we get the people of Doria to Mistveil. Rafael, you are faster than we are, so head to Valyn and Westley and help them send people our way. Patrick and I will guard the tower from any attacks." I barked out commands, and neither of them told me no nor tried to tell me to get myself to safety. At least I have two friends who trust that I can take care of myself. A conch horn blew in the distance, dragging our attention to the city. Rafael took off the second the sound stopped. "What the hell was that?"

"A call to war."

CHAPTER 48

LUNA

Arrows and fire rained down from above the city, people fleeing towards the beach without a second thought. Victoria was pointing people in our direction, and we were getting them through the portal as fast as we could. Daemons began cresting the dunes once more, heading our way. Patrick was the first one at the base of the dunes, swords clashing with daemon claws as he spun around them. I could see his eyes light up as the surrounding sand danced around him as a veiling shield protecting him, yet blinding the daemons as they charged wildly at him.

Two people I recognized only from being aboard the Birkenhead, came running up towards me. Their arms waving people along as they ran down the sandy shore to where I was standing. The first woman—a petite blonde—stopped just short of running into me, planting her hands firmly on her knees as she tried to catch her breath. The second woman—a taller, red-head—stopped right behind the blonde, gently patting her on the back in the most soothing of gestures. I watched as a small family stopped short of the portal, turning to face my new guests.

"Thank you for saving me and my family," the elderly woman in the small group sobbed to the two women. The blonde was still trying to catch her breath, but offered a small smile to the family as the taller one comforted the woman.

"It's our duty to the people, ma'am. Please, you and your family need to hurry through the portal. You'll be safe on the other side." She consoled the woman while helping the family up to the portal and through it. Her short red hair swished at the nape of her neck as she walked back over to where I was ushering more people through the portal and monitoring Patrick. He was doing an incredible job of keeping all the daemons from pushing past him to where people were running for safety. "I swear to the gods, Elsa, if you don't go through that portal and get to safety, I will toss you through it." She propped her hand on her hip as she spoke.

"Ease up, Lyra. I am not leaving you," Elsa panted as she finally caught her breath. "I know you, and you won't leave until the last person goes through the portal safely. So, I will stay here until you are ready to go through it yourself." The blonde—Elsa—propped her fists on her hips, mocking Lyra's stance before sticking her tongue out at her childishly. Lyra just rolled her eyes and sighed. I really shouldn't be listening in on their private conversation, so I instead turned my focus onto the rest of the beach. Scanning the crowd of faces looking for those I might recognize, I saw Victoria shouting out orders to a group of people that were making their way towards the portal. Westly was now beside her, swords out, fighting daemons off the far side. Behind her, Jasmine and Undine were keeping all threats from the sea at bay. I couldn't see Valyn or Rafael, but I could see the tall waves cresting high above the dunes and through the city streets as Valyn purged the city of the rot of the daemons. Shadows dancing in the waves that I saw were the only sign that Rafael was with Valyn, and that they were both safe.

Be careful. Please. I whispered through the bond to Valyn. Warmth instantly flooded me as his love radiated back to me. I took that as him being safe and moved on. Lyra stepped up in front of me, saluting as she spoke. "Princess Luna, my name is Lyra Thilman, and this is my wife, Elsa. Captain Victoria sent us to assist with the evacuation of our people. Queen Cassandra and Prince Valyn evacuated everyone in the city that was closest to the castle. The queen is also through and safe. Prince Valyn is just keeping the daemons at bay in the streets as we get the last few families to safety." Elsa nodded at me as she moved quickly into the crowd to pick up a child who had fallen while trying to keep pace with her family.

"It's nice to meet you both." I smiled at them as Elsa rejoined us. "I'm really glad you two are here. The only thing these people need to know is that they have to focus on Mistveil to end up there and not somewhere else. If anyone argues with you, I give you full permission to toss them through and let them end up where the hell they end up." A smirk graced Lyra's lips as she looked at Elsa, who turned three shades redder.

"Yes ma'am. I highly doubt anyone will fight with me." Her grin widened as she patted the daggers at her sides. Touche. Both women excused themselves, making their way to either side of the portal, calling out orders for a single file line and to move quickly, helping the elderly and the youth. I took this as my time to help Patrick. I rushed through the crowd, ducking and weaving through bodies, until I was right behind the veil of a sandstorm. He was still swinging his blades with perfect precision; I was kind of envious of his skills.

My presence must've drawn his attention as the veil parted, leaving just enough room for me to move through the storm without a single grain of sand daring to touch me. "Luna, what are you doing?!" Patrick shouted over the growls and grunts of daemons as they flung themselves at him. "Who is helping with the evacuation?" The sandstorm closed up behind me as I made my way to stand beside him. I smirked as my fingers clenched tight around the hilt in my hand. The daemons jumped back, halting their advances as the blade sang as I slashed it through the air in front of me. I was pleased that I didn't have to form a weapon, no; I had the god-killing blade this time.

I looked at Patrick before drawing my attention to the mob in front of us. "Lyra and Elsa took my place by Victoria's orders. I can't just stand by and let you do all the fighting now, can I?" I smirked as he scoffed. The weight of Otius's blade felt lighter than it had any business being. The behemoth of a blade shouldn't feel as light as a dagger, and even easier to swing. My hand twitched as I watched all the daemons that were just attaching Patrick fall back, chittering amongst themselves. Their eyes darting between the two of us, landing on Patrick and licking their lips. I took a step forward, readying myself to charge at the biggest one in the middle. I took off into a sprint before he could say anything. I lunged at it. Blood and fabric dripped from its maw, sparking a whole new rage inside of me. When the steel of my blade slid through his flesh, white flames ignited him from within it, exploding out of it. The blast wiped out the entire front row of daemons from existence as if they had never existed.

I heard Patrick curse under his breath as daemons began swarming him from the opposite side in a wild rage. He swung at several of the beasts with one blow of his sword, flinging bodies and blood across the beige sand. Growls, howls and screams filled the air as we raged at the onslaught coming our way. The flapping of wings above us momentarily drew my attention to the sky; luckily for us, it was Rafael coming in as the cavalry and not an airborne attack.

"Sorry it took so long, Princess. Your husband doesn't like to listen." Rafael said as he nodded his head to the other end of the beach where Valyn was now backing up Westley. Seeing his silver hair dash across the battlefield made my heart flutter. The next step I took, however, had me almost face-planting the sand. Thankfully, Rafael was within arm's reach and hoisted me up to my feet, holding me upright. "Can you fawn over him later, please? We have our hands just a little full over here." He gestured to the mob of daemons charging at us.

I felt my cheeks heat to a bright red and hurried out of his grasp. "Sorry. Thanks for not letting me fall and die." I said as I plunged my blade through the heart of a tall daemon, this one looking like it had been freshly released from a dungeon.

Its skin wrapped tightly to the bones beneath, its eyes sunken into its skull was something of nightmares. Not to mention the smell of rot and decay pouring from its open wound. Rafael must've taken that as a sign that I was fully capable of refocusing my attention because he launched himself through the mob, dragging smoke like daggers across the throats of each daemon as he passed them.

The mob quickly thinned out after Rafael's little trick. Patrick thinned out the sandstorm that was wrapped around us as I tried to peer through to see the status of the evacuation. Lyra and Elsa were finishing up with the last ten or so people. I let out a breath of relief. Once they were through, we could evacuate ourselves and regroup in safety. I glanced down the beach to find the others swarmed by more daemons. Valyn was covered in blood, some red, some that filthy blackish blue. Westley wasn't any better off. Victoria's long silver hair was matted close to her face as daemon blood splattered across her. They needed help.

"Rafael! Finish these last few off and protect the portal! Get Lyra and Else through it! Patrick, you're with me!" Without waiting for them to agree, I tore down the beach, sand kicking up under my feet as I ran toward Valyn. I caught a flashing glimpse of Teal and Mocha sprinting from the sea to the others.

My heart relaxed once I could make out Jasmine's features. Rage twisted on her face as she shot arrows of water from her hands at the daemon that was bringing down a blade right on Victoria. She turned her rage on the daemons cresting the dunes by Westley, sweeping them up in a thunderous wave and dragging them all into the sea to drown. Undine had lined the shoreline with small whirlpools, keeping the daemons in the sea from following Jasmine and crossing onto land and causing us more issues. A small mercy.

I felt it before I saw it. The tremor that shook the ground, slowing me down. I watched as the ground around my mate shook and crumbled as it tore away from itself. His bright turquoise eyes met mine as a scream tore from me, his eyes widening in fear as he fell into the earth herself.

Darkness formed a wall around me before I could reach Valyn, blocking my view of the others and the scene unfolding. I felt something bump into my back as Patrick pressed his back into mine, alerting me to his presence but making sure we weren't caught off guard. A deep rumble of laughter echoed off the wall of shimmering blackness that surrounded us. I immediately recognized the laugh and cursed under my breath. Fucking Marcloff was here, and I didn't sense him. I focused on the sound of the sand gritting beneath our feet as we circled back-to-back staring into the darkness. We weren't alone; now we just have to figure out exactly where he was hiding.

"Think you can force the sand through it and make a hole?" I whispered to Patrick as I felt the sand whip up around my legs.

"I've been trying, but the sand won't budge against whatever the hell this is." He bit back, his voice sharp but still hushed. Dread filled me as the darkness seemed to move closer and closer with each passing second. Otius's blade vibrated in my hand, sending a rippling shock through my body. Reminding me I am the solution we need to get out of this alive. A white light—bright and warm—surged through my core, filling every fiber of my being. It was like the blade was calling me, begging me to extinguish the creature in the darkness and be free again. I heard muffled yelling from behind me, but I couldn't make out the words. Incoherent screaming was all I could hear, but I could see everything clearly now. I could make out the figure stalking us through the darkness, the group of people rushing down the beach, carrying what looked like a lifeless body over their shoulders, and the daemon who swore to stay close and protect me. I watched as he thrashed against the darkness to get through. Two more winged beings came to his aid, striking at the darkness as if it would relent to them.

"Get down and cover yourself in the sand. Use your power to keep yourself protected. No matter what, stay hidden. That's an order," was all I barked at Patrick before I raised my blade high, pouring all of my white flames into it and striking the shadowy figure. Marcloff's laugh echoed louder, coming from behind me, no; on all sides of me. Before I could adjust, a sharp pain laced through my skull as I was slammed repeatedly into the ground. Otius's blade shot from my hand, skittering across the sand, just out of reach. Something was holding me down on the hard, gritty sand. I could feel Patrick's body beneath my hands as I clawed at the sand, reaching for the hilt of the blade.

Another laugh rippled through the darkness as my fingers grazed the hilt of the god-killing blade. Before I could fully grip it, a black-soled boot slammed down on the center of the blade, snapping it into pieces as if it were made of wood and not some rare steel from centuries ago.

"Princess, you look like you've just seen a ghost." Marcloff was looking down on me as I paled at the sight of the remainder of the once might blade. The pain in my skull intensified as he gripped me by my hair, pulling me up to dangle almost lifelessly in front of him. "You thought you were the only one who could manipulate the darkness?" He smirked as he flung me hard against the wall of darkness. I tried to get up. I tried to search deep within me fast to get to my feet and get my scythe to come to me, but pain held me down in place.

Helpless.

I tried to stagger to my feet as Marcloff circled me. His boot met my ribs with a loud crack, dropping me back to the ground, forcing all the air from my lungs. My vision betrayed me as I tried to focus on the many blurred versions of Marcloff I saw sauntering my way. He squatted down, grabbing my hair once more, forcing me to look him in the eyes as I gasped for air. His eyes shone bright as his grin turned like that of a Cheshire enjoying the hunt of its prey. I spat weakly in his face, the only act of defiance I could muster at the moment. He laughed once more as backhanded me across the face with his free hand, my hair still firmly gripped in the other. He looked at the necklaces around my neck, the locket Virgil had given me and my grandmother's moon pendant, and ripped them from my neck, tossing them to the ground. "You're going to make a nice little offering, Princess." He looked into the darkness and gave his order. "Grab her and let's get out of here."

Icy, bony fingers shot out from the darkness, clawing at me as they pulled me into the darkness. I tried to scream and kick, but I couldn't get free. Sand and darkness swallowed me up, but at least Patrick stayed safe, hidden in the sand from Marcloff. If the others around the darkness are who I think they are, he'll be safe. Defeat consumed me as the darkness dragged me further down. Endless silence and darkness stretched before me. I will not die at this man's hands, nor will I be a sacrifice. I let the darkness take me, slipping into an icy calmness as Kaos words rang in my head.

"The King of Darkness is waiting for you to return."

CHAPTER 49
NIKLAUS

Arriving in Mistveil in the middle of chaos wasn't as jarring as I expected it to be. I guess all those late nights helping at the Mor and at the small healer centers in Oakenhall prepared me for the chaos of an on-field medical center. The priestesses scurried about as Maggie and my mother shouted out orders to the others. Where to put people who were coming through critical. Where to place people who just had cuts and bruises. Most importantly, we needed to find a place for the children if their parents had been injured, but the children were safe. I glanced around at the families looking out of the medical tent we were in. The giant portal that reached from Doria to here on the shores was wide open. People were flooding through, but most who weren't injured watched the battle raging on the other side. Most were watching to see if their loved ones had made it through or if they had fallen. After Luna's random demands for healing while I was heading here, my head awas all sorts of foggy. I needed to get to her.

"Don't get distracted, boy. This isn't the time to sully about," Maggie said as she passed me with nothing more than a quick glance outside of the tent. I was surprised when my mother said Maggie would leave the Mor and tend to those in need from the tent. I decided on following her and see what she needed from me. She weaved through all the bodies around us with such grace and poise. The tent was humongous, wide enough to space out eight rows of beds, each four deep. Glancing around the rows, I looked for faces I might recognize, someone from the summer realm that I would recognize at all. I had all but given up when my eyes caught sight of a very pregnant Alyssa Moore.

"Lyssa!" I called out as I made my way through the throngs of people to her bed at the end of the last row. "Are you alright? Baby still moving?" It took Alyssa a few moments to gather her thoughts.

"Niklaus? Is that you?" She asked, squinting her eyes as she took me in. It hadn't dawned on me before now that she might not recognize me. It's been roughly two decades since she had seen me last, and I was not the same person anymore.

"Yeah. Are you alright? Can I give you a once-over really quick to make sure your baby is doing, okay?" I asked, keeping all the questions, I really wanted to ask in my head instead of bombarding her with them. "I mean, if someone hasn't already done it."

"I just got here. Westley and Patrick are fighting on the shores of Doria, so Peter got me, Maria and the kids all out safely. He stayed close to the portal to help get people through on this side." Alyssa spoke softly in between contractions. Peter was always a good guy, taking charge of situations and putting others before himself. I figured when he lost his leg that he would sideline himself and put himself and his family first. I guess he did technically.

"Hopefully Westley will get through and here before your baby arrives. Until then, are you having any contractions? Any pain or discomfort?" I asked, gently helping her to lay down. "We can move you to the Mor. Just say the word."

"Niklaus, I am not moving from this spot until my husband gets here." She growled as she clenched her fist. I offered her my hand, which might've been a mistake, she took it and squeezed as tight as possible. I honestly thought she was going to break it. After a minute she eased up. "I'm sorry. The contractions are about ten minutes apart, but that's just me guessing."

I looked across the tent to find my mom and Maggie hands deep in someone's chest, I couldn't ask them for help. My eyes scanned the rest of the tent, finding priestesses tending to various different wounds, all too busy for me to ask for help. "The Prince of Spring is helping out in the trenches. I never thought I'd see the day." A thick skothi accent dragged my attention to behind me. A petite, brunette stood there, glancing between Alyssa and myself.

"Bethany, you're a sight for sore eyes." I let out a sigh of relief. "Just so you know, I do have the healers gift. I'm not completely useless like everyone thinks I am. Can you sit with Alyssa while I go check on the status of her husband? I need to see if he made it through yet."

"How far along are you?" She questioned Alyssa, who was beginning to squeeze my hand again. Dear gods, if this is any indication of what childbirth on the males' side is like, my hands going to be broken when Luna gives birth. If that's what she wants.

"I'm over a week past my due date. My doctor wasn't going to push for labor until next week, but something tells me our little one will be here any time now." She huffed out between gritted teeth. My hand was beginning to go numb by the time she let me go.

"Niklaus, go do what you have to do. I'll take care of her. I really think we should move you into the Mor—" Alyssa opened her mouth to refuse, but Bethany kept talking—"but I understand your desire to stay. Let go of his hand so he can be of more help to you." Alyssa released my hand. I mouthed thank you to Bethany before sprinting from the tent and out to where the mass crowd of people were gathered awaiting their loved ones.

Silver hair caught my attention, bobbing and weaving through the crowd running toward the tent. It was Valyn, instead it was Victoria. Her eyes widened as they caught sight of me, pivoting from her current path straight for me. "Valyn got hurt! We need help getting him to the tent." I looked behind her to where Westley and Jasmine were carrying a limp Valyn through the crowd. I quickly grabbed where Westley was holding Valyn up. I pulled him more onto myself, so Jasmine didn't have to deal with a ton of his weigh on her shoulders.

"Westley, Alyssa is in active labor and refuses to leave the tent for the Mor until you arrive, so get your ass in there will ya." It didn't take much more for him to turn on his heels and run to the tent where I had just come from. Hopefully now she will listen and get inside. "What the hell happened, Vic?" She was barking orders at some of the soldiers who were standing about. I saw Yuri being carted off into the tent with Elana hot on the heels of those carrying him. She was looking around, taking note of everyone she saw. I had only met her twice before and she always remembered the finer little details of all our interactions, never so much the conversations being held around her.

"A darkness swept over the beach. The next thing we know the ground is quaking beneath our feet, ripping apart around Valyn. Thanks to Westley's quick thinking we were able to get him out, but he was unconscious." As she spoke, my eyes darted around the area. "Where is Luna?"

Jasmine shook her head when I glanced at her, but it was Victoria who spoke. "Last we seen her, she was running across the beach in our direction. There's a funnel of darkness on the shoreline. She has to be inside it keeping whatever attacked us at bay. Rafael was trying to get inside of it when two others showed up." She shuddered as we made out way into the tent. My mothers head shot up as we entered with Valyn, placing him on the closest cot we could find. She rushed over to him and immediately started working on him. I could feel the broken ribs, and the tears in his muscles. Those would all fix easily with my mom working on him, so I turned my attention to the portal.

"I'm going to go get her. She shouldn't have been left behind." I snap as I reach for the opening in the tent. A hand grabs me on my arm and pulls me back inside. I whirl, not expecting my mother to be face to face with me when I turn. Her eyes are fierce, her blonde hair a mess in a pulled-up bun atop her head. I can see the weight of today on her. "I have to find her." I whispered.

"If you stop helping people here to go look for her, you know that will just piss her off more than anything. Heal your brother, Maggie is busy and I am needed to help with other wounds. Focus on the damage to the ribs first, then repair the muscle." She turned from me without another word. Victoria and Jasmine huddled together in the corner, whispering to one another as the tent filled up with more injured bodies. "If you two aren't here to help, then go outside. Find something to do there." I snapped as I turned my attention to Valyn. His pulse was weak and I could feel the teether of life clinging onto him like strings holding together a satchel. Whatever else had happened when he fell, they didn't know about it.

Jasmine went to say something, but Victoria ushered her out of the tent. I'm going to need to apologize later. I felt for my bond, the lifeline to Luna. It was faint, but it was still within reach. I knew better than to distract her from whatever was going on, so I held the opal light that led me to her close as I began working on Valyn.

CHAPTER 50 VALDIS

Trickling news for Floria and Doria was flooding my phone as I made my way into my father's office. Gabrial and Kieran were already inside, bickering with one another as I entered. Vanessa was standing next to my father, watching coverage that I didn't even know we had access to. Bombings and fires filled the screen, smoke obscuring half of the coverage from Floria, but my eyes were glued to the active bombings in Doria. Luna was there, and I could see her powers flourishing on screen.

"We should be there! Why are we watching on the fucking monitors?!" Gabrial barked at my father, who barely reacted at his outburst. He turned his attention to me as I gripped my phone tighter in my hand. "Why aren't you fighting this?!" Kieran and Vanessa both looked at me as well. Pity and sorrow in their eyes. They knew she had ordered me to stay put. She ordered me to continue with helping Talissa and the others find a way to take Marcloff out for good and not just put him in a long slumber.

"His wife gave him an order. She sees the bigger picture that clearly you don't see, boy." My father finally spoke. Pity flickered across Gabrial's face as he looked away from me. I wanted to be there. I needed to stand by Luna and help her, but she had already given the warning to everyone. Stay the fuck away. Bastian, Damian and Niklaus were all rerouted to Mistveil to help get the citizens of Doria out and to safety. Fennik had called Bastian for help, but Luna overrode the call. Fennik had help from the Crimson Army. She needed everyone she could get in Mistveil. Fennik seemed to understand at the time, but he's been radio silent since. I hope he's alright. If something happens to him because she called off aid, she won't forgive herself.

"What can we do to help?" Vanessa asked as she tapped away on her phone. "Vanalli and Erina are prepping the Mor and some of the local bed and breakfasts for the influx of citizens. Should we open our doors as well for those who aren't afraid of us?" She paused, glancing down at our father, who looked as though he was frozen.

"Fuck." Kieran grumbled as he saw what our father did on the screen. "Marcloff is in Doria." His whispered words hit me like a bullet to the chest. Gabrial grabbed his swords from the table by the door, Kieran not far behind him. I couldn't disobey an order from Luna even if I wanted to, and they both knew that. Vanessa looked between me and our brothers.

"Stay here and help them find a way to kill the bastard. We got her back." Gabrial said as he and Kieran vanished from the room as if they weren't even here to begin with. I wanted to follow; I wanted to get to Luna and make sure she got out of there safely. Now all I can do is trust that my brothers will get there in time and join the fight before it's too late. My phone vibrates in my hand, drawing my attention to the small screen in my hand. A message from Bastian pops up on the screen.

I can't get to Fennik. Get to him... NOW!

I knew I needed to stay put, but if he was in trouble and something happened to him, that would be the end of everything. Luna can't lose a mate in this war. Not to Marcloff and not to one of his minions. I quickly tap out a response asking for the coordinates of where he is and get an equally quick response. I look over at my father, who is still watching Luna on the screen, keeping track of her movements and making sure she stays safe. Vanessa turns right as I walk out of the large room. I can hear the clacking of her heels on the marble flooring behind me.

"She told you to stay put. You can't not listen to her, you know!" Vanessa is fast, quickly on my heels before I can tell her to fuck off. She grabs my arm, but I twist out of her grip.

"Bastian sent an SOS text telling me to get my ass to Floria and save Fennik, so unless you're going to fucking come with me, go back in there and keep an eye on my wife." I snap at her. Vanessa stops short, biting her tongue before she says something that she might actually regret. She pauses, looking back at the door to our father's office.

"Give me five; you're not going alone." Without another word from me, she heads back into our father's office to inform him of what's going on and to hopefully get out of those ridiculous fucking heels before we leave. If Bastian doesn't want to speak with me mentally, then I won't risk talking to Fennik that way either. We can't distract Luna. I tap out a quick message to Fennik.

Calvary is coming. Don't die on me, autumn prince.

Floria was covered in fire, and smoke by the time Vanessa and I got there. The Crimson Army was out in waves, taking out as many daemons on the front lines as they could. I saw Elijah from across the field, taking out a very large grimlock with some bright-ass fire power. There were people on the battlefield whom I didn't recognize. More and more people from across the autumn realm came to Floria to join forces with Fennik and Elijah when duty called. Alstrom was the closest to my sister and me as we made our way into the city itself. He stopped us halfway through the gate.

"Boy, I wouldn't go in there if I were you. Daemons can't step foot in Floria since Luna cleansed the land. They walk in and poof!" The large man made an exaggerated sound effect, tossing his arms up in the air before looking at my sister. "I wouldn't want to see anything happen to either of you."

"Fennik needs help. I've already been on Floria soil since then, and so has my sister. We will be fine, but thank you for caring enough to warn us." I say in thanks. We had heard word that Floria had become a holy ground after Luna's cleansing. I guess our intel was correct. Vanessa smiled at Alstrom and walked confidently through the gates. As we suspected, nothing happened to her. We aren't normal daemons. Alstrom looked like he was about to pass out as she blew him a kiss and stalked over to the castle. I patted him on the shoulder before following my sister through the streets and towards the castle. Luckily for the two of us, most people here knew who we were and gave us a wide berth as we passed.

The streets were filled with able-bodied people, all of whom could shield the young children and the elderly from harm. They tried to usher the children into the larger buildings to keep them in one spot. The elderly, on the other hand, were arguing about how they could be of assistance to those fighting. It took only a matter of moments before I felt the energy around us become charged. I looked at my sister, and I could see the disgust on her face as she looked to the sky. A smile curled at the edge of her lips as she snapped her fingers. No one around us had noticed, or if they had, they weren't letting on. As quickly as her fingers snapped, several dragons' wings snapped, plummeting them and their riders straight for the streets.

Florians rushed from the streets and into the closest shelter they could find as the sky rained dragons and daemons. One by one, each daemon burned bright. The dragons, on the other hand, would need to be dealt with on their own, but they were as good as dead by the time Vanessa was done. No one saw her claim their minds and boil their brains from the skulls. My sister is terrifying, and I am eternally grateful that she is on our side. I would hate to be her enemy.

Alric was running towards us the moment we turned the corner heading to the tunnel where Fennik was. I didn't like that demi-god. There was something that I didn't trust about him. Clearly my sister was sensing from the way she all but jumped out of his way when he reached us. Alric tried not to notice it, but she made it very obvious. "Fennik told me to run since it didn't sense me. He's trapped in there." Vanessa cocked her head to the side like a dog trying to figure out if it wanted to rip someone's throat out or let the person pet it. She tasted the lie on his lips. Demi-gods smell distinctly different, like any god, but with something muddling the scent and dulling it. There is no way whatsoever that what is in that tunnel didn't know he was there. Unless... he's turned on us. Vanessa looked at me the moment it clicked in for her. We can't trust this man. No matter who his son is and how well we know him. His father is not to be trusted.

"We got him. You just worry about helping Elijah on the outskirts." I said as I pushed past him, intentionally bumping my shoulder into his. I could feel the deception rippling off of him. A satisfied feeling that now has me more worried about Luna and her safety. What if Valmor is hiding something from us? Could he be like his father and playing deception? I didn't get that from him after being around him for so long, but he also kept his distance and made sure not to touch me. I'm going to have to force an altercation with him when we're done here. If I sense it, Zekon and Talissa need to know. Alric wasted no time running off from us and through the gate.

"Do you think he is actually going to help Elijah?" My sister asked as we picked up our pace to the tunnel entrance.

"No. I always knew he couldn't be trusted. You get the same feeling from Valmor or Elucia?" Vanessa had spent some time with Elucia recently and with Valmor far more than I have. She just shook her head and ran ahead of me. Maybe Alric is acting alone. It still doesn't ease the worry forming in my stomach. Vanessa stopped dead in the entrance of the tunnel, her normally ivory skin, paled even more than usual as she looked inside. She turned away from whatever she was seeing and dropped to her knees, screaming. I ran up to her and looked into the tunnel.

My blood ran cold as I watched a jabberwock fling blood across the tunnel, shredding its prey to pieces. Jabberwocks were myths. Nothing more than a story to keep the children of Hellis at bay. We were told they could devour any and all beings. Regardless of race. No fae, no daemon and no god was safe from a jabberwock. Now here I stand looking in the eyes of one. It looked more like a wolf and a serpent hybrid to me. The face of a wolf, with the tongue and tail of a serpent. It stood tall on two cloven hooves, looking down on me as I entered the tunnel. I took in the blood dripping from it's maw onto the moss covered stone beneath its feet. Its arms had fur until it reached what would be its wrist where dark black scales took over, forming the talons at the end. I refused to look at the mess of flesh and clothes that was now on the floor.

An icy chill ran down my spine as rage built up in my chest. The creature chittered before letting out the most disgusting disembodied laugh I had ever heard. And then it spoke. "Little daemon prince. Come to the rescue of the little fae. Poor little fae. Poor little daemon prince. You will die here, Valdis Noire of Infernia." My blood ran cold as the creature before me spoke my name. How the fuck did it know me? Vanessa came up behind me, her rage as palpable as my own as she ran and plunged her dagger into the beast's eye, ripping it from its socket with a satisfying popping sound. A horrible scream tore from its throat as it lashed out at her, cutting her leg with its talon. "You little daemon bitch! Vanessa Noire of Infernia. You will die here with your traitorous brother!" It howled as it swiped out at her again. Vanessa managed to evade this attack, flipping onto her back and rolling back towards me.

"How the fuck does it know who we are?!" She yelled at me over the creatures howling and screaming. I shrugged my shoulders, running at the beast with my swords out at my sides. I slashed out at its right leg, clipping it right at the heel. Something warm and wet drenched my pants. The horror of realizing that I was now in the blood of the Jabberwock's victim ripped at my chest. That momentary realization cost me. A sharp pain laced through the top of my head as blood trickled down my cheek. Fuck me.

Vanessa charged at the creature again, but at this point I was seeing two of her. By the screams of it, she took its good eye. Another satisfying pop echoed off the walls and further down into the tunnel. I could feel the whole place shake from the stomping that the creature was doing. Vanessa had successfully blinded the fucker. Now, we just had to take it down. I shook my head, trying to clear the haze from my sight. It took a little while for my vision to clear and for me to stand, but she was doing really well at blocking its flailing. I gripped my swords tighter and sent a prayer up to my beloved. I was going to take this thing down; be it for vengeance or comfort. Vanessa must've realized my plan and kicked the beast in the chest as it got closer to her. It slipped on the blood and fell backwards. Now was my time to strike. I crossed my blades in front of me and ran at the beast, scissoring my blades through its neck, severing its head from its body.

The thumping of its body on the stone echoed throughout the tunnel. No more shrieking, no more taunting. Just eerie silence. Vanessa moved closer to the clothes and flesh that lay in a heap on the ground. I could looked. I could let the truth of who that was settle into me right now. Her sobs were all I needed to confirm who that was. Dear gods, I hope she is wrong. Please don't let Fennik be dead.

CHAPTER 51
VALYN

Thick plumes of black smoke clouded the once-white sandy shores. Daemon blood oozed onto the cobblestone sidewalks everywhere I had looked. I had just made my way back to the beach where Luna and the others were getting people to safety. I saw her running toward me, her arm reaching for me. Then it happened so fast I didn't know what was going on. A darkness had swarmed me like the entire world was eating me alive. I could hear her screams until I couldn't. Pain writhed through my body as I hit the walls of the earth as I fell.

Then suddenly, it all stopped. My body hit a solid wall of earth and I blacked out. That was the last thing I could remember before waking up in this tent only moments ago. Where the hell am I? How am I still alive? I opened my eyes to see a sweat soaked Niklaus panting heavily above me. Sweat dripping from his brow onto the cloth he was using to keep the sweat from running into his eyes. "You're awake. Good. How are you feeling?"

His voice was like a drum thrumming loudly in my ears, but I could tell he was just talking, not yelling. I propped myself up on my elbows and looked around. The movement making me slightly dizzy. "I feel like I've been spinning for a good three hours. What the hell is going on? Where are we? Where's Luna?" In that moment of clarity, my eyes shifted around the room, searching for my mate.

Niklaus looked out of the tent and then back at me. "I've been told she's still in Doria, fighting and getting people to safety. Rafael and Patrick are with her." I could see his jaw tighten at the thought of being here and not there with her.

"Damian and Bastian?" I questioned as I tried to get up from the cot. Niklaus just put his arm out for me to grab as he helped me find steady ground beneath my feet.

"Sorting through who is injured and who can help get things done. They just got here a little while ago. Bastian said he sent Valdis to help Fennik in Floria." Niklaus took a deep breath before continuing. "Floria and Doria both got hit at the same time. Fennik obviously couldn't leave his people's side."

"And she would be pissed off if he did." I finished the rest of his sentence for him. We both knew Luna put the people before herself and wanted us to do the same. It didn't matter what else would happen.

"Nox and Virgil arrived just before Damian and Bastian. Everyone has been trying to find a home for the displaced citizens of Doria. Damian suggested Daglidell. I think that might be the consensus moving forward. Once we know how many people are capable of moving, that is. Unless you have some other idea of where they can go." Niklaus pulled back the flap of the tent and helped me through.

Throngs of people littered the land, huddled together as they looked back at the opening of the portal. No one was coming through anymore. They watched as three winged men attacked a dark mass on the shores. I looked at Niklaus, who was staring intently at the three beings.

"Is that Rafael?" I asked him. He just shrugged his shoulders.

"You would know better than me. You spent more time with him. But something tells me that's Kieran and Gabrial with him." Niklaus was watching each of the men striking at the darkness, but not able to cut through it.

"We can't just stand here and do nothing. We need to go there and help them." I said, releasing Niklaus's arm and stumbling forward. Two rough hands grabbed my shoulders halting my advance.

"You're not going anywhere. Niklaus has been working on you since Victoria, Jasmine and Westley brought you through.

You're in no condition to go running off." Bastian was being the voice of fucking reason. Seriously?

"She's there! How can we sit here and not go to her?" I spat out, trying to pull myself from their grasp.

"Because if she finds out that you were injured again and went through the portal into danger, she might just hurt you herself. She's not weak, and she doesn't always need saving. We need to respect her wishes and focus on those here who need us most." Damian spoke up as he let go of me. There was the voice of reason that I was waiting for.

Bastian finally let me go as Virgil and Nox made their way through the crowd. "Glad to see you're alright." Virgil said with a smile that didn't fully touch his eyes. I get it, as much as we've all come to accept one another, he still loves her. Nothing will kill that love. She was the love of his life, and we swept in and essentially stole her from him. Fuck. Maybe we are as bad as their stories claim we are.

I shook my head and let that thought die where it began. Nox was grumbling something that I clearly wasn't paying much attention to. He held the attention of the others and I saw my opening. I ripped off from the others and booked it straight for the portal. Shouts roared from behind me, but I watched as Victoria moved others out of my way so I could go save the day. Jasmine pulled three little children with her as I jumped through the portal home.

I'm coming for you Luna.

By the time my feet hit the sand, the twister of darkness had vanished, and with that the others. I ran through the sand, slipping and losing balance as if the sand itself was trying to stop me. Something glimmered in the sand, catching my eye as I made my way to whatever it was. It was protruding ever so slightly out of the sand where the once black inky whirlwind was. Anyone else wouldn't have noticed the three little objects buried in the sand, and if they did, they would've thought they washed up from the sea. But I knew what they were, and it put me on my knees.

Luna's locket, which Virgil had given her, was sprawled out on the sand next to a triple moon silver pendant that I had recognized her wearing recently. Bright red blood pooled around the necklaces and the silver pocket watch that lay beside it. I recognized the watch immediately as the one I gave to Patrick when he joined the Navy and my team. I gave everyone a token to commemorate their beginning. I began frantically searching the sand for blood droplets, a trail of some sort that would lead me to them safely, but there was nothing. No sign of Luna, Patrick or the three daemons who were frantically trying to get into the void to save her. A body sized hole in the sand was all that was left with the trinkets that now sit out as a taunt.

The sand bit into my hands as I dropped to my knees. They're gone. There was not a single sign of life anywhere. Worse yet, either one or both of them are injured. I frantically called on my bond, trying to find the teether of light that would lead me to the little giggle on the other end, the sass, hell even the angry would take away this heartbreaking silence. But there was nothing there. None of what I've grown accustomed to. A giant hole ripped open in my chest.

Tears streamed down my face, darkening the sand below. I clutched the necklaces and the watch in my hands and forced myself back to my feet. I could hear more daemons shouting in the distance, and I knew I had to leave, but I wouldn't go down without a fight. Stuffing the necklaces and watch into my pocket, I grabbed my sword from its sheath at my side as a daemon crested over the hillside behind the beach.

Its flesh was half rotted from its body, the stench of decaying corpses reached my nose, threatened to have me vomiting before anything. It laughed and charged at me, its flesh falling off of its body as it ran. I swallowed down the bile and smirked in return, charging full speed at the creature. Its hands extended into long razor-sharp claws as it lunged at me. I dodged to the right bringing up my sword through its ribs and twisting. A sharp howl escaped from its maw. I knew that was a sign that more would be on their way. I quickly ripped the sword from the creature's body, black blood spurted all over me as I kicked its legs out from beneath it and took off running. I could hear the howling and screeches from behind me, but I didn't look back. The clouds above the sea were pitch black, aside from purple lightning ripping through the clouds occasionally. There was no rain, no thunder, just the bright light streaking across the sky in silence. I looked out to the sea once more, Undine was nowhere to be found and maybe that was a blessing that she got out of here safely. The portal came into view and I charged forth harder. The dock was barely standing at this point, and the portal was going to sink to the depths of the sea at any moment.

I turned one last time to look back on my home. The fire ripping through the city, the daemons giving chase through the sand but slipping and falling. Today was the last day I would set foot here for a long time. A tear slipped from my eye as I knew what I had to do. Calling the waves to save us one last time, I destroyed the dock as I jumped through the portal to Mistviel.

Doria has fallen into the hands of Hellis. And I had lost it all.

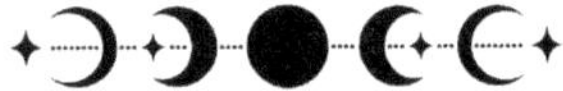

The ground hit hard and heavy under my ass. Jasmine and Victoria were standing above me looking through the portal watching the sea claim it. How the water didn't tumble through was beyond me and my comprehension. With the sound of the crowd gone, I looked behind me to see the field had emptied out in my absence. Bastian, Damian and Niklaus were all standing there. Their eyes focusing hard on me, clearly pissed off at my antics.

I reached my hand into my pocket and pulled out Luna's locket, her pendant necklace and Patrick's watch and placed them on the ground in front of me. The true realization washing over me in a wave that took me under my own sea of shame and guilt. Tears still streaming down my face as I had to face everyone around me.

My brothers were the first ones in front of me, taking in what I had just put down on the ground. Their rage was palpable and

I couldn't blame them. Guilt tore at me. I wasn't there for her. I couldn't save her. Why wasn't I by her side the whole time? I broke.

"I lost her... I couldn't protect her... Forgive me..." I sobbed and begged as my brothers looked down at me. Bastian took the locket in his hand and turned it over. He clutched it in his fingers as he turned away from me. No doubt deciding if hitting me was worth it or not. Damian gripped me up from the ground and held me by the collar of my shirt up in the air.

"You were supposed to protect her!" He roared in my face. Niklaus dropped to his knees, letting out the most gut-wrenching scream I have ever heard from him. Not even the shit we did to him as a kid had him break like this. Nox and Virgil ran up behind them, taking in everything. Peter wasn't far behind them.

"Where is Patrick?" he asked before noticing the pocket watch on the ground. "Valyn, where the fuck is my little brother!" I hadn't noticed Elana step up as Damian threw me hard on the ground.

"Patrick and Princess Luna were engaged in a battle on the shore, according to people who were escaping. What I gathered was that they were protecting the last bit of the citizens as they were escaping. No one knows who they were fighting, but they said they had vanished in a dark cloud of smoke. One we clearly all saw through the portal. This isn't on Prince Valyn," Elana said, putting herself between me and everyone else. Victoria stepped up beside her, making sure no one started anything else. She knew I was broken, but she would have words with me later. I know she's angry, but she won't berate me in front of others.

Bastian walked up to Virgil and put the locket in his hand before walking off. Not saying a single word spoken. Bastian had just drawn his line in the sand with me. I was dead to him.

I thought Niklaus' scream broke me, but I was so wrong. Virgil screamed as if his heart had just been ripped out of his chest and burned in front of him. Nox barely caught him before he hit the ground. Erina and Drake came running through the field with our mothers and father. I watched as Erina stopped next to Virgil and consoled him. I watched the realization hit everyone's faces as they looked around for Luna. She was nowhere to be found.

Erina moved swiftly from Virgil to me and I could see the rage setting on her features, but it was the cold ice that formed around my hands gluing me to the spot that sent dread through me. "Where is my daughter?" Her voice echoed through me as she stood high above me looking down. The last necklace was still sitting in front of me, it glimmered and shined brightly, causing me to look away.

"You should know better than to blame this boy. Your Luna is more and more like your mother and sister than you. She figured out the tower. She knew what had to be done. You need to think to yourself whether you'd rather rage on her mate or those that actually took her Erina." A musical voice spoke out from the blinding light. A woman appearing out of nowhere stood between Erina and me. Her silver blonde hair was neatly tied back into a long ponytail, but when she turned, her bright orange eyes stopped my breath. Flecks of obsidian melted in the magma that was her eyes, and I saw it. The little pink star mark under her left eye. Holy shit!

"What are you doing here, and why does he have your necklace?" Erina was seething. I knew she was made at me for not being there for Luna, but this rage was something different.

"I gave Luna my necklace a little while back when I paid her a visit." She turned to look at me and smiled. "I'm glad my great granddaughter was able to keep you and the others alive. Now it's up to you and the others in your mate group to go find her before it's too late."

"I don't even know where to begin." I whispered. I looked past the goddess before me to where my brothers were standing. "I highly doubt I'll have help."

She must've known where my thoughts were wandering because she looked at Niklaus and Damian with scolding eyes that rivaled Luna. "If you all keep blaming one another for Luna putting others before herself, you'll fail. Not just your people, but you'll fail her." The words cut deep. I've already failed her.

"Illisandra, you have no right to put that on the boys." Erina chimed in. My mother standing eerily quiet behind her.

"You're wrong, little Erina. Your choices have all failed you. Your daughter is strong willed, hardheaded, but she sees the world for what it is. Dangerous and unjust. She will be the end to this war whether you, her father, her mates, their families, and even your parents and siblings want her to or not. There is a reason she is now known as the Goddess of All, Erina. Your sister was supposed to be the ending of the war, but she had a secret she didn't want the world knowing until it was safe. Luna has already proudly announced what your sister kept as a secret." Erina looked confused in the moment, but I got it.

"That mating bond to a daemon king," I whispered. All eyes fell on me at that moment. The ice that held me melted as Erina looked stunned at my confession. "Luna didn't hide that she is mated to Valdis. Valdis will take over as King of Infernia when Alastar steps down. Talissa didn't want the public knowing of her and Zekons mating. Zekon was feeding her intel from behind enemy lines. It was a risk for both of them. But that means she wasn't at full strength." My voice trailed off when it hit me. Talissa could've ended the war long ago if she had just been vocal and Zekon was by her side.

"You figured it out. You're very smart, Prince of Summer. Now go find my great-granddaughter before something happens." Illisandra was gone in the same blinding light that she had appeared in. Erina was still seething, but it was my mother who stopped her from lashing out again. Her voice was soft, but loud enough for us all to hear.

"I told you what I saw. You didn't believe me. Now you have no choice but to believe me. Luna is the savior of light. We all have to prepare for war."

CHAPTER 52
LUNA

My head felt like I got hit with a metal war hammer. My ears were ringing, my vision blurry. What the hell happened? I pushed my hand to my head and felt sticky wetness in my hair. Fucking great, I'm bleeding. I closed my eyes and thought long and hard about what had happened right before I blacked out.

Visions of bombs and fire flooded through my memories. The city of Doria falling to the hands of Marcloff. At least the people of Doria are safe in Mistviel, the one thing I got right. Save the people, distract the warlord from killing innocents. Victoria and Jasmine were fighting as I was running with Patrick to join them. Valyn was fighting with Westly, then the ground opened up. Fuck! Where is he? What happened? What about the others? Did Patrick listen to me and stay hidden?

Clinking of metal on metal dragged my attention back to the space in front of me. My vision was still royally fucked, but I could make out a tall figure standing just out of reach. "Finally waking up?" Ugh. You have got to be fucking kidding me.

"Marcloff." I spat. His laugh rumbled through the floor beneath my feet. "Where the fuck am I?"

"You haven't already figured it out? I won't tell you who helped me, but I must say I've never seen the ground so stubborn to let someone go before. It wanted to keep you all to itself. Such a shame you didn't win this one though, Princess." Marcloff's tone was mocking. My vision slowly began to focus on the tall man in front of me as he ran his fingers across the gold bars. Fuck. I was trapped.

"You can't keep me here. I can get out." I pulled myself up from the floor, trying to drag the rage from deep within me, but something was off. I faltered backwards onto my ass. Again, Marcloff just laughed at me.

"You really don't get it do you? You are my prisoner. This cage was forged from the same metals that Otius's blade was forged from. It's rare, but not extinct like he thinks it is." Marcloff gloated, a smile cresting his lips. A stone dropped into the pit of my stomach. I can't touch the cage. "By all means, grab the bars. Please. Otius's blade may be destroyed, but something tells me the damned thing wouldn't have worked on you anyways."

I tried again to focus my power to come to the surface, but nothing. Ophelia was refusing to leave me. They all were refusing. Out of fear or worry, I didn't know. Maybe once he was gone, they would come out. I know they didn't fear him, but maybe they feared leaving me alone with him. I backed up to the center of the large cage, taking in the enormity of it. There was a bed, a crudely looking toilet and a wooden divider for what I am assuming would be for privacy and a bathtub. Three chests lined the inside of the cage by the only point of entrance and exit. I tried reaching out to the guys, but nothing was getting out. I couldn't hear their voices, and I bet they can't hear mine. The normal banter didn't flood my bond, neither did the sweet scents of them. It was just silent and lonely. I am so fucked and not in the way I would like.

Marcloff walked away from the cage and sat on a throne like chair outside of the cage and watched me. I knew he was waiting for me to panic and lose my shit, but I wouldn't grant him the satisfaction of seeing me break. The door behind him opened, cascading a reddish light across the floor. "Excuse me sire. You are needed elsewhere." A tall thin man appeared behind Marcloff. His features shadowed beneath a black mask. He sounded much older than I would've expected by the way he walked. I couldn't tell if this man feared Marcloff or respected him.

"What did I tell you?" Marcloff gripped the arms of the chair so tight you could hear the cracks in the wood beneath him hands.

"I know sire. This cannot wait. You have a visitor, one who is threatening to tear the place apart if you do not come to see her." I watched as Marcloff's jaw ticked at the mention of someone else demanding his attention. He relaxed and smiled at me.

"Looks like you get to be alone for a brief moment. Good luck trying to get out. The doors are heavily guarded by those that I trust with my life." He got up from the chair, crossing the distance to the cage. "Welcome to Limbris, Princess."

He turned on his heels whistling as he made his way to the door. And just like that he was gone.

And with him, so was my hope.

Thank you for reading!

If you've made it this far... THANK YOU!!! This book has been a long process and it's taken me even longer to get out. Luna and her mates have their work cut out for them as their story slowly comes to an end. Don't worry though, there is more to come with Luna and her mates. There are two more books coming!

I would like to thank my boyfriend, JD for putting up with my late night writing, and my music listening with headphones and slightly ignoring him while I write. He's a trooper and I am grateful that he's one of my top supporters. I also want to thank my kids for cheering me on, even though they are NOT allowed to read it. My family is super important to me and I am thankful that they support me the way they do.

I want to thank all of my friends who put up with me constantly asking them to read my books, and for those who have given me feed back. Jessica, this is for you! Thank you for putting up with my insecurities with how this book was going. I am really grateful to have you in my life.

I want to thank my ARC/Street Team. I'm pretty sure ya'll have seen me stressing out the most over all of this. I just hope that it's worth it for you all.

Finally, I want to thank all of you. For giving this little indie author a chance and for reading my series. It means so much to me that people are actually enjoying my writing. I know it can be a little crazy at time and my writing can sometimes be off or I miss something, but thank you for not giving up on me.

The next chapter in the Cerulia series will be coming out in 2027, but for now, I can give you this little token.

The next book will be called.... A Realm of Stardust and Shadows!

Be on the look out for a few novellas coming later this year. Who knows, maybe one of your favorite characters will get their own book.

Thank you again for reading!

Krystal Harding

ABOUT THE AUTHOR

Krystal Harding is a devoted mother, a full time barber with the ambitions of becoming a full time author. She loves to write fantasy, romance (fantasy and dark) and epic fantasy with epic world building and a vast wealth of enchantment and adventure throughout all of her books. When she isn't working or writing more, she can be found reading or making stuff for her books or her shop. She is a gamer, a writer, a mother and a creative mind fueled on caffeine and fantasy realms.

Her inspiration come from years of falling into different worlds through books and movies from Dragonlance to Dungeons and Dragons, from folklore and mythology to the magical worlds of old. Krystal grew up, like most elder millennials, on The Lord of The Rings trilogy, Harry Potter, Eragorn, The Vampire Diaries and Twilight. Krystal loved also finding books and movies that others didn't know about or didn't like.

Her love and passion for reading started at a young age and flourished over the years. She instills the importance of reading onto her children, teaching them that while some games can teach lessons, books teach many more.

Connect with Krystal

Website: www.authorkrystalharding.com

IG, TikTok and Threads @krystal.harding.author

Or on her Facebook Author Krystal Harding

Join the community at Krystal's Korner

Also by Krystal Harding

Cerulia

A Realm of Wind and Rain

A Realm of Fire and Earth

A Realm of Flowers and Light

Seven Deadly Sins

The Book of Wrath

Behind the Scenes

Join My Newsletter!

Join my newsletter for an exclusive behind-the-scenes look into upcoming events, releases, my writing process and sneak peeks of all the works that I have going. Also, get first pick at joining my ARC teams!

AuthorKrystalHarding.SubStack.com

www.ingramcontent.com/pod-product-compliance
Lightning Source LLC
LaVergne TN
LVHW010629110826
845149LV00014B/2811

* 9 7 9 8 9 9 0 4 0 9 3 4 7 *